# BUSTY

'You're lovely,' I tell her, 'really lovely. I've got to see you.'

As I speak I've started to pull up her jumper, real urgent, like I'm about to come. She squeaks, but there's no real fight in her and up it comes, over a nice lacy bra, white, with those two round little titties sitting in their cups like a pair of puppies in a nest, with their little noses poking through the material.

'Beautiful,' I tell her, and before she can stop me I've caught underneath her cups and pulled 'em up, flopping out those darling boobies right into my eager little hands.

# BUSTY

*Tom King*

The LAST
WORD *in*
FETISH

*enthusiast*

This book is a work of fiction.
In real life, make sure you practise safe, sane and consensual sex.

First published in 2006 by
Nexus Enthusiast
Nexus
Thames Wharf Studios
Rainville Road
London W6 9HA

*www.nexus-books.co.uk*

Typeset by TW Typesetting, Plymouth, Devon

Printed in the UK by
CPI Bookmarque, Croydon, CR0 4TD

ISBN 0 352 34032 0
ISBN 9 780352 340320

# Foreword

Lust is life. I think my voluptuous body and my enhanced female features are physical expressions of the lust that resides in me. An insatiable lust for life and sex. For the experience of ecstasy. Those moments of deep intensity and connection, like during an orgasm. I have become a living embodiment of how beautiful, pleasurable and intense my lust for life and love can be.

I have had many opportunities to wonder why men and women are so intrigued by breasts. Besides some rather dry psychological interpretations, my conclusion is that breasts simply embody a sheer goodness in every sense: warmth, nutritious comfort and sexual excitement. They are positioned on the chest, which is also the seat of the heart.

Love is expressed by affection, caring, nurturing, warmth and tenderness. All of which we experience from our mothers' breasts at the very start of our existence. I believe big breasts symbolise love, womanhood and femininity. I would not suggest that small breasts equal less femininity, but big breasts seem to be a natural statement that their function is solely to give love. Breasts are pure pleasure and big breasts are an abundance of pleasure.

My boobs started growing at a very early age. I was a very shy teenager and the attention on my ever-growing breasts was difficult to handle. With my breasts growing beyond the double D cup before I even turned 20, something else had to grow along with them – my sexual consciousness, my erotic awareness, my understanding of the sexual nature of men.

I had to learn to live with my enormous breasts, to accept them as part of me. Searching for a purpose and role in life, I could not exclude my breasts from my decisions. I realised that, if there was a reason for anything, then there was a reason for why I had been blessed with this body. And I accepted my legacy as a personification of the female goddess. From that day on I stopped hiding inside baggy clothes and thick sweaters. I stopped being ashamed of my body and embarrassed by its beautiful sexual nature.

My breasts give me an incredible amount of sexual pleasure. The more my partner pays attention to my breasts, from the base to the explosive sensitive tips, the more aroused I get. Therefore I absolutely love the physical attention my breasts receive. The sexual attention and admiration I receive from men sparks a strong response in me. A powerful arousal which, of course, I cannot always allow to run free, but nonetheless I enjoy it.

When men worship me because of my breasts I feel that I am an embodiment of the goddess that has become lost in our time, but still remains a part of our collective human soul. Nature, love, the physical pleasures, the luscious celebrations of our senses, all struggle to find space in our modern lives, yet our longing for such is ancient. Loving breasts is a deep, primordial instinct.

I am honoured by the masculine attention, because I see and feel that behind the fascination there is more than a mere physical interest. The massive response I get because of my body is an expression of a deep longing for what breasts symbolise. When men worship my body I know that they are longing for the very height of femininity, and desiring the Goddess, and adoring all that she stands for.

Lust is life. Enjoy!

Chloe Vevrier

# Author's Introduction

I can never get enough of girls' breasts.

It doesn't matter how many I enjoy, how many I see, how many I touch, I can never get enough. I know I could never be content with one woman. However perfect she was, she would still have only one pair of breasts – and that could never satisfy me. Anyway, there is no such thing as perfection. There are qualities that a woman's breasts should have, yes, but no single ideal.

First, let us consider size. Big is good. Big ignites that spark in my brain. Small breasts have a certain sweet appeal, it is true, but a big pair will send the blood pumping to my cock and leave my throat dry with desire. Big is womanly, big is desirable. On a slightly built girl a pair of apple-sized breasts can look exquisite, so let that be our starting point for size. If the girl is bigger, then her breasts must be bigger in proportion: while a fragile, elfin little thing may have apple breasts and be beautiful, a big fat motherly woman needs big fat motherly breasts, at the least. Note that I draw no crass fashion-driven distinction between the virtues of the elf and the earth mother: each is desirable as long as her breasts meet that minimum standard in proportion to the rest of her body. The maximum? In my dreams there *is* no maximum. Often I imagine breasts out of all realistic proportion to their bearer's body – colossal breasts, bigger than her bottom cheeks, bigger than the full roundness of her hips and thighs together, bigger even than her entire body. To put it bluntly, let us say that if a woman's breasts are each as big as her head then I will be in Heaven.

Shape is no less important. Perhaps it is more so – and here the concept of the ideal breast breaks down completely. Certain shapes hold little appeal. Breasts should be full, heavy, prominent. Sagging bags of skin hold no appeal – *rondeur* is everything. To fully understand, we must classify, although it must always be understood that no two women's breasts are exactly alike, and that much of their charm lies in the infinite variety. Using a somewhat arbitrary scale, and drawing a discreet veil over the actually unappealing, six shapes cover the spectrum of desire.

'Buds' are breasts that are still swelling towards maturity, or those that maintain the appearance of doing so since many women never lose this early shape. Like small breasts, buds hold a certain sweet charm, but only that of the still-tight rose: the full bloom presents the display of true glory.

'Bumpers' are breasts of mature contour but broad-based and firm, rising high and proud from the bearer's chest. These I appreciate rather more, although bumpers can never achieve that heft of pendulous weight that feels so good in my hands.

'Apples' are full but not too big: round and upturned, their shape carries a touch of cheekiness. I find slightly built apple-breasted girls adorable, intensely feminine, although in a fashion redolent of the maiden rather than the mother.

'Bouncers' are, I suppose, the classic form, the sort of breasts that those of us blessed with both artistic talent and a strong obsession will draw in female figures in erotic cartoons. Jessica Rabbit has bouncers, and damn fine ones too. Bouncers must be big, heavy and, above all, round.

'Melons' take us a step further, to the woman whose breasts are so large that she seems awkward, vulnerable. Bouncers may be as big as their bearer's head, but melons are even bigger.

'Udders' are typical of the fine, mature woman: they are massive, pendulous yet still full and meaty, the breasts of a woman used to giving milk.

Each shape has the potential for glory, and no one type is inherently superior to another. The same may be said for breasts' colours. From the palest milk-white to the darkest ebony, every human skin tone has the potential to delight. I could never – on the basis of colour alone – choose a white girl over a black, nor a black girl over a white, and were I lucky enough to have one of each I would still yearn for the varieties in between: the olive of the Mediterranean and the rich tan of the Indian girl, the subtle tones of the Far East, the distinctive and curious ochre of the Native American. All are sublime. The colour, however, should be even, excepting only the nipples and, in certain cases, the demarcations of tan lines.

Texture is a consideration often neglected, though it is essential to the sensual pleasure of touching a woman's breasts. Resilient flesh and silky-smooth skin is perhaps the obvious combination although the ultra-fine down characteristic of natural blondes has a certain appeal. Some girls I have known possess a rubbery pneumatic texture, which can be rather pleasant. But then, so is fleshy softness, not to mention the engorged sensation that comes only when the bearer is in milk. Silicon-assisted firmness feels and looks odd, although I would never dream of criticising any woman who, cheated by nature, has chosen to accept science's aid in achieving mammary magnificence.

Nipples come in many different shades and sizes and my only preference is that they should suit the breasts that they adorn. Buds should, and generally do, come with pale soft cones. Apples look nice with their nipples small, neatly formed and slightly turned up. Bouncers need good-sized nipples, with broad areolae and prominent teats, while melons should have the same but even more so. The nipples on udders can be as large as you please, and if possible should be dewy with milk. In general terms, the bigger the breast, the darker the nipple should be. This is as nature intended, for a woman's nipples usually darken with age and with pregnancy.

Thus and so, there is no ideal, rather a magnificent variety of choice. Imagine, if you will, a parade of girls with glorious breasts, each pair exquisite in their own right: perhaps a pale and slender elf with a pair of ripe little apples, a strapping Jamaican dancer with a pair of bouncers that seem to defy gravity, an elegant Italian model with firm, high bumpers thrusting from her chest, a sweet little butterball, heavily pregnant with her swelling udders weeping milk – and more, as many as you please. Could you content yourself with just one? No, and nor could I.

My personal display preference is for the girl or girls to be bare, as nature intended, without adornment and without concealment. Yet there is no denying the allure of presentation. Slow, teasing exposure is a delight, as is the sudden unexpected flash. But for me at least the revelation must at last be complete: she must go bare. Which is not

4

necessarily to say completely nude, but bare-breasted. Prior to that delicious moment of exposure, we have a wide choice of delights with which to whet our appetite.

Bras nowadays come in a multiplicity of designs, and, thank God, their primary purpose is to display rather than to conceal. The shapeless armoured monstrosities of the past may presumably still be purchased. But any glance at a modern lingerie catalogue will reveal a wonderland of lace and gauze, of silk and fine cotton, of cunning artifice for providing lift or hinting at rather more than nature has seen fit to provide, for holding apart or pushing together according to the bearer's need.

All I ask is that the bra should be appropriate to its purpose. Breasts are the very essence of femininity, so let bras too be feminine, delicate, elegant, perhaps at times mysterious, at others a little silly. Let us have silk for the smouldering beauty, lace for the coquette, leather for the siren, fluff for the kitten and feathers for the clown – metal, even, for those rare women who can carry it off, for, as womankind has a multitude of aspects, so should the way she displays her breasts.

Breasts are round, so let bras too be round, round, round. Seams are a nuisance and spoil the natural curve of the breast though they are clearly necessary at times. However let them be kept to a minimum. Anything that distorts the divine shape is anathema so please, for the love of God, let us dispense with the conical bra. Who thought of that? Some mad surrealist? An alien? Nipples may be conical, maybe, but breasts are round and they should stay that way.

It might seem to be stating the obvious to assert that a bra should fit, but this is not necessarily the case. Although, in my opinion, too large a bra merely looks slovenly, I will gladly grant that this may be to some men's taste. Too small a bra is a different matter: with the right girl the effect of abundant flesh spilling uncontrolled from an inadequate constraint can be deliriously arousing. This is also true of bikini tops, which are essentially specialised forms of bras.

A bikini top should display a girl's mammary curves, allowing the natural shape of the breast to be appreciated beneath a single layer of unadorned material. For my money, a bright colour chosen according to the girl's coloration is best. Yellow and pale green are nice on dark-skinned girls, white on the very darkest. Blue and dark green are best on a blonde, while red looks delightful on any young woman. Black works best for a redhead. As with bras, a bikini top should fit snugly but not tight against the breasts that it conceals, although a deliberately inadequate bikini can achieve an overtly sexual or playfully foolish look, both of which work well on the right woman.

Nowadays one might be forgiven for assuming that the bra is the natural garment for a woman's first and most intimate layer of concealment for her breasts. But it is in fact a modern invention, dating back less than a century. It is also very much a product of contemporary Western mores and obsessions. Our Edwardian and Victorian ancestresses wore chemises, exquisitely delicate garments of lace-fringed cotton cut like a diminutive blouse and designed to reveal the upper swell of the breasts above the edge of a corset.

Similar garments have been the norm through most of history and in most corners of the globe, except for those times and regions in which felicitous climate and joyful lack of moral restraint have allowed women to go bare-breasted. The best examples were the Ancient Minoan priestesses whose garments were cut not merely to allow their breasts to remain bare but actively to display them as objects of pride and adoration. Now *there* was a sensible culture.

In our dank and chilly northern lands such delight-ful displays are hardly practical. Indeed, it would be cruel of us to expect our darlings to go bare-breasted in any but the most clement of weathers. There is also the matter of the dead hand of Christian morality, which lingers still. Yet who knows? Clothes have steadily been growing more revealing throughout my lifetime and with the help of a little global warming I may yet live to see bare breasts bobbing in the local high street. Wishful thinking? Certainly, but consider how just a few short years ago the idea of girls deliberately showing the tops of their knickers above the waistband of their low-slung jeans would have been considered an outrageous impossibility.

If bras have their charm, so does their absence. Naked breasts beneath a top have undeniable appeal, and are still rare enough to produce a pleasant shock. In such cases, nothing beats a fine pair of bouncers on a relatively young girl and it is fun to debate on the relative merits of seemingly innocent or accidental display versus unabashed showing-off. Personally, I like both.

Indeed, I get much pleasure from the sheer variety of girl's breasts and this extends to the outer gar-ments that conceal them. Only the most shapeless jumper or the heaviest of overcoats lacks appeal. T-shirts are a delight, either tight to display the full *rondeur* of the wearer's bust or loose so that it merely hints at her contours as she walks. Blouses too are fine, allowing as they do a variable display of cleavage or a tantalising glimpse between two buttons – of lace trim, of softly curved pink flesh, perhaps

7

even of a nipple. Tight sweaters are also good even though they provide a thick covering because they still display that quintessentially female shape.

However formed, however displayed, breasts to me are infinitely desirable. They are a divine gift to a woman whereby she may arouse her men and, in my case, at least, provoke an all-consuming passion that can ultimately be released only through orgasm over the objects of desire. This brings me to another factor in the appreciation of breasts: a woman's attitude to her own breasts.

I have heard remarks from two well-known and well-endowed women (I mention no names) whose fame derived at least in part from their mammary magnificence. Both said more or less the same thing: that they were unable to understand the fuss over what were to all intents and purposes large lumps of fat attached to their chests. This astonished me at first, but after some reflection I reached the only tenable conclusion, namely that both females were not in fact human beings at all but a species of shapechanging alien sent here for some inscrutable purpose.

Naturally I am being facetious. Yet I really do find this attitude astonishing, and also as destructive to the erotic urge as a bucket of ice water applied at the moment of supreme pleasure. How can a woman not enjoy her own breasts? Are they not crucial to her sexuality, second only to her genitals? Is it not arousing to display them, to have them touched, kissed, suckled?

Fortunately, after considerable research, I can answer the above questions with certainty. A minority of generally somewhat sexless women do indeed seem to have little or no appreciation of their breasts, but this is not the case for the majority – far from it. Most women find their breasts exciting as an element of sexual display and also erotically stimulating for their own sake. If you are privileged to watch a woman masturbate, I will lay short odds that she will do so with one hand to her vulva and the other to her breasts, generally, in my experience, with her arm held beneath them and one nipple between finger and thumb.

My cousin, a pretty girl with a fine pair of bumpers set off by long tawny blonde hair, used to masturbate like that. She and I were never lovers as such but we came to a mutual understanding whereby we would lie together and tell each other dirty stories while we masturbated. Occasionally her hand would stray to my cock or mine would move to her breasts but that was the limit of our contact. Our pleasure was in fantasy, and in watching each other.

Exact circumstances varied but, so far as memory serves, her private technique never did. She would make herself comfortable on her bed, sometimes naked, more usually in knickers with her nightie or her top and bra lifted to expose her breasts. As she liked to see my balls I would either lie head to toe beside her or sit in a chair, my nether regions exposed to her as I brought myself erect, stimulated by her body and whatever we had chosen to talk about. After a while she would place her arm under her breasts, supporting them and stroking herself as she watched me. Only when she had tweaked her nipples erect and I was straining to attention would she slip a hand between her thighs, still pinching and pulling at her nipples, but now with increasing urgency until she came. By then I was usually finished myself.

In telling the above anecdote, I trust that you will not think me boastful. Rather, consider it a tale shared between fellow enthusiasts for our mutual delectation. With this in mind, I hope that you will few further excursions into my experiences, ...nts focused always on the joy of girls' breasts. ...s with my cousin, who had best remain nameless as she is now a respectably married mother, I am often quite happy with visual stimulation and the use of my right hand. Yes, given the right conditions I prefer encounters of greater intimacy. But in my memory all such conjunctions are equally sweet, and those of a purely voyeuristic nature only a little less so.

I have always loved to watch girls on the beach and I cannot resist taking a sneaky peek in the hope of catching a glimpse of their naked breasts when they are changing. On such occasions, I find that my pleasure is in direct proportion to their embarrassment. The bold girl who strips naked as if she were in the privacy of her own bedroom is certainly a stimulating sight, but far less so than her shy sister who wraps herself in a huge towel beneath which she undresses with clumsy motions and pulls her swimsuit on with as much haste as she dares. Ideally, she employs rather too much haste – and drops the towel.

Perhaps my happiest memory of this sort occurred not on a beach at all but beside a deep pool on the high moors. I recall the day perfectly: bright sunlight and that sultry heat one can only hope for during a few days each summer, the river beside me sparkling and chattering, the scenery more like something created by Thomas Hardy or possibly J. R. R. Tolkien than by God. Except, that was, for the girl standing on the water-worn slate some little way downstream from me, who had more in common with a cartoon from *Mayfair* or *Penthouse*.

Just to watch her was amusing and not a little arousing. She was beside the pool – her boyfriend was already in the water – and was attempting to undress beneath a barely adequate towel. No doubt she would

10

normally have managed perfectly well. But on seeing me approaching she became flustered so that as she attempted to take her knickers off they caught on her big toe. Instead of untangling them, she merely pulled harder, lost her balance and sent herself hopping across the rock on one foot, the towel gone, her fine apple-sized breasts bouncing free on her chest to create a sight at once utterly ludicrous and highly erotic. I thought so, anyway, and, after bidding the couple a polite 'Good afternoon' and getting a dirty look from the girl in return, I found myself a private space among the rocks in which to masturbate.

A more calculated piece of voyeurism involved a girl who used to live in the houses that back onto my own. I have no idea if she was merely careless or a deliberate exhibitionist, but either way she had the curious habit of always shutting her bedroom curtains *after* she had undressed. She was also regular in her habits, retiring to bed each weekday night between ten-thirty and eleven o'clock, which enabled me to be ready and waiting with my own curtains almost closed and a powerful telephoto lens set up on a tripod and trained though the tiny gap that I'd left.

The girl was well endowed, with a juicy pair of bouncers that wouldn't have been out of place in one of the raunchier pornographic magazines. She would usually strip to her bra and panties, allowing me to get myself erect as she went about her business. By the time she felt ready for bed I would usually be feeling fit to burst, and could generally time my orgasm to that perfect moment when she finally undid her bra and let that magnificent pair loll forward out of her cups. Sometimes I would wait a little longer, to watch her remove her panties and put on a fresh pair for bed, all the while with her breasts gloriously naked. Occasionally she would even pull

...ns closed while she was still bare-breasted, ... me a last full-frontal flash before the show ...ed. Sometimes I think she knew damn well that she was being watched.

An amusing postscript to this story occurred the last time I saw her before she moved. I had taken up my normal position at ten-thirty sharp, cock in hand and eye to my lens. Her light was already on and her curtains were wide open as usual. But rather than the customary sight of her moving about her room as she began to prepare for bed there was a most curious apparition: two pink objects, round and smooth, set some little way apart, were bobbing up and down to an even rhythm, each becoming visible in turn. These were clearly human in origin, and my mind being the way it is I immediately thought that I was witnessing some bizarre exercise involving the display of a pair of truly colossal breasts. This was not the case. The girl had found herself a boyfriend, and what I was looking at was the alternating motion of his bald head and his bottom as they fucked.

A rather more intimate and enjoyable memory of round pink things of exceptional size comes from an early relationship. This girl was the daughter of our local confectioner. She was a bubbly butter-fat blonde of seventeen with a fine rolling stern and magnificent udders of extraordinary size for her age, made all the more impressive by her petite five foot and two inches or so of height.

She was rather more experienced than me and at the time I was still a little in awe of women – and, of course, completely in awe of their breasts. Nevertheless, this girl was blessed with that wonderful feminine sympathy than makes one think of nurses and Sir Walter Scott's *Marmion*, and she led me gently along the path towards the heaven of full sexual intercourse. Unfortunately, when she decided that the time had come – after a woodland picnic – and straddled me in the grass to engulf my head with her gigantic breasts I found myself unable to rise to the occasion. The sheer shock of having so much heavy pink breast-flesh unloaded into my face had made me come already.

One thing I learned to appreciate by going out with the confectioner's daughter was that for the true breast enthusiast one cannot afford to allow one's choice of partner to be dictated by humdrum fashion. Breasts may look better above a slim waist, true, but if one is to revel in the *real* glories of genuinely big melons or the grandest of udders their bearer must always be at least a bit plump. Silicon-assisted breasts, however large, simply do not cut the mustard for me, although I confess to a certain horrified fascination when faced with these unnatural monsters.

Aside from my sweetshop sweetheart I have encountered a good many plump girls with superb chests: if forced to make a top ten of my finest I expect eight or nine of the places would be occupied by women whom society would view as overweight. So, generally, would the girls themselves, which creates an exquisite irony: because they reckon that they do not have fashionable figures, those girls with the most to offer in the breast department are often considerably more eager to please than their arguably more fashionable but actually less desirable sisters.

I recall Leone, who lived in a constant state of embarrassment about her breasts. She was short, as the best breast-girls often are, and was endowed with as fine a set of bouncers as one could hope to find anywhere. Her waist was slim, but she had big bones, full hips and a large wobbling backside. In many ways she was the essence of femininity, and she was also highly sexed, with nipples so sensitive that she could almost achieve orgasm simply by having them sucked and stroked.

Having her breasts admired and played with not only turned Leone on, it made her feel confident. So much so that I think I can safely say that I've never known a girl so easy to get out of her bra, nor so prepared to tolerate hours of close attention to her breasts, a process that generally culminated in me coming over them as she herself masturbated.

It is also remarkable how often a girl will be happy to indulge you with the pleasures of her breasts – or indeed to play with another girl's breasts for your entertainment – when she would draw the line at more conventional sex. Many is the girl I've persuaded to lift her top and bra while I masturbate, so long as it is clear that I will demand nothing more. And why not? She can't get pregnant and she is safe from sexually transmitted disease, while like my darling cousin she may well appreciate the view that I myself provide for her.

I knew an Irish girl once, Naomi, with a fiery personality and a pair of bouncers of exceptional *rondeur*. She invariably had a boyfriend, often more than one at a time. Naomi made a point of letting me know that she was not interested in me sexually, yet more than once I persuaded her to take her top off and let me masturbate over her, even, on one memorable occasion, to fuck her breasts and come in her cleavage.

But enough of my personal reminiscences. Breasts, for me, are a central part of my life. I know it's an obsession. I don't care. I want to surround myself with breasts on every side, in every way. It's my life, and if other people don't like it then they can simply go their own way and I will go mine.

14

Nor is it simply a matter of my physical sex life. I collect, I classify. Any erotic material that focuses on breasts is a delight to me, although I would like to think that I am at least moderately discerning in my choices. I have extensive collections of magazines, videos, DVDs and so forth, also artwork and sculpture. In this I have no shame. Some of it is pornographic, some artistic. For me the distinction is trivial at best. Breasts appeal to me sexually and aesthetically, and if this makes me a pervert, or any of the other things that I have been called over the years, then so be it. I want my newel posts to be full-chested caryatids, I want the statuary fountain in my garden to be three magnificently developed nymphs sporting naked in the water, and until the authorities drag me away to the camps that will no doubt soon be erected for social deviants like me they shall remain that way.

Thinking of that fountain reminds me that one thing that has always delighted me is the notion of having a group of bare-chested girls together, especially lined up in military style. I suppose every Englishman remembers the classic moment in *Carry On Camping* when Barbara Windsor loses her top – although sadly she doesn't actually have much worth showing – and possibly this episode is relevant. In any event, I have always wanted to be able to line up ten or twelve girls, or a hundred for that matter, all in identical clothes, and have them pull up their tops and bras on command. One day, perhaps, I shall.

Another curious delight is the Japanese *manga* artwork that shows impossibly large-breasted girls who are often deeply embarrassed by their mammary development. I find this idea of a girl being so well developed that she becomes clumsy, even helpless, strangely compelling. On a more practical note, there is considerable pleasure in the notion of those girls who are sufficiently big enough to make buying bras a challenge or even an ordeal for them, and I love the idea of a girl being obliged to go braless simply because nothing will fit her.

Better still is the idea of a girl's clothing giving way under the strain: the buttons of her blouse popping, the catch of her bra failing, cotton and elastic splitting to let her flesh spill out in naked, rounded magnificence as her face goes pink with embarrassment while I stare, drinking in each tiny detail of her nakedness and her shame. Sadly such events are in reality rare to the point of non-existence. But one can dream.

You may be thinking that my attitudes make me something of a chauvinist, or that my obsession with a particular part of the female body means that I see women as objects rather than people. To an extent this may be true, and I certainly don't deny taking pleasure in representations of breasts – just the opposite, in fact, as I have already mentioned. Yet although I am a confirmed bachelor I feel that I may at least claim to treat women with an old-fashioned respect that is generally appreciated. Damn it, any woman with her head half screwed on knows full well that just because we men appreciate their bodies doesn't mean we don't also appreciate their minds. How much nicer, after all, to have a girl giggling with pleasure or blushing in shame because she is bare-chested than for her to exhibit the indifference of a mannequin?

So yes, I admire women's breasts. I adore women's breasts. I worship women's breasts, and not surprisingly I treat them as one should treat objects of adoration, gently and with care. I am always aware, too, that even the most magnificent pair of breasts is incomplete without the woman who bears them.

To finish, then, a cautionary tale. Women's breasts are sensitive, and should, in my view, be treated as such, with a loving reverence surely most appropriate for such succulent glories. To me, the idea of inflicting pain on a woman's breasts is nothing less than sacrilege, although I know that some men like to do so and some women appreciate having it done. One such man was a friend known among his fellow breast enthusiasts as 'Mr Clampit' for the pleasure that he took in attaching nipple clamps to his partners' teats. He was persuasive and moderately attractive so not infrequently had occasion to break in some new girl to his particular penchant. One such was Amanda, an opera singer blessed with a pair of melons as full and powerful as the lungs beneath. His lust inspired, Mr Clampit had soon got past the stage of wining and dining her, enjoyed the first removal of her bra – always a great moment, that – and at length managed to persuade her to try his lightest pair of nipple clamps. She agreed, her nipples were duly clamped and she found the experience rather stimulating. Encouraged, Mr Clampit moved up the scale, so to speak, applying larger and sterner clamps, crocodile clips, nipple chains and more. Each in turn brought Amanda to new heights of breathless pleasure, until at last he dared to suggest his cruellest torment: electrified clamps. These were duly applied and the current turned on – at which point she floored him with a right hook.

Thus the reader will appreciate that my experience is not entirely negligible. In putting together this slim volume I have interviewed a number of busty girls and collected stories from friends both female and male, some true or but mildly embellished, some pure fantasy. As to which is which, you must judge for yourselves.

These accounts I have divided into three groups: those from women, those from men – and those from both women and men whose tastes in matters mammary are, shall we say, somewhat strange. Between these narratives are the comments and confessions of a number of busty girls, their names changed and with a few minor alterations for the sake of narrative fluency, but all genuine to the best of my knowledge.

# Tales from the Girls – The Offer

As I climb into the bath I'm wondering if I should accept Liz's offer. It is a hundred pounds for one evening's work, and I could certainly use the money. But that's not the real issue. The real issue is whether I mind going topless in a bar.

I slip into the water and immediately feel the strains and cares of the day begin to slip away. The office is a pain, the same thing every day. My employers are not going to approve if I do it. But then, maybe that's a good thing. After all, why should they know? What's it got to do with them, anyway? Maybe I'll do it.

Then again, maybe not. It's embarrassing enough having such a big chest as it is, without having to show myself off to a load of lecherous City boys. On the other hand, maybe a lecherous City boy is just what I need. Maybe they'll like my boobs. Maybe one of them will like my boobs so much that he'll ask me out. Just think, no more office.

I settle down into the water, looking at myself with a critical eye. My feet are small, my legs and hips in proportion, my waist slim even if I do have a tiny little tummy, so why must I have such enormous boobs? They rise out of the water like two gigantic pink blancmanges, each topped with a cherry, or a pair of well-filled water balloons. No, let's face it, like what they are: two embarrassingly, indecently large titties, each slightly bigger than my head. Why me? I mean, who else has tits bigger than her head? Nobody I know.

They do draw attention at least, but not always from the right people. All those comments about melons, men asking if I've got two footballs up my top, and every joker thinks he's the first one to say something like that to me. Doubtless there'll be more of the same if I go but this time I won't have a top, I'll be showing everything I have topless. The word itself carries a little thrill, the excitement of disapproval, which makes me smile.

I wonder how men see me. Perhaps simply as a giant pair of boobs. The thought briefly turns my smile to a grin. It can be funny at times, after all, with the state some of them get into over my chest, and here I am, showing them off the way they'd like me to, but in private. They're mine and I can do what I like with them, whenever I like.

It's rather exciting to think of those men slavering over what I can play with whenever I like, and I'm starting to feel tempted to do it. I take the soap, feeling a little silly but naughty too as I rub the bar between my hands to work up a good lather. Soon the bubbles have begun to run down my hands and fall onto my chest, creating a pleasant slippery sensation and tickling a little as they pop. One patch of foam falls onto a nipple, and that tickles enough to make me giggle.

I *am* going to play with myself – why not? My hands go to my breasts, rubbing the soap in, which feels nice, warm and slippery, my skin smooth and sensitive, the curves of my flesh enticingly sexy. Now is when I appreciate having big boobs, when they're in my hands and they feel large and heavy and ripe, making my whole body deliciously sexual. I've closed my eyes to enjoy the sensation of touching myself, and when I open them again my breasts are half covered by a froth of soap bubbles with my nipples sticking through at the top, both of them hard.

I start to tease myself, very gently running my fingernails around my nipples, deliberately slowly, until my tummy has begun to jump and I'm wriggling to the tickling sensation. I'm just glad it isn't anyone else doing it or I'd go nuts. Or am I? Maybe it would be nice to have a man teasing me, perhaps holding my hands away from my chest as he slowly torments me, making me giggle and squirm until I'm completely helpless.

It *would* be nice. It would be *lovely*. Once I was really turned on I'd let him climb into the bath with me and fuck me between my soapy tits. I bet there are plenty of men who'd like to do that to me, sliding their cock up and down in my soapy, slippery cleavage until they come on me and I can rub their spunk into my nipples while I bring myself off with my fingers.

My hands are still on my breasts, my fingers spread wide as I rub the soap over myself, bumping my hard nipples. I push them together, admiring the deep wet cleavage that I can make, all pink and curvy with a froth of soap bubbles in the groove between, the groove in which my imaginary man would be rubbing his cock. It is nice to have big tits. Other than Liz, hardly any of my friends could make a decent titty-slide for their boyfriends.

I start a new fantasy, imagining myself being hired by my girlfriends to have my tits repeatedly fucked, maybe as birthday presents for their boyfriends or husbands. Obviously it would never, ever happen. Most of them wouldn't leave their boyfriends alone in the same room as me – although it's hardly my fault that I'm built the way I am. It would be nice, though, to turn up dressed for sex and show off my boobs while one of my female friends sucks her husband hard. I'll rub baby oil all over them, especially into my nipples, just the way I'm doing now with the soap, making my cleavage all slippery, folding myself around his erection and letting him titty-fuck me while his wife looks on, smiling indulgently.

Now I'm lost to pleasure and I wish that I had three hands so that I could soap both my tits at once while I play with my pussy. There's a way around it though – clumsy but it gets me there. I tuck one leg back, pressing my heel against my sex. It's awkward and it makes me feel faintly ridiculous, but I'm too far gone to stop. I start to rub myself with my foot while I continue playing with my boobs, stroking the plump soapy globes as I follow my fantasy.

No wife or girlfriend is ever going to let their partner titty-fuck me. But maybe, just maybe, that sort of thing goes on at the club where Liz works. I know the girls go topless and that when the evening gets going boobs tend to get groped and that the girls aren't supposed to mind, but that is all. Maybe it goes further. Maybe Liz and I will be offered more money for extra services.

It's a truly dirty thought, and I know that I could never do such a thing – it would be too degrading. That doesn't stop me fantasising though, and in my imagination Liz and I are kneeling side by side on the floor, our boobs bare in our hands, well lubricated with olive oil, the men from the club lining up to pop

22

their cocks in our mouths and to titty-fuck us, one after another, cock after cock after cock, until I am dizzy with sex and covered in sperm, rubbing at myself just as I'm doing for real.

I come, groaning in ecstasy with my back arched tight to thrust my boobs up higher still through the soap bubbles and against my clutching hands. It's a special orgasm, and as I come down slowly I know that I'm going to take Liz up on her offer.

When the day comes, I don't feel so confident. It's one thing to lie in a nice warm bath and imagine myself parading my titties for a group of lust-filled City boys. But actually doing it is a different matter. For a start I'd assumed, foolishly perhaps, that topless meant just that and perhaps I'd have to wear high heels and a pretty skirt too. What I hadn't expected was the black satin maid's uniform, although I'm willing to bet that no *real* maid ever wore anything of the sort. For a start the spike heels are almost impossible to walk in, while the skirt is so short that I only have to bend over the tiniest bit and my knickers show, my big white frilly knickers. There's a gauze underskirt too – my bum looks as if I've sat down in a meringue – and white fishnet stockings with a suspender belt. The upper part of the dress has a corseted waist with lacing at the back to pull me in with lace at the top, and that's it. My tits are bare, nestling in two filigree mesh cups, held up and pushed out.

That's easy to describe but standing in the little changing room we've been given and looking at myself in the mirror is making me wonder if I can go through with it. My boobs look huge, vast, colossal, and the way the lacing pulls me in makes them look bigger still. My nipples are erect and won't go down, sticking out like a pair of overripe raspberries and just asking to be pinched.

If it wasn't for Liz I think I'd quit. But she's dressed just the same as me and she doesn't seem to mind at all, bustling around and sorting everything out with her tits also bare. I tell myself that I'm being silly and settle down to helping her, loading glasses onto trays and opening bottles of champagne. I can already hear the men gathering outside, their loud masculine voices raised loud and confident, doubtlessly waiting for a good eyeful.

Liz picks up her loaded tray and I have no option but to imitate her, my throat dry and my tummy tying itself in knots as she opens the door one-handed with practised skill and sails through. I follow – and then I'm doing it, standing in a room full of men with my tits out. I feel hideously self-conscious, and I'm sure they think that I look utterly improper, although of course that's ridiculous since they're paying for me to go topless as their maid. More likely they're all thinking what a little tart I must be to take the job.

I do my best anyway, smiling sweetly and bobbing curtsies as I offer them champagne. Some of the men are embarrassed, others are openly admiring or coarse, making remarks and the same stupid jokes I've been hearing since my schooldays. A few take no notice of me whatsoever, talking earnestly about their jobs as if having a topless girl serving them drinks is a completely everyday occurrence. Maybe it is.

There is at least plenty of drink, and Liz encourages me to help myself. I do, and after a few glasses of champagne things don't seem so bad after all. My smile is no longer forced and I'm starting to tease the men who are now seated around a long table, bending to let my boobs loll forward as I serve, or pressing myself against their arms. One or two begin to get cheeky, squeezing my bottom as I bend to serve, stroking the curve of my breast, even touching my nipples and remarking on how big and stiff they are. I let it happen, as Liz has asked me to, and slowly but surely I start to grow aroused.

By the time they're on the main course I'm beginning to wonder if it might not be nice to go home with one of them. Several are good-looking, and there's a dark-haired man who can't be more than a year or two older than me but who exudes confidence. I wouldn't mind going to bed with him at all. Another possibility is a blond man much the same age who seems particularly friendly and quite sensitive too, always saying 'Thank you' and talking to me instead of to my tits. Then there's the company's president who must be twice my age but who carries himself with effortless authority and is still in good shape as well.

I start to flirt with my chosen three, although as Sod's Law will have it they're not among those who're taking the most interest in me. All three respond a little: the blond man shyly, the dark man with amusement, the president with a fatherly affection that somehow really turns me on. I'm starting to like having my boobs bare too. It makes me feel wanted, and special, and, although I know that's mainly the effect of the alcohol, I don't care.

By the time they've finished their dessert and Liz and I are serving out brandies I'm back to my bath-time fantasy, imagining that she and I are the final course, made to kneel side by side for the men to titty-fuck us – all thirty of them. I tell her and it makes her laugh. She slaps my bottom, telling me off for being a dirty girl. I tell her that she's no better, and I'm trying to slap her back when the company president starts his speech in the other room. We're left giggling together and I imagine the men coming in to find us fighting on the floor. We wait for the speech to finish.

Now is my moment but it's atually a complete anticlimax. Liz and I have to clear everything away and wash up, so before we're even close to finished all the men have left, including the three I would willingly have gone to bed with. Or that's what I think until the president reappears. He speaks to Liz, glancing at me from the corner of his eye. I smile, wondering what's going on, and then he comes across to me, his expression one of paternal warmth. But there's something else in his look as well.

'Please don't take this the wrong way,' he says. 'But I understand that a little something extra might be on offer?'

I swallow hard, because I know exactly what he means. He wants to titty-fuck me. Part of me feels horribly insulted. Another part wants to do it, desperately. He's waiting for an answer, but all I can do is smile and look down at my shoes. My boobs are bare, right in front of him, my nipples achingly hard, their stiffness betraying my feelings. All I have to do is go down on my knees, and I'm doing it.

He gives me an indulgent little smile as I kneel. Liz obviously expected me to take him somewhere private because she is looking surprised. But she stays put, watching as I take out his cock with my trembling fingers. He's quite big, quite thick, rather nice really, and I begin to tug on him as he makes himself comfortable, leaning back against the table.

His hand goes to my head, guiding me gently. A moment later I've taken him in my mouth, unable to resist his calm, authoritative manner. Now I'm sucking and his cock swells rapidly in my mouth. I'm playing with my boobs, all the while intensely aware that Liz is watching me. Soon he's hard, a pillar of wet pink flesh straining up from his fly. I move up a little and fold my titties around his hot shaft, completely encasing him in soft heavy breast-flesh. He sighs, something about me being big – and then he starts to fuck my tits.

I stay as I am, squeezing my breasts around his cock and watching its head bob up and down between the pillows of flesh, just as I'd imagined it in the bath. Now it's for real: I'm getting my titty-fucking and it feels good, good enough to make me want to slip a hand between my thighs and bring myself off as he slips it to me. I'm just about to start fingering myself when he comes, his cock erupting all over my tits and in my face, sending a shock of surprise and delight through me.

That's it. I'm left to clean up my boobs after he's given me just a peck on my cheek to thank me – that and the information that there'll be something extra in my pay packet. I'm not sure I want it, but my emotions are too raw and I don't say anything. The company president has got me immeasurably horny, while I was drunk too, and I'm confused by what's happened. He's used me, really, just as a cock slide, but it's turned me on so much. It was my fantasy too, I know, and I hold that thought as Liz and I finish clearing up.

Liz invites me to crash at her flat, which is much closer than mine. As I sit in her armchair, now wearing nothing but a bathrobe and with a big glass of brandy in my hand, I'm still feeling confused and horny. Liz is full of life and laughter, teasing me for being embarrassed at first and a slut once I'd got a few drinks inside me.

'I am *not* a slut!' I protest. 'You suggested it!'

'Maybe,' she says. 'But what was it you were thinking about in the bath? All of them, one at a time?'

'No,' I reply trying to defend myself and get to her at the same time. 'I imagined half of them, one at a time. *You* dealt with the others.'

'Oh yes?' she answers. 'How?'

'The same way I did,' I tell her, 'between your tits.'

Liz gives a little purr, deep in her throat. 'That might have been nice.'

'You see? You're as bad as I am!'

'I never said I wasn't.'

'And I suppose you never do what I did?'

I'm hoping she does because I want her to tell me, in detail.

'Once or twice,' she admits. 'It's a bit of a perk for the president, that's all.'

'Which you decided you'd like to watch me give to him?'

'He wanted you, and it's about time somebody else took a turn. And besides . . .' She stops and shrugs.

'And besides what?' I demand.

'And besides, I'm not really that interested in men.'

I know, or at least I've guessed, because Liz is very attractive but she never seems to have any boyfriends. It's never really bothered me but suddenly it's personal. I *did* like her watching, I *do* need sex – and I'm wondering if she'd be willing. My own thoughts shock me, but my body is telling me a different story. There's an ache between my thighs and my nipples are suddenly hard again. Can I ask? Dare I ask? Maybe not. Maybe.

'So, with the men,' I say cautiously, 'not the real men, but the ones I was imagining in the bath, you said you'd like to help me? I mean, how come, if you don't like men much?'

I stop, leaving Liz to fill in the blanks, but she doesn't answer.

'Is it because you like to see me like that?' I demand.

She's already seen me topless, she's even helped me to dress in the ridiculous maid's outfit, she's even seen me getting my tits fucked. Now she starts to answer. But then she stops, hesitant, biting her lip. I take the sides of my robe and draw them gently apart, showing her my breasts. But this time there's no excuse, no men who we can pretend we're doing it for. Just us.

'You can, if you like,' I tell her, my voice low, soft.

'Do you really mean that?' Liz asks, her own voice so hoarse that she sounds as if she's choking.

In answer I start to play with my erect nipples, running my fingers around them so that they tickle and grow harder still. She's staring, her mouth a little open, her face as full of lust as that of any man I've ever shown myself to. I meet her gaze and cup my breasts, lifting them to show her how full and round they are. She nods and stands up.

'You *do* mean it, don't you?'

I smile. Liz lets her robe slip from her shoulders and then she is in my arms, cuddled close with her breasts pressed against mine. I want to hold them – they're nearly as big as mine – but not as badly as she wants to hold me. We're groping clumsily at each other for a moment before we slip down to the floor, our knees touching, she stark naked, me with my robe open. I reach out for her, taking her breasts in my hands as she in turn explores me, both of us enjoying the other's body in devoted silence. It feels strange, stroking those same smooth curves and the bumps of stiff nipples but on another woman rather than myself. It's nice, though, and my excitement is rising as I touch Liz and she touches me.

My nipples tickle as she begins to tease them and now I've started to giggle. With that we roll together again, tight against each other with our hands moving over our bodies without restraint but always coming back to our breasts. We're kissing, too, pecks at first, then open-mouthed, and as our tongues meet I know we're going to go all the way. I want Liz as badly as she wants me.

I roll her over onto her back, straddling her and laughing as I dangle my breasts in her face. Liz takes one of my nipples in her mouth and my eyes close in pleasure, delighting not only in being suckled but in being suckled by another woman. I know I'm drunk. I know that I may regret this in the morning, for now I'm hers and she is mine. There is no resistance as she takes hold of my hips and draws me slowly forward until my pussy is pressed to her mouth and my bottom is against the pillows of her breasts. I give a little wriggle to encourage her – and then she is licking me.

Now I am truly lost, with Liz's tongue flicking among the folds of my sex. Another woman, licking me – a thought so deliciously naughty that I can already feel the twitches of an approaching orgasm. I take my breasts in my hands, feeling their weight, stroking them over and over to excite my skin and caress my aching nipples. Liz holds me firmly by my bottom, pulling me to her face and licking harder, her eyes open, her stare glued to my breasts as I ride her mouth to an exquisitely long orgasm.

I've come, and now it's her turn. Now I have to lick Liz's pussy, or whatever it takes to get her there. What it takes are my boobs. No sooner have I finished coming than she is wriggling up beneath me and pulling me down onto her. My breasts swing out into her face, slapping against her cheeks as she rubs herself into my cleavage. Her thighs are open too, her hand between them, masturbating fiercely as she kisses and licks and sucks me, revelling in my bare titties. As she comes beneath me with a long groan of ecstasy I realise that men are not the only ones who can be obsessed with women's breasts. I also realise that next time I want to get off by soaping my tits in the bath I'll probably have some help.

# Being Busty

Laura, like most if not all busty women, finds the attention that her chest attracts both welcome and unwelcome, according to circumstance. Male admiration and arousal are fine, when that is what she wants, but she also finds that her ample 36D bust sometimes makes people, male and female alike, pigeon-hole her as a bimbo.

This is not in line with her personality. She finds it irritating and this means that she can feel a sense of embarrassment about her large breasts. But sometimes, in the right company and with the stimulation of a little alcohol, that very sense of embarrassment can turn to her advantage. As she says – 'Sometimes it feels nice to have attention paid to my breasts, as long as it's being paid by the right people. Usually that means just my boyfriend, and more recently my husband, but there have been a few exceptions.'

### Laura's Confession

'I remember every detail of that evening as if it was yesterday. We'd been to a pub called the King's Head: me, Dai and Matt. It was late by the time we left, well past normal closing time, and to get back to my place we had to walk up a long residential road, which was very quiet and not very well lit. We were all drunk and I suppose the boys had got randy while watching all the girls in their skimpy clothes in the pub.

'They were teasing me about the size of my tits, demanding that I flash for them. Because I was in the right mood and found them both attractive, the idea turned me on too. I wanted to do it, and when I was sure it was safe I jerked up my top and bra to show them – just quickly, mind. That turned them on even more, and they began to take liberties, pinching my bottom and touching my breasts, right there in the street. Normally I'd have hated that but as it was I couldn't help but respond, teasing them by running ahead and giving them quick peeps – because I still had my bra lifted under my top.

'That made them even more eager. About the fourth or fifth time I did it they chased me. They caught me, of course, and before I really knew what was happening they'd taken me in between a big van and a wall and stripped me – not naked, but topless. I did struggle, properly, despite secretly wanting to lose, and it's hard to describe the thrill as my arms were held behind my back and my breasts were laid bare, or when the lads finally jerked my top and bra right off and I was left topless in the street.

'They wouldn't give me my things back, either, and they made me walk home like that, with my hands over my tits. I should have been furious but I was so turned on. Several people saw and it just made my feelings stronger. Back at my house it was obvious that something was going to happen, and both of them were egging me on. They'd let me have my top and bra back just before we reached the house, in case my parents were in, but nobody was about. They wanted to see my tits again and they'd soon talked me into doing a striptease for them.

'That was something else. I don't think I've ever felt so excited as when I peeled off in front of them, with both of them playing with their cocks and feasting their eyes on me as I teased them while I took off my blouse and bra. I got bolder, too, coming close to let my breasts hang forward into their faces so that they could kiss me and suck my nipples. I even went all the way to nude, ending up sitting between them on my bed to give them a helping hand with their cocks while they played with my breasts.

'It felt so exciting, and I felt so powerful at the same time, holding their erections in my hands while they felt me up – they just couldn't get enough of my breasts. Matt was going out with somebody else and really shouldn't have been playing away. But Dai kept on coming back, at first just to play with my breasts while I wanked him off. Later, though, we ended up going out together properly for nearly five years.'

# Tales from the Girls – Home
from School

What have they done to me?

I feel all shivery and I want to touch myself between my legs. They've made me horny, that's what they've done.

Not that I'd ever admit to it, not to them. To myself I have to – and I know what I'm going to do just as soon as I get home. I'm going to touch myself off. Until then I'm going to think about what they made me do.

They followed me into an empty classroom. They said I had to do it. They said it was either my bra or my knickers, my tits or my pussy and bum. They stood round me and told me I had to do it: show them my tits or show them my pussy and bum. They said that if I didn't they'd make me and it would be everything – my bra pulled up and my knickers pulled down. I could have run. I could have told them to get lost. I didn't. I showed them my tits.

I can't stop thinking about it. How it felt to unbutton my blouse in front of them. How it felt to undo my bra with all of them staring. How it felt to pull up my bra cups and show myself off. How they couldn't take their eyes off me. How Charlie Turner said I had the nicest tits in the school. He meant the biggest. Maybe he meant the nicest, too. I was hoping that he'd ask to touch them, but I lost my nerve and covered up. Now I'm wishing I'd been braver.

Normally I go by the shop. Not this time. This time I hurry straight home. Nobody is in. I knew they wouldn't be but it's still a relief. I hurry upstairs and lock myself in my bedroom. Now I'm alone. Now I'm safe. Now I can be myself. My school shoes are a pain, boring and uncomfortable too. I kick them off and walk to my mirror, imagining what the boys saw. What was it Danny said? My tits look like they're trying to get out of my blouse.

He's right. They do. My buttons are straining and it really is time that I got a bigger blouse – a bigger bra, too. I take off my jacket and spend a moment looking at my reflection, from the front and from the side, trying to imagine how the boys see me, how the size of my breasts gets them so horny. Some of them had erections, I'm sure they did. Danny and Graham too, and George. George looked *big*.

I should have done a deal. I should have made them take out their cocks in exchange for a peep at my tits. That would have been fair, only then maybe they'd have expected more. Maybe they'd have wanted me to wank them. That would have been dirty. That would have been lovely.

Moving away from the mirror, I take my skirt off and lie down, thinking of how it could have been. I always get attention because of my breasts, from the boys and from men too. It is nice, really, to be so big, to get so much attention. That's what men like, isn't it? When it comes down to it. Big tits. That's what they like to see, to feel, and, if mine are a bit awkward sometimes and rub, they still feel nice, sexy. I'm going to play with them, and with my puss. I'm going to make myself come.

I sit up a little and undo my blouse, one button at a time, imagining that the boys are watching again. They'd be turned on, all of them, their cocks stiff in their trousers as they watch me do it, one button at a time, revealing the long pink cleavage between my tits, showing my bra. For definite they'd be turned on. Every guy I've ever let touch them has been turned on, like Johnny Fisher when he took his cock out on me and made me kneel down so that he could put it between them. He got so worked up, calling me his angel and everything. And he made me suck him, the dirty pig, but it was nice, and a lot nicer after, when I got home and touched myself off in the bath.

My blouse is open and I shrug it off, imagining them egging me on to go further, maybe to go topless or strip nude. That would have felt good, daring too, to be naked in the classroom, stark naked, with all seven of them enjoying the view. With my blouse right off I lie back on my bed, my eyes closed as I start to stroke myself through my bra. I feel so big, and so sensitive, making me want to pull up my legs and let them fall open.

It feels nice in just my underwear and the first little shiver of pleasure passes through me as I let my knees part. That's how far I'd go at first, the way I am now, down to my socks and panties and bra. The boys would be getting excited, demanding that I take off more, demanding that I strip naked, telling me they'd do it for me if I didn't do it myself. I'd give in, after just a little teasing. First I'd take off my shoes and socks, very slowly, then I'd reach back, just as I'm doing, to unclip my bra to let it loose. Then I'd pull up my cups, quickly, and cover my breasts again, playing peek-a-boo with my tits to get them even more excited.

I've done it: my bra's up, my naked breasts are in my hands, full and warm and sensitive, my nipples are already getting hard, poking up between my fingers as I give myself a little jiggle. They are big, annoyingly big sometimes, but not now, not with my fingers spread out over my skin and rubbing my nipples to make them go properly stiff. Now they feel nice, and it's good that they're big, because it makes me feel dirty. I close my eyes and pinch my nipples a bit until it's making me wriggle, all the while imagining them watching me get my nipples hard for them.

After a while I peel off my socks and panties, imagining myself doing it in front of them. My bra goes too and now I'm stark naked on the bed, the way I wish I'd been in the classroom. I wish they'd been like Johnny, too, knowing exactly what they wanted, telling me to strip nude, then pulling out their cocks and demanding I jerk them off or let them do it between my tits.

I wouldn't mind at all. I'd do it straight away, taking all my clothes off to go nude for them. I'd let them feel me up, as long as they liked, touching my tits and my bottom, even putting their fingers in my pussy. I'd let them kiss my tits too, and suck them, put their cocks between them the way Johnny did. At that thought another shiver runs through me and I arch my back, pushing up my naked breasts and wriggling my bottom against the bed covers. It feels so good to be stark naked and playing with myself.

Now I have to do it. There is no choice, because I'm feeling too dirty to stop. My tits need touching again and I ache between my legs. I think of Johnny and the way he made me feel, scared and dirty all at once, so that I could never stop myself. It hurt so much, that first time he did me properly, when his mum and dad had fallen asleep after lunch and he made me strip off for him. It felt good nude, and it felt good when he told me to suck him hard because he was going to put it in me. I was ready but, even though it hurt, like a bee sting inside me, I never cried out and I never told him it was my first time.

Now he's with Karen and I'm left rubbing myself on my bed. That won't do. I'm not coming over *him*. Jack maybe, the ringleader, but Jack's just a dirty kid, making me pull my top up in front of all his mates so that they can have a good stare. It *did* feel good, being bare in front of them all, but it was scary too. Not that they'd have gone any further. They didn't have the guts. I wish they had: maybe they could've touched me up, or made me suck their cocks, or taken turns to do it between my tits.

Boys are so dirty – but I wish they were dirtier. I wish they had made me do it. I wish they'd made me strip nude. No, even better: I wish I'd refused to go along with their dirty little game and they'd done me anyway. Yes, that's right, *that*'s what I'm going to come over. I slip my hand between my legs to find my pussy sensitive and wet, ready to be rubbed off. I start to do it, stroking my breasts at the same time and imagining how it might have been.

I'd have refused and they'd have done what they'd threatened to do, pulled down my knickers and pulled up my bra. Just to think that to myself feels so good that it sends another shiver through me, and again as I say it out loud – 'Pulled down my knickers and pulled up my bra.' They'd have gone further, too. They'd have stripped me nude. They'd have held me down on a desk and had a good feel, stroking my tits and saying how big I was, sucking my nipples. They'd have held my legs apart too, and fingered my pussy.

And then ... then they'd pull their cocks out, getting hard over my body, nice and hard over my body. And they'd make me touch them, putting their cocks in my hands and making me jerk at them, putting them in my mouth and making me suck, climbing on top of me and making me squeeze my tits together so that one of them could rub his prick in my breast-cleft. How they'd laugh to see me taken like that, held down naked on the desk, George maybe on top of me, his long dark cock between my breasts as I squeezed them together, fucking my cleavage.

I'm there, one hand down between my legs, the other on my tits. I'm wishing that I could touch myself all over all at once, in all the nice places, or that the boys were there to do it, all seven of them, their hands all over me, their cocks out for me, enjoying me in every way there is. They'd really have me, stripped off naked so that they could enjoy my tits, just as I was enjoying them, stroking my skin and pinching my nipples, putting their stiff cocks between my breasts and inside me, in my mouth and up my pussy, between my tits and in my hands, seven cocks to satisfy.

My back is arched as I come, my tits pushed firmly together as I imagine how it would be: George's cock between them, long and hard, as I suck on Danny and Jack holds my legs up to fuck me – not just to fuck me but to fuck me in front of everybody. That's perfect, it's what I want, to be made to strip for them, and as I buck and wriggle on the bed I'm saying it over and over again – *pull down my panties and pull up my bra* – *pull down my panties and pull up my bra* – *pull down my panties and pull up my bra*. Then I'm screaming: *Fuck me, fuck me, fuck me!*

I'm done, lying panting on my bed, my thighs still apart, my fingers deep between my sticky pussy lips, my arm still curled around my tits. As I come down slowly I'm smiling, wondering if I can entice the boys into that empty classroom again. And what might happen if I do . . .

# Being Busty

Amanda was never particularly self-conscious about her beautifully formed 34C chest. Not being extravagantly busty, and also being tall, slim and naturally blonde, her breasts were simply part of a body that she took for granted – save for the occasional feeling that she was privileged to be so attractive. Boyfriends gave them plenty of attention, but not to the exclusion of the rest of her body. Until she went out with Neil, that is.

Amanda had always been the girl with whom all the men wanted to be seen: her previous boyfriends had generally viewed her as something of a trophy and had also been intensely possessive. Neil was different. To him, the opinions of others didn't matter. Instead he was concerned almost exclusively with the beauty of her breasts – and not merely for his own enjoyment, but for hers, and to some extent for that of others.

'Neil taught me to appreciate my breasts,' Amanda says. 'He knew more about bras than I did, not to mention corsets, tops – anything, really, to help me show myself off. He also made me realise just how much pleasure I could get out of my breasts – not just being touched and sucked, but having my nipples clamped, getting my chest bound with rope, experimenting with hot wax and tiger balm, all sorts. He used to love to show me off too, which I really liked. Most of the men I'd been out with before him wanted to hide me away, but not Neil. He liked to go driving and have me sitting beside him in the passenger seat with my top pulled up and no bra, so that all the lorry drivers would see. It really turned me on – not just the exposure, but the feeling of looking sexy without being restricted.'

## Amanda's Confession

'It has to be one of the occasions with Neil, but there are so many to choose from. He drove me from the outskirts of London right up to Manchester with my breasts bare, and he took me to a cricket match with nothing on under a really flimsy top – basically he made me bare my breasts or show myself off in all sorts of places and situations. Maybe the best times were those when the exposures were made to look accidental.

'On one occasion he offered to take me shopping for lingerie, which he loved to do. I didn't mind at all, given that he was treating me and that being made to show him my breasts in the changing cubicles always turned me on. This time he had something even more wicked in mind. It was one of the shops in Oxford Street where the changing facilities are just one big room, and while men aren't really supposed to go in you get plenty of them hanging around for a peep or pretending that their presence doesn't matter.

'I don't mind, really, because I've got enough confidence in my body, but what Neil did was far worse than just a bit of peeping. He helped me choose things, mostly sets of lacy or see-through bras and knickers. He told me to change into them. But instead of him taking a peep into the changing room I had to come out, in nothing but fancy underwear, and give him a twirl so that he could see me back and front. I had to parade up and down the shop and basically make a complete exhibition of myself. Of course there were plenty of other couples there as well as a few single men – the seedy sort: you know, you're never sure whether they are there to buy lingerie as presents or just lurking around for a good stare.

'By the time I'd done this about five times I was feeling intensely aroused, so much so that I was wetting the gussets of the knickers I was trying on. That was embarrassing, as you can imagine, so I made Neil buy everything he'd seen me in. He did it, but on the way home he was telling me that I should have been made to go further because he'd spent so much. His idea was that I should have been made to offer oral sex to all the men who'd been hanging about until I'd made enough money to pay him back.

'That really got to me in a way that's hard to describe. I felt really quite insulted by the idea that I should prostitute myself to all those horrible men, even though it was just fantasy, but I felt excited at the same time. My arousal won – as it always seemed to with Neil. Back at home I put on my prettiest lingerie, a tiny bra-and-knickers set that was really just a few scraps of lace. He blindfolded me and made me kneel on the floor. Then he came in and out of the room, repeatedly, putting his cock in my mouth each time while I pretended it was different men.

'I was ready in no time. But Neil really drew it out until I was so eager that each time he came in I'd be cupping my breasts and rubbing them on his cock and balls in between sucking him. He gave in eventually and mounted me on the floor with my

44

knickers pulled aside so that he could get in. But he didn't come like that – and nor did I. Instead, he did something really dirty, rubbing between my breasts until he was ready and then coming into my bra cups and smearing the semen over my nipples. By then I was too excited even to think about him being so lewd with me and I masturbated like that, kneeling on the floor with one hand down my knickers and the other covering my breasts and bra with his semen.'

# Tales from the Girls – Do I Dare?

Do I dare? To get them out. To show the boys.

I know it's a really stupid thing to do. I know it will only lead to trouble. But I want to do it. I think about it so much, always a little playlet in my head, a playlet with a thousand different details, but always the same theme. I want to pull my bra up in public.

Sometimes I imagine playing it safe. There's a Lenny Kravitz video where a girl lifts her top as she dances. She's pixelated in the version I've seen but it still turned me on. Not the sight of her, you understand, but imagining myself in her place. And why not? I could do it, maybe at some riotous pop concert where other girls are doing it too. Oh so good: my top up, my bra up – and out come my titties for all the world to see.

Sometimes I imagine being naughty. A pop concert is a bit too predictable, really. The platform of a lonely station would be better. I'd be the only one there and when an express came through up it would all come and I'd show them off as the train sped past, just a glimpse for the passengers but oh so horny for me. There would be bound to be CCTV – there always seems to be – but so what? The camera operator could have a flash too.

Sometimes I imagine being dirty. I'd be in a park when some guy would flash me, opening his overcoat to show off a great big cock. In real life I'd run or I'd kick him in the balls, but not in my imagination. In my imagination I'd take one quick look and haul up my top, showing him what I've got just like he's showing me his equipment.

The best I really get to do is flashing them at Sam, usually in the boring privacy of indoors but sometimes in an alley when nobody's looking, or in the car. Unfortunately he gets so jealous – and I don't even dare admit I want to show them off for all the world to see. He'd freak, but that doesn't stop me thinking about it.

When I've flashed for him and he's got turned on, while I'm sucking his cock or rubbing my titties around it, when he's pumping away on top of me or I'm on my knees and he's giving it to me from behind, I'm thinking about it then. I'm thinking how nice it would be if more people saw me, lots of people, men of all ages – and some girls too: that always makes me feel so horny. While I rub my clit in the loo afterwards (Sam hates to think I don't come on his cock) I always think of how my flash might have been more public.

The last time was when we were coming home from the pub. We took a short cut, up between the houses and over the railway, and on the little bridge I pulled my top up for Sam, showing myself off in the rich yellow light of a street lamp, bare and excited in front of him. He touched me, taking one breast in each hand and squeezing me, quite hard, before telling me to put them away and that I was a slut. I love him to call me a slut, but I wish he'd help me be one for real.

Back at his flat he took me straight to the bedroom. Off came my clothes in double-quick time – too quick, really – and he sat on the bed and told me to suck him hard. I liked that, because he hadn't undressed, just pulled it out to stick it in my mouth while I was nude, nude on my knees and sucking cock while I teased my titties and my pussy too, stroking myself until Sam was hard and I was wet and ready.

He put me on the bed, first on my back so that we could kiss and cuddle as we fucked, then on my hands and knees, the way he likes me best, with my bum in the air and my titties dangling down. I like that too. I like to get so that my nipples rub on the coverlet as my titties swing to his thrusts. What Sam likes is to see his cock go in and out, and my open bottom. He says my bumhole opens and closes when I get excited, so really he's even ruder than me, which is what I'm thinking as we fuck.

I wish we knew a couple, a couple we could really trust. I'd flash for both Sam and the other man, his girlfriend too, and I wouldn't mind if she showed off her tits as well, or her bum. It would be fun. That's what I was wishing then as Sam started to grunt and shove himself harder and harder into me. I was thinking of how we might have met up with a couple in the pub, how we might have come home together, how I might have flashed for them on the bridge, drunk and laughing as I showed off my titties, offering to let this other man touch, to let his girlfriend touch too if she wanted.

When Sam came he asked if it had been good for me. I said it had, and it was true. It *had* been good – but it hadn't been enough. I ran to the loo and locked the door, pretending to clean up. But really I sat down with my eyes closed and one hand on my pussy, the other stroking my tits and pinching my nipples.

Sam's come was running out of me and that felt lovely, all over my fingers and all over my pussy as I rubbed. I put some on my tits too, giggling at my own naughty behaviour and wishing I could do it in front of him.

Soon I was high enough to come, thinking of my imaginary couple again and how much fun we might have had. I thought of how the alley had been empty, and how she and I could easily have kept our tops up as we walked home, the boys admiring our naked chests. I thought of how we could have gone totally topless, more daring still, unable to cover up if anybody appeared. I thought of how good it would have been to be seen by a stranger, to have left him with his head full of images of our bare titties.

When I came I thought of the boys taking us home and having us side by side as we leaned forward over the back of the sofa with our bums up high and our titties swinging, bare to both of them. I imagined her wanting to touch me, telling me how big I was even as her boyfriend pumped into her, feeling me and sucking me as I was fucked. It had been all I could do not to scream the house down.

I wonder if I should tell Sam. Maybe just a hint. After all, what harm would it do? I'd love it, and we'd give somebody a thrill: maybe another couple, to start them thinking about new and exciting kinds of sex, maybe a single man, to leave him hard and needing to come over the mental image of my body, maybe somebody lonely, maybe somebody old or disabled, anybody who'd appreciate a naughty treat. I'd really like to do that, because I'd feel naughty and I'd feel good at the same time.

And why not? I have nice breasts, fairly big and very firm, turned up a little too, so that my nipples stick up in the air when I flash, if I'm hard, which I usually am. Why shouldn't I share what I've been given? Somehow it seems mean to keep it all to myself and to Sam. I should show myself off to lots of people, have my pictures put up on the Net or even published in a magazine, displaying myself, naked and proud of what I have. Unfortunately I know what Sam would say – 'You're mine, Nina, and mine alone.' Then there'd be a row.

I have to do it, though, sometime before I get much older, before I have children. Sam wants that and so do I, but not yet. I'm too young and so is he. We should be having fun. We should be showing me off, parading me topless on the beach, putting me up to strip in clubs, flashing my tits in the street. I want to dance in a cage above a crowded floor in nothing but my panties. I want to be taken to dinner in a see-through top. I want to stand proud in nothing but teeny-tiny bikini pants and be crowned Miss Boobies or whatever naughty, smutty title it might be. Above all, I want to be taken flashing.

You see, I have it all worked out. A girl can do that sort of thing safely as long as she has back-up from a man or two. If Sam would only support me we could drive to another town and spend a happy evening showing me off in bars – if we can find the right sort – in the streets, best of all in parks. I don't know what it is about parks, but I really want to show my tits in a park, with plenty of men around to see.

Sam won't. It's not even worth asking, but I know a man who will. Davy will, I'm sure, and I wouldn't even be being unfaithful to Sam, not really, because Davy is gay. Sam hates gay guys – he won't even look Davy in the eye – so I know I'm safe there. I can easily get time to talk to Davy as well, because he works with me at the salon. He's big as well, and very fit, all sinew and muscle, the perfect protector. All I need is a little chat and an excuse.

I keep putting it off. But every time I have sex with Sam I'm thinking of how it might be. Every time I lie alone in my bed with my fingers wet and sticky between my thighs I think of how it might be. At last we have a row, Sam and me, because I said I wished I was as bold as a girl we saw on TV, dancing in nothing but a tiny red bikini. She wasn't even bare on top, but Sam said she was no better than a prostitute. I couldn't help but take it personally because I truly wanted to be like her.

So I wait until Davy and I are having a drink after work and I talk to him. He's easy to talk to, always joking and teasing, never judging. It still takes a lot of courage, but when I tell him what I want he calls me a bad girl and slaps my bottom, his eyes full of laughter. I tell him I'm serious and he looks surprised. He asks about Sam. I try to explain, stumbling over my own words as I confess to my darkest desires. But Davy understands, the wonderful, lovely man understands.

He tells me how it felt to realise that he was gay, how hard it was to accept his own needs and how much harder he found it to come out of the closet and be open about them. I understand, because we are the same at heart even though what he has already done was so much harder for him than what I aim to do. We get thoroughly drunk together, long after the others have gone, so drunk that he has to support me home. Davy's arm is around me, and as he kisses me goodnight I want to let my mouth open for him and to have him touch my breasts. I feel confused as I masturbate myself to sleep, fantasising over what we've planned to do.

Davy is going to take me to Dublin Park and stand guard for me while I flash my tits. There's a railway

51

running alongside, apparently, and I can hold my top up and let every single person on the train have a good stare as it goes past, without any risk at all. There are often dirty old men in the park and if one flashes me I can flash right back and retreat to the safety of Davy's arms. There are often couples – gay and straight – having sex in the bushes and in the car park, and he'll pretend to be my boyfriend and have me with my tits out in front of whoever cares to look. I want to do it all, and more.

It takes a while to sort things out, and I do feel guilty about going behind Sam's back. Not much, because if he wasn't such a stiff it would all be wonderful, but he is, and it isn't. I fix up a visit to Auntie Gwen who lives just a few miles away from Dublin Park. I even visit her for lunch and meet up with Davy afterwards, feeling slightly drunk after all the sherry she's poured down me and rather naughty. By the time I've taken a few shots of courage in the pub I'm feeling more than *slightly* drunk – and *very* naughty.

Davy steers me out before I can flash my breasts at the hunky barman and across the road into Dublin Park we go. It's big, much bigger than I remember from my single visit as a child. Davy knows it well, and as we walk between the neatly cut lawns and smart little beds of pansies he tells me how he used to come cruising here before he came out to his parents and friends.

If what *I*'m doing is naughty, cruising is ten times worse. Davy used to go into the bushes in the wilder part of the park and meet other men, complete strangers more often than not, to suck their cocks and have his sucked in turn. It thrills me to think of going down on my knees in front of a strange man and taking his penis in my mouth, maybe after I've flashed him, and definitely with my top and bra pulled up to leave my breasts naked as I suck.

Listening to Davy talk I realise that he needs to suck cock in the same way as I need to expose myself. I like to suck Sam, and he loves me to do it, sure. But for Davy it's more than that, it's a drive, an obsession, an urge that he can only satisfy with multiple partners. That's something I understand, and I take his hand as we leave the formal gardens and head into the open parkland beyond.

Most of the park is no good for what we're up to. It's mainly wide spaces of grass set with huge old trees and criss-crossed with asphalt paths, cracking where the trees' roots have pushed through – like the veins in a truly monster cock, Davy says. He's obsessed with size as well as sucking. Beyond the open space is where we want to go, a long strip of rough ground running beside the railway.

We agree that the first of my dares should be the safest: flashing a train. Davy knows the perfect place, where a cutting opens out among scrubby trees and bushes. My tummy is fluttering terribly as he leads me there, but my nipples are hard too and my pussy feels swollen and eager, wetting the gusset of my panties. I'm going to do it, I'm promising myself I will, but it still takes courage.

As we walk through the woods we see several men. Many of them are in tight clothes such as cycling shorts and torso-hugging T-shirts that show off their muscular legs and arms. One gives Davy a knowing look, then turns away in disappointment as he sees me. Others are older, plainly dressed. Davy says they will be married men looking for sex with younger guys. It's common, he says. Only one man looks *really* seedy, and Davy jokes that he has come into the woods to wank himself off.

I think of this man lurking among the bushes, jerking at his wrinkled old cock, perhaps fantasising over the thought of me in my tight top. It's a disgusting thought, frightening too, but there's no denying the compulsion it gives me to pull everything up and let him wank over my bare tits. I know it's a dreadful thing to think, unspeakably dirty, and yet so many times I've imagined displaying myself for the pleasure of men who really appreciate me, who need me. And wouldn't that be exactly what I was doing?

The seedy guy is cautious of Davy and moves quickly away as we push into the deepest part of the woods, near the railway. Once I think I catch a glimpse of two people together through the trees, one on his or her knees in front of the other – almost certainly *his*, but I can't be sure. Then we're at the railway and quite alone, with just the tracks stretching away in either direction, the air fuzzy with heat haze above the hot steel. The embankment is thickly overgrown with sycamore, shielding us completely, except from any passing train.

We wait, talking in low, nervous voices until the tracks suddenly begin to vibrate. Davy gives me a wink and a pat on my bottom as he sends me forward to the fence. I climb up onto the lowest strand, leaving my upper body in full view from the tracks. Davy has retreated in among the bushes and I'm alone, with the tracks humming louder, the clatter of the approaching train, the blunt blue-and-white nose pushing out from the tunnel at the end of the embankment. I grip my top, my heart hammering as I prepare to jerk it up and spill all my tit-feast out. But at the last moment my nerve fails me and I'm left shivering with reaction and need.

I tell myself it was the wrong train, a local, which might just conceivably have somebody I know on board. What I want is one of the big red express trains travelling at full speed, thundering down the tracks like an impossibly big stiff cock, aimed between my breasts and up my pussy. Yes, I'll wait for an express. Then I'll do it, I swear.

Again the tracks begin to hum, the other set this time, nearer to me. I look down the track to where it vanishes around a curve, praying it will be an express that appears and praying that it won't, simultaneously. I hear it coming, louder than the previous one, a roar of enormous power. The bullet-shaped red nose thrusts out, my hands grip my top again and I've done it, catching it up with my bra to reveal my naked breasts, high and proud and bare in front of the astonished driver, who is staring open-mouthed as the train bears down on me and thunders past.

I keep my top up, held high, my face set in a delighted grin as carriage after carriage clacks past, each with a row of faces at the windows, blurred and racing past. But they've seen me, lots of them. As I climb down from the fence I'm shaking badly, and feeling hornier than I've ever been before. I never want to cover myself up. I want to stay bare and on display for ever, my titties on show, enjoying the delight of men in my nudity, letting them wank over me, perhaps providing a helping hand or having them put their cocks in my mouth, even offering the use of my cleavage for them to fuck in.

Davy is standing behind me, grinning. He can see the state I'm in, from my trembling body and rock-hard nipples. I cuddle him, my whole body shaking with need, for both comfort and sex. Gay or not, I badly want him to take his cock out, so badly that I'm even wondering if he'd let me suck him if I asked politely. It's what I need, to suck a man's cock as I kneel with my top and bra pulled high over my naked chest, and I want to do it right away.

'More?' Davy asks. I nod urgently as I detach myself from him.

'You are well bad,' he tells me, and again he takes my hand, leading me back through the woods.

I cover up, pulling my top down but leaving my bra dishevelled underneath. It shows, as do my straining nipples. Anyone who sees will know, and if they respond the right way then up will come my top and out will come my tits. I promise I'll do it, for any man who smiles at me, any man who gives me the slightest encouragement. Once more I'm a little afraid, not sure that I really can do this, but again I'm telling myself I must, for the first man I see.

We reach a little path. Somebody's coming towards us: male, tall, well built, black, his satin-smooth ebony skin bare at the legs and arms, his torso bulging with muscle beneath his Lycra bodysuit and his crotch bulging with what looks like an enormous set of cock and balls. Davy thinks the same and gives him an appreciative glance. But it's not returned, and he's not my man.

I'm about to apologise to Davy for cramping his style when another man appears, a businessman from his appearance, maybe thirty-five, in a smart grey suit and a pink tie. Maybe he's cruising for rent boys, maybe he's just taking a walk. I don't care. He's handsome, he's smiling at me, and I want to show him my tits. Up comes my top – before common sense can get the better of me – and I'm flashing, tits out in a public park, something I've dreamed of so many times, something I've masturbated over until my pussy's sore.

The man's eyes open in surprise. He gives Davy a nervous glance and hurries past, but not before he's had a good eyeful. I leave my top up, turning to give him a little wave as he looks back, astonished. Now I really feel pleased with myself. He'll be wanking over me just as soon as he gets home. Maybe he won't even wait but will go in among the bushes and do it right now, jerking frenziedly at his cock as he thinks of my naked breasts and the shock of me exposing myself to him. Again I want to come, badly. I cover up and take Davy's hand once more, nuzzling my face against his shoulder.

'Take me to that car park you were talking about, Davy. I want to do something naughty, really naughty. Remember you promised to pretend to be my boyfriend? Well, I want you to take me into the bushes where people can see and pull up my top and my bra – and suck on my titties.'

I'm nuzzling him all the time I'm talking. All Davy does is give me an arch look and take a firmer grip on my hand. I don't think I've ever felt so full of apprehension before, not even the night I lost my virginity. I've been flashing, and now Davy's taking me somewhere for more, and worse. He's going to play with my breasts in public, and if it doesn't turn him on then maybe it will turn somebody else on, somebody who'll want me to go down on him, bare-chested in the warm summer air, playing with my pussy until I come at the same moment as I get a mouthful of thick salty spunk.

The car park is at the far end of the rough ground, beside a steep slope where the railway runs past the embankment. High red-brick arches rise among the bushes and small trees, making it the perfect place for people to watch from if there's anything going on in the cars. There will be at night, Davy assures me: couples will be deliberately rude, safe in their locked cars as men watch from the bushes. I can just imagine it as I lift my top and bra to free my breasts so that I can offer them to his hands and to his mouth. I wriggle with pleasure, all the while thinking of lust-filled faces peering in at my dirty little display.

We have no car and it won't be dark for hours. But I don't care: I want it, and I want it now. Davy leads me in under one of the arches to where a heap of earth and broken brick is piled up against a wall. He pulls me up to where we can be seen from the car park. But it's empty apart from a burned-out wreck left by joyriders.

'They'll be along,' he assures me. 'Now, what would you like me to do?'

'I want my top lifted,' I tell him, already breathless with need. 'I want my top lifted where somebody can see. Act as if you're my boyfriend and you want to play with my tits. That's OK, isn't it?'

'That's fine, sugar,' he tells me. 'But if you want anyone to come, best to get dirty.'

I nod, biting my lip at the prospect of being watched, even if it will only be pretend voyeurism. We climb down a little so that we won't be too obvious but anyone lurking nearby will still be able to see. Again I wonder if Davy would like to have his cock sucked by me, even if I am a woman, and this time I have an excuse to ask.

'Can I pretend I'm pulling your cock?' I ask. 'Maybe even suck you?'

I'm going to say more, but Davy puts a finger to his lips, hushing me. Then he makes a faint movement with his head. I glance in the direction he's indicating and my heart jumps as I see that there's a man in the bushes, the man I flashed at. He is standing very still, his eyes wide and round, his hand pushed deep into his trouser pocket. I'm scared for a moment by the sheer intensity of his gaze. But Davy is with me and he knows what to do.

Gently, he pushes me back against the brick. Davy takes hold of my waist, pulling us together, his lips seeking mine. I respond, knowing that this is what is expected of a couple and no more, that Davy is only faking. Yet, as my mouth opens under his and our tongues meet, it feels very, very real. It's nice, too, but nothing like as nice as what he is doing with his hands. He's taken my top, gripping it at either side, and he's lifting it, lifting my top – with a man watching us.

Up it comes, a little bit at a time, baring my tummy, the whole of my midriff, the undersides of my breasts, then all of them. I'm bare: my chest is showing, my tits are out, exposed in the park as a boy snogs me and a man looks on, squeezing his cock through his trousers as he watches. It feels so good, so good that I could almost come. The slightest touch and I would – the urge to push down my jeans and panties and rub off in front of Davy and the man is close to overwhelming.

It's getting better too, as Davy stops kissing me and goes lower, nuzzling my breasts with his mouth, kissing my nipples, sucking on them until they're both pointing up and sticking out as far as they can go. I'm wriggling against him, unable to contain myself, my eyes closed in bliss and my teeth biting hard on my lower lip. His hands leave my breasts but his mouth stays there as I hear the soft rasp of a zip. Again my heart jumps as he takes one of my hands and guides it down – to his cock.

Davy's already hard, rock hard, and if he's fantasising about gay sex to get himself that way then I don't care. I just want to touch him, to suck him, to rub my tits all over him while the man in the suit watches. As if Davy can read my dirtiest thoughts he is pushing me down. I go, onto my knees in the dirt, my mouth gaping for his lovely cock and taking it in. My hands go to my chest, catching hold of my bare titties to hold them up, deliberately showing off how big I am to the man in the suit.

A glance to the side shows that our watcher has his own cock out, a hard pole of pale flesh protruding from his open fly. Now there's another man too, further back and indistinct among the bushes. I bounce my titties for them and turn my head a little so that they can see Davy's cock in my mouth. It feels so dirty, so wonderfully dirty, tits out and sucking cock in the park – something only an utter slut would do.

That's me, through and through: a flasher, an exhibitionist, the sort of dirty bad girl who gets her tits out for fun and likes to suck men's cocks in public. I like to come as well and now I'm going to. A quick wriggle and my jeans are down, adding my taut panty-seat to the show. The pair I've got on are small and bright red, very tarty, and they leave most of my bum showing behind. That's good, how it should be. But it would be better still if I was bare-bottomed, with my panties pushed down in the same way that my bra is pulled up.

I do it, stripping myself behind, and now I'm naked from my neck to my thighs, showing everything. The man in the suit will even be able to see between my legs, to catch a glimpse of my pouty pussy as I rub myself, which is what I've begun to do. I'm sodden, and I'm going to come soon, with luck before Davy does, because while I'm quite happy to be given a mouthful of spunk I really want him hard in my mouth when I reach my own orgasm.

He's cool, though, looking down with a pleased little smile as I mouth eagerly on his erection. I start to get dirtier, kissing his balls and taking them briefly in my mouth, kneeling up to rub my titties over his straining cock, reaching back to smack my bottom and pull open my cheeks, thinking of what a filthy little slut I am as I deliberately exhibit my anus to two strangers. Two strangers, one of whom is coming closer.

'Would she give me a hand?' he asks, his voice thick with nervous excitement.

Davy shrugs. 'That's up to her,' he says. But I'm already nodding and reaching out to take hold of the man's hot thick penis.

Now I really am in heaven, sucking one man and wanking another as I rub myself towards climax. I can feel my tits bouncing on my chest and I badly want to touch my nipples. My pussy is aching and I want to be entered. My bumhole has begun to tighten and I'm thinking how rude I must look from behind. I'm going to come – my thighs are tightening, my bottom cheeks are clenching.

The man whose cock I'm gripping in my hand comes, quite unexpectedly, showering my face and Davy's cock. Better still, some of his jism splatters all over my bare tits. A few last tugs and I've let go of him so that I can rub his spunk into my nipples, clutching at myself and trying to suck Davy deeper so the mess will go in my mouth too. I'm in climax, my body jerking to the rhythm of my fingers as I masturbate, working my dirty little cunt and my naked titties and Davy's gorgeous cock all at once. At the very, very peak of my orgasm he comes too – right down my throat.

As Davy pumps his spunk down my throat I'm still rubbing myself, gradually slowing down. After a moment I take my hands away from my pussy and take one breast in each hand, smearing the watcher's spunk over both heavy globes as I swallow Davy's sperm. Slowly my ecstasy is subsiding, but I'm still on a plateau of bliss, and I don't release Davy's cock from my mouth until he gently detaches himself.

I rock back on my heels, grinning. The man I wanked off has gone, but he wasn't alone. Not just one but two others have been watching, the seedy-looking man we saw earlier and another, an overweight business type in a brown suit. I flutter my fingers at them, smiling, but they retreat in embarrassment. I'm not embarrassed – I'm ecstatic, because I have just done for real what I have only fantasised about for so long.

Davy knows how to handle me, perfectly. There's no show of bruised ego because I used my fingers to bring myself off, no sudden indifference, just a soothing cuddle and a kiss on my cheek. He helps me tidy up too, and with him there I feel completely safe. The only surprise is that he got excited with me and I can't resist teasing him as we walk back across the park.

'I made you come, Davy!'

'One little cocksucker's as good as the next,' he answers, and I don't even feel offended – just the opposite.

'So you really liked it? You weren't thinking about that black guy we saw?'

'Yeah, and you too. You're dirty, and I like dirty.'

'But I'm a girl.'

'And? Truth is, I'm a bit of a tart.'

'I suppose that makes me a tart too?'

'You said it, girl.'

I smile. I don't mind at all. 'So would you like it again sometime?'

'Any time.'

I squeeze his hand. To hell with Sam. I'd rather be Davy's tart.

# Being Busty

Meshia has always been acutely conscious of her large breasts and has always wanted to show them off. At less than five feet and slender with it, her tiny size makes her 30E chest look even more impressive and she dresses to enhance her shape. For her, nudity is freedom and the exposure of her breasts is as much a gesture of defiance as a sexual display.

'Maybe it's a rebellion against my background,' she says, 'or maybe I'm just a natural show-off. Maybe both. Whatever it was, while other girls were thinking of finding a suitable husband or starting a career I wanted to be stripper. I know that's outrageous, and that you always hear about girls only doing that sort of thing because they have to, but me, I just wanted to get my clothes off in front of as many men as possible. I did it too, and the first few times it was a thrill like nothing else. Unfortunately that wears off after a while, and in any case not everybody you meet in strip bars is very nice. I posed for men's magazines as well, and did topless waitressing. But again, the thrill soon fades. I don't really like doing it for money, either, because for me it's all about freedom, and you can almost hear people thinking what a poor little thing I am to have to earn my living by getting my tits out. Maybe one day I'll do a streak, at Lords or somewhere. That would be fun.'

## Meshia's Confession

'What would you like? I've been such a bad girl, stripping for money and showing my tits to strangers. But like I said, it just doesn't really feel the same if I'm doing it for money. It's weird, because I get a bigger thrill from knowing that somebody is watching me undress but doesn't realise I'm showing off than I do when I'm up on stage and hundreds of people are watching me strip naked.

'I think the horniest thing I've ever done, when it comes to showing off my tits, was before I even quit home. My bedroom was at the back – I shared it with my sister – and you could see right across to the rear windows of the houses in the next road along, just across the backyards, which weren't very big at all.

'You could see right in, and we were always careful to keep our curtains shut, not so much because we minded showing our bodies, at least as far as I was concerned, but because we knew what a fuss there'd be if anyone saw us naked. Some of the houses had students in them, though, and on this particular occasion I saw this guy almost directly opposite me, just sitting at his computer.

'I was in a state over something, I can't remember what. But anyway, I was feeling rebellious and the thought of letting this guy see my tits really appealed to me because I knew my family would be furious. I had my light on and it was dark outside so he could see right in, and for once I left the curtains open as I started to undress. Obviously I pretended that I hadn't realised he was there, but he was soon watching. Just knowing that his stare was fixed on my body as I undressed was really getting to me.

'All I'd meant to do was undress, making a point of taking my top off by the window so that he'd see. I did that, and got right down to my knickers, but it just made me even hornier and I started to move around the room, doing normal stuff, but in just my knickers so that he could get a good long look at my tits. Before long I was really in the mood, so I lay down on my bed and pretended to read, changing position occasionally. He was still watching, with his curtains only half drawn so that he could peep through a gap but I could see his head move and I knew he was there.

'I kept thinking about how I'd stripped for him, and how improper that was, especially when I'd pulled up my bra to show everything. For you to realise how daring that was, think how it feels when your upbringing teaches you that it's wrong even to show your *face* in public. But there I was, my tits bare, lying on my bed in just my knickers.

'In the end I just had to do it. I pulled off my knickers and opened my legs to him while lying on my back. That felt so horny, such a dreadful thing to do, to show anyone other than my husband my naked body and let them peek between my legs, but it felt far too good to stop. Soon I was playing with my tits, being deliberately rude with myself, and rubbing between my legs. I took ages, getting more and more obscene, holding myself open between my parted thighs, sucking my fingers when I'd been touching myself, all sorts, even at one point sitting up and lifting my tits so that I could suck on my own nipples. How bad is that!?'

# Tales from the Girls – On Show

The bikini is tiny, far too small for me. It would have been indecent when I was thirteen. Now it's quite simply ridiculous. The bottom part is a thong, which will leave my bum cheeks completely bare, and as for the front, well, let's just say I'm very glad I waxed. The top is worse: two minute triangles of bright-blue material held together by what look like bits of string. It's not going to cover me properly. It's barely going to cover me at all.

'You cannot do this to me!'

'Oh, can't I?' he answers. 'You just have to say the word, Sarah, just one word.'

I make a face but I don't say anything. How can I? I'm the one who asked for this to happen and I *do* want it – only now that it has become real it has also become frightening. Yet I'm determined not to back out, not now.

Connor is grinning as I take the bikini from his fingers. I glance up and down the beach. Nobody is looking, or they don't seem to be, but I'm imagining men everywhere, watching me, concealing the directions of their gazes behind their shades, or lurking among the rocks and behind every one of the straggling bushes along the top of the low cliff behind us: binoculars, telescopes, cameras with telephoto lenses, all trained on me as I stand there holding the pathetic scraps of material, all the instruments' owners knowing full well what I'm about to do. I reach for my beach towel to undress beneath it but Connor snatches it away before I can get hold of it.

'Uh, uh,' he says, wagging a finger at me. 'Undress like you just don't care, all the way until you're nude. Then put the bikini on.'

I swallow hard but I know he's right. It's good for me. Stripping naked on a beach as if I just didn't care will help me break free from the taboo I've suffered under for so long. I *do* care, though, I care so much. Every gentle admonition from my mother, every disapproving glance from the nuns, every preachy little comment, all of them are running through my head at the same time. My body is a temple. Modesty should be a woman's first virtue. A decent girl never shows too much. My tight bra is making me look like a cheap tart.

That was the worst of it, because I couldn't help it. My bras were *always* too tight. I just grew and grew, so fast that it seemed I'd barely got back from the shop before I was bulging out in all directions. It wasn't my fault. I didn't choose to have a pair of breasts like melons, or footballs, or balloons, or any of the other things the boys used to compare them with. It's just the way I am, but nobody ever seems to see that. The way the nuns used to talk it was as if I was being deliberately provocative just by having a big chest, that it somehow made me a slut.

The trouble is, I want to be that way. I'm proud of what I have and I'm keen to make the best of it. It's not easy, but maybe this is the right way to drive a bulldozer through my inhibitions: to strip on the beach and spend the day as near to naked as I can get away with, in public, where people can see me. And two fingers to the penguins.

My defiance does not make it any easier as I fumble my jeans open. I don't know what to take off first, what will be the least embarrassing item. My shoes, yes, my shoes and socks, obviously. I sit down on a big rock and pull them off. Connor watches, grinning. He is enjoying my embarrassment. He always does. I stick my tongue out at him, which goes a tiny way towards soothing my feelings.

What next, my jeans? My knickers will show. My top? My bra will show. It has to be my jeans. I push them down, the blood rushing hot to my cheeks as my knickers come into view, and hotter still as I make a complete mess of getting the jeans off, catching one toe and hopping about on the sand for a few seconds as if I'm demented before falling on my bottom. Now Connor is laughing, and I've got sand all over the seat of my knickers. It's wet and sticky, so I can't even brush it off.

What next? My top has to go, because it's that or my knickers. Then I change my mind. Yes, my knickers must be discarded next because they're uncomfortable and because my top is long enough to cover my pubes and leave just the bottom of my bum cheeks showing behind. I push my knickers down, quickly, praying that nobody is looking at what must surely be one of the most embarrassing things a girl can do: taking down her knickers in public.

Now what? I'm bare from the waist down, my bottom is already showing, yet I can't bear to take my top off. My bra will have to go. Yes, that's right, pull it off down one sleeve and I'll be spared the embarrassment of removing it more publicly. My hands go back to its catch, but I'm shaking too badly to open it through my top and so I have to go underneath the garment concerned, standing there fumbling with the triple bank of hooks, my bare bottom exposed to the entire world. Finally the hooks open and I can ease my arms out of the straps and tug my bra off. My breasts feel bigger still, and heavier, as they loll forward onto my chest, but at least they're covered. Not for long, though.

What next? There is no longer any choice. It has to be my top. I look pretty rude as it is, with my bum cheeks showing and my breasts blatantly bare underneath the top. My nipples have gone hard, to my utter consternation, and they're showing really badly. Of course, they'll be showing *completely* once my last piece of clothing is off, but it has to come, it has to come.

I take a deep breath and then I've pulled it up – and off. At last my breasts are bare, naked in the open air, with people in view, lots of people. Several of them are looking, men and women, no doubt with lust and curiosity respectively. I am burning with embarrassment: my cheeks are aflame, my chest is prickly with sweat, my lower lip is trembling. Yet there's a sense of liberation too, a wonderful sense of liberation.

That doesn't stop me hurrying into my bikini. I grab the bottom first, then realise this was a big mistake as my breasts swing forward beneath my chest, unencumbered by any restraint so that they're hanging down on blatant show to anyone who wants a look. I'm sure I'm flashing my pubes from behind too, and I wriggle quickly into the tiny garment – only to realise that I've put both feet in the same hole. I end up hopping about in the nude with my tits bouncing every which way as I struggle to stay standing. Finally I get it right.

I feel relief, but only for a moment. Behind, I'm as bad as before, with the strap pulled tight up between my cheeks and just a tiny blue triangle where my crease opens out. My bottom cheeks are completely bare, naked and pink and wobbly, on show to the entire beach. In front it's worse: the patch of material that's supposed to cover me is so tight that my vaginal lips bulge through, every detail showing, only in royal blue instead of baby pink.

There is no time to make adjustments. I pull on the bikini top in a flurry of embarrassment, pushing my arms through the straps and tying them behind my back. Just as I feared, it's tight, ridiculously so. The cups barely conceal my nipples and, as with my lower lips, the shape of my stiff buds shows through in embarrassing detail. It's squashed me rather too, so that there are plump pink bulges of breast-flesh sticking out in all directions. It doesn't feel secure either, and I'm sure that with the slightest wrong movement my tits will bounce out.

Stripping was bad enough but I'd fondly imagined it as the worst of my ordeal, which would be over as soon as I got into my bikini. I was wrong. Naked is naked – embarrassing but natural, the way I was born as I've always told myself despite years of having it drummed into my head that my bare body is inherently indecent. With my bikini on I may not be naked any more but I'm something far worse. I'm exposed.

Naked is not necessarily sexual. Being in a bikini that's far too small for me is. Why else wear such a thing if not to draw attention to the most sexual elements of my body: my pubic mound, my big cheeky bottom and, most of all, my huge breasts? Everyone is going to see, and everyone is going to know, male and female alike, that I'm on show.

'There we are,' Connor says cheerfully. 'That wasn't so bad, was it?'

It was. It was terrifying, but my nipples won't go down and there's an all too familiar ache between my thighs. Maybe I'm helping myself get over my taboo, maybe not, but I am definitely turning myself on. I want Connor to take me back to the car and have me on my knees with my tiny bikini bottom pulled aside at the back to let him in. Or maybe I could simply crawl away somewhere private and masturbate. That would shock the penguins, wouldn't it just?

My next ordeal is to put on my sunblock, rubbing Factor 30 liberally into my pale skin so that I don't end up looking like a freshly boiled lobster. Obviously I have to do it properly, covering every inch of exposed flesh, but it is intensely embarrassing to stand there rubbing at my bottom and breasts in full view of all those who've already watched my awkward little strip. It intensifies my feelings of arousal, too, despite myself. But then, that has always been my curse: a high sex drive combined with a strict moral upbringing.

Once I'm fully creamed I sit down on the big rock again, feeling extremely conspicuous and not sure what to do with myself. Just in the time it's taken me to change quite a few more people have arrived on the beach, spilling out from the path between the dunes which we took, or from further along where a slipway comes down from the road. I'm very glad not to be nearer the slipway, because it looks as if something is going on, maybe a competition of some sort.

'What shall I do?' I ask.

'Act naturally,' Connor advises. 'Just do whatever you would normally.'

Normally I'd be in a nice secure one-piece black swimsuit. Even like that I feel conspicuous, but after this experience I don't suppose I will any more, a piece of knowledge that just seems embarrassing until I realise that it represents a small victory. I'm getting there, maybe, but there is still a long way to go.

'I need to do something,' I protest. 'But I think you'll have to make me, otherwise I'll just sit here feeling embarrassed.'

'OK,' he says. 'Let me see. Yes, I could just do with an ice cream. Fetch me an ice cream.'

'Where from?' I ask.

He points towards the slipway. At the top of it, not on the beach at all but parked beside the coast road, is a square, brightly coloured van. It could be an ice-cream van. It's probably an ice-cream van. All right, it's *obviously* an ice-cream van, because it has a huge plastic ice-cream cone on top. It's also at the far end of the beach, maybe as much as six hundred yards away. I'll have to walk through the crowds, wait in the queue, order my ice cream with my breasts straining out towards the vendor, who is sure to be some dirty old man, that or a slick Jack-the-lad type – anyway, just the sort to make remarks about a girl's breasts and think it's funny.

'Here's some money,' Connor tells me, holding out four pound coins. 'I'll have a double, with a flake and clotted cream on top.'

I take the money and set off down the beach.

It should be such a simple thing, something with no stigma whatsoever attached to it, for a girl to walk the length of a beach in a bikini, purchase two ice creams and walk back. OK, so maybe I am showing a bit more flesh than most people, but that's hardly indecent.

Yes, it is. It's not just indecent, it's obscene, with my bare bottom cheeks wobbling behind me as I walk and my huge breasts quivering in my tiny top, my flesh already spilling out and threatening to burst free completely at any moment. Everybody is looking at me, and I know what's going through each of their heads.

A sandy-haired young man in red shorts wants my bikini top to burst, the tiny straining bit of string stretched between my breasts simply to give in and snap, letting them explode out, fat and pink and bare. If it does he's going to sneak off among the dunes and pull his cock to orgasm over the thought of my naked breasts. Maybe he'll do that anyway.

The elderly woman in the floral swimsuit is full of disapproval, thinking what a tart I look. She'd probably like to give me a lecture on how to dress decently. Maybe she'd like to make me touch my toes so that she can apply one of her husband's flip-flops to my bottom. If she did that my breasts would definitely fall out, either when I bent or as she spanked me, and that would certainly give the youth something to wank himself off over.

Her husband has rather different thoughts. He'd like me naked, naked and at play, so that he can have a good stare at my bouncing breasts and later on take his withered old cock in hand for a crafty tug. Better still, he'd like to take me in among the sand dunes and pay me a fiver to do it for him – with my breasts out, obviously. Dirty old pig.

Two girls in the same modest one-piece suits that I normally wear are rather harder to read. Both have surf boards. They look sporty. Maybe they pity me for my inefficient and overly sexual body. Maybe they're jealous, because both their boyfriends follow my every move as I pass.

The further I go, the worse it gets. I'm leaving Connor behind, and the sense of security he provides fades a little with every step. What privacy I had at the quieter end of the beach is vanishing too, my embarrassment growing steadily keener as the beach grows more crowded. By the time I reach the slipway I'm positively boiling with embarrassment, which grows still more intense as I approach the van. There are people on every side of me, of both sexes and all ages, and every one of them seems to be staring.

I'd seen that the ice-cream van was parked beside the road, but what I hadn't seen was that it was opposite the main car park, and exactly opposite the area reserved for coaches. A vast German vehicle has just pulled up and is starting to disgorge its passengers, elderly men and women in shorts and floral shirts, in dresses and hats. Every single one of them seems to have at least one camera and be determined to take photographs.

There is no choice for me but to join the end of the queue, but at least I can choose which way to stand. I can either flaunt my bottom to the Germans and my breasts to the ice-cream vendor, who is even slicker than I'd imagined, or flaunt my breasts to the Germans and my bottom to the ice-cream seller. Some choice that is, but what I end up doing is turning slowly on my feet in an effort not to allow either party to see too much. But I succeed only in flaunting everything to everybody.

Several people are ahead of me in the queue: a man who must have more children than Jacob to judge by the number of ice creams he wants, another man who only wants one but has left his money on the beach, a girl who keeps changing her mind, an old woman who objects to the prices and in the end goes away with nothing. I wait as each of them is served, never once losing my awareness of the way I look, and that my bare bottom and almost bare breasts will now probably be adorning photo albums from Berlin to Bavaria.

Finally my turn comes. I give my order in a clear voice as the greasy vendor allows his stare to linger on my bulging breasts. He doesn't even bother to be sneaky about it but stares openly and makes a remark about not having melon flavour today. I give him what I hope is a withering look, but he takes no notice whatsoever. When I ask for Connor's ice cream he takes a double cornet, places a round scoop of ice cream in each side, sticks the flake between them at a jaunty angle and smears clotted cream liberally on top, including on the tip of the flake, so that what he eventually passes to me resembles nothing so much as an erect cock flanked by two monstrous testicles – an erect cock that has just produced a copious ejaculation, no less. He winks at me and speaks. 'That's free for you, love. Just drop back when I'm closing up, yeah?'

'Not if this is all you've got,' I reply, holding up the phallic ice cream in attempted mockery of his dimensions.

I think it's quite a good put-down, made straight off the cuff – that is, until I turn around and find myself looking into the steely eyes of a woman in tweeds clutching a handbag to her front as if she thinks I'm going to try and snatch it.

'Disgusting!' she mutters as I pass. I can feel her stare following my wobbling posterior down the slipway as I beat a hasty retreat, my face burning with blushes.

The ice creams are in my hands but my ordeal is not over yet. I have to get back and I have to walk carefully, because one over-enthusiastic step and my breasts will be out: with an ice-cream in either hand that would be extremely awkward. The beach is more crowded than ever, with the entire German coach party milling around at the bottom of the slipway. I have to push my way through, asking them to excuse me again and again, with my ice creams held above my head. They take no notice, repeatedly brushing against me, the fabric of their clothes or their hot reddish flesh rubbing against my breasts.

I make it through, and I've gone a good fifty yards past the last of the Germans when I realise that all the jostling has displaced one of the cups of my bikini top. My left nipple is showing, a half-moon of rosy pink flesh exposed. They're no longer erect, fortunately, and I quickly tug the material across, dislodging one scoop of Connor's ice-cream, which lands exactly between my breasts.

The sudden cold makes me gasp, but there is nothing I can do except jiggle my chest frantically in an effort to dislodge the ice cream as it slithers slowly down my cleavage. Mistake, big mistake, as both my breasts fall out, bouncing free of my hopelessly inadequate bikini top to sit big and naked in the sunlight. Panic, blind and unreasoning, grips me and I run down the beach with my bare boobs wobbling, on show to all and sundry, my cleavage slippery with ice cream and my nipples once more sticking up hard and urgent, on blatant display and blatantly sexual. Æl*!①(*)①.$②Æ At last I get enough of a grip on myself to stop and transfer both ice creams to one hand so that I can adjust my minimal clothing. As I pull the little blue triangles of material over my breasts one-handed it seems as if ten thousand people are staring at me. Plenty are, certainly, and no surprise. My nipples have by now grown achingly stiff from the cold of the ice cream, poking up so big and hard that they're bumping up the material to leave little slices of rosy flesh showing at the sides.

I am in an agony of embarrassment, very real embarrassment, and yet it is having an awful effect on me. My vagina feels sensitive and urgent. I know I'm wet, and now I'm wishing I *hadn't* waxed, because with the material pulled up tight between my hairless sex-lips I know that a tell-tale damp patch will be showing.

Maybe if I go into the sea? No, I'm going to look a prize idiot walking waist deep in the water with an ice cream in either hand and my cleavage all sticky, aren't I? I have to walk on, carefully now in order to avoid further embarrassment, although given the state I'm in that's a pretty hopeless task.

I do quite well, leaving the worst of the crowds behind until all but a few only have my wobbling bottom to stare at instead of my far more embarrassing ice cream-smeared breasts. Unfortunately the ice creams have by now begun to melt, forcing me to lick around the tops of the cones to stop them dribbling, which is what I'm doing when I put my foot in the moat of a sandcastle left by some thoughtless child the previous day.

Over I go, flat on my face in the sand, one ice-cream lost, the other squashed against my face and chest. Out come my boobs, hanging under my chest like a pair of enormous and extremely sandy udders as I scramble up into a kneeling position. I pop them quickly back in, but they're covered in sand. As I stand up it feels as if I'm having my nipples sandpapered, while the whole of my chest, my neck and around my mouth is coated with a sticky mixture of ice cream and sand.

One look at myself and I realise that I have to go in the sea, and quickly. I feel unspeakably foolish as I walk down to the water's edge, and I now have the full attention of everybody on the beach, including Connor, who is looking at me and trying not to laugh. I can't really blame him, and I manage only a wry face in response as a wave splashes over my feet.

The water is freezing, far colder than it has any right to be on a blazing July day. It's bad enough on my feet, and my tummy is already fluttering in anticipation of being immersed. The worst bit, though, will be when the water reaches my breasts. I try to wash by splashing water on myself, but it's still freezing and it only makes the mess worse. I'm definitely going to have to rub the sand out of my bikini top to stop the agonising scratching sensation on my nipples.

There's only one thing for it: a plunge. I go in up to my knees, trying to pluck up courage and gasping each time a wave sends cold water onto my dry flesh. The two sporty-looking women are nearby, their bodies sleek and muscular beneath their wetsuits, apparently indifferent to the cold. One sees me and says something to the other, who laughs. That decides me.

I run forwards and hurl myself into the water in what is supposed to be a racing dive but which still creates the most enormous splash as I hit the surface. The cold strikes me with a jolt and I'm immediately gasping for breath. As the wave goes out I'm left thrashing in the shallows like some sort of berserk whale. Then the next one has tumbled me over and my bottom is sticking up out of the water before I finally manage to right myself. I'm still gasping as I kneel in the surf but at least I'm now clean, with my bare boobs sticking out fat and pink and glossy with water, pointed right at the beach. My bikini top has come off.

There's water in my eyes and it takes me a moment to realise. As soon as I do I duck back under the water, searching frantically for the wretched top. I can't find it. The water is cloudy with sand and the waves make it harder still to see. I'm not even sure if I'm in the same place where I dived in, or where my top came off. Again I start to panic, scrabbling desperately around on all fours with my boobs wobbling bare under my chest. Then I see it, right on the surface, a few yards along the beach.

I slap my hands over my breasts and run to get it, struggling into the tiny cups as quickly as I can. Until now, wearing it had seemed the most embarrassing thing on earth, making my breasts achingly prominent and overtly sexual, but not any more, not compared with having them bouncing nude and free for general viewing. Topless is worse than completely naked, reminiscent of bad girls in seedy bars, the sort I've always been taught to look down on – and who I envy so very much.

Covered once again, at least after a fashion, I run for where Connor is still sitting on his rock, laughing openly now. I stop only when I reach him. Not only do I not have any ice creams but I have just been through the most embarrassing experience of my life. I am also soaking wet. He lets me have my towel, watching me dry myself, his expression full of that open yet cool admiration I always find so appealing.

'No ice creams then?' he asks after a while.

'I dropped them – you saw me,' I point out, trying not to think about the way my breasts swing forward as I rub at one shin.

'Maybe I should make you get some more?' he suggests.

'No, please,' I answer. 'I don't think I could bear to walk past all those people again, even fully dressed, and the ice-cream man is a real slimeball. He made a pass at me!'

'Sensible chap.'

'Connor!'

'Well, I'd make a pass at you, dressed like that. Hey, do you reckon he'd give us some free ice creams if you offered him a titty-fuck?'

'Connor!'

'I think you should. You want to get over your inhibitions, so why not? I think a good titty-fucking would do you the world of good.'

'Connor, stop it.'

'Not with him, maybe, if you're really not into him, but with me, and then maybe with a few other guys, anyone you fancy. We can go behind the rocks and take turns with you. Think how you'd feel, with those lovely big titties out and wrapped around some man's hard cock while I watch.'

'Stop it, you're turning me on!'

He is: his words make my already extreme excitement even more intense and as I wrap the towel around myself the concealment brings me more disappointment than relief. I take it off again and as I reveal my body a little tremor runs through me. Now I really am winning, because while I'm still intensely embarrassed I'm also so excited that I can cope with it. All I need is Connor to push me that little bit further, and he knows me well enough to read the signs.

'Anyway,' he says casually, '*I*'m going to titty-fuck you if nobody else is. If we go in among the rocks we'll be safe, I reckon. Come along, and out with your tits. You're going topless.'

I turn to him, trembling with reaction, badly wanting to do what he is suggesting but really not sure that I have the courage.

'People will know!' I hiss, because if he does take me in among the rocks and I'm wearing nothing but my bikini pants it's going to be pretty obvious what I'm doing.

'Good,' he says. 'I love that, when all the guys are looking at me and are as jealous as hell because I've got you, and I'm going to fuck you.'

He clicks his tongue on the word 'fuck', sending another jolt through me. It's so crude, just like me showing off my breasts, something I should avoid. Certainly I should never be with a man who says such things, but I've loved him from the moment we met. Now he's going to take me somewhere private and fuck my breasts. Fuck them.

'Now get those titties out,' he orders.

I stand up, trembling badly now, wanting to do it but not sure if I can. Part of my mind searches desperately for an excuse, or at least something to delay my fate.

'I'd better put some more sunblock on,' I tell him.

'Good point,' he responds. 'Make sure you use plenty on your nipples.'

He's right, of course, but I have well and truly dropped myself in it. Now I not only have to remove my top in full view but I have to cream my breasts. I'm going to do it, though. I reach for the tube of sunblock with trembling fingers and squeeze some into the palm of my hand.

I do my legs. I do my tummy. I do my back and get Connor to deal with the parts I can't reach. He does my bottom too, enjoying himself as he creams my bum cheeks in full view of several other people, but I'm too far gone to stop him. Now is the moment, it has to be – my arousal is high enough for me to cope as my hands go behind my back. He is watching, and gives a gentle nod as my bikini strap comes loose.

One last tug and I've done it: my breasts are bare in the hot sun. I'm topless, a bad girl, a naughty little tart showing off her boobs on purpose. It feels so good, although I'm still intensely embarrassed. I want to stroke them, and I can – the sunblock is the perfect excuse. Connor hands it to me, watching as I squeeze a generous portion out onto each breast and begin to rub it in.

People are watching me play with my breasts, and if they don't realise that what I'm doing is sexual they must be idiots. My nipples are standing to attention like guardsmen, my chest is flushed scarlet and it's all I can do not to squeeze my thighs together and sqirm with need. There's an awful lot of breast-flesh to do as well, and my titties feel bigger and more prominent than ever, only now in a nice way, a sexy way. If it wasn't for the onlookers I would go down on Connor right away, sucking him and folding my breasts around his cock while I masturbate. It's what I want, and it's what I'm going to get, just as soon as we're alone together.

When I'm finished he takes me by the hand, leading me up the beach towards where a rocky headland juts out into the sea. Plenty of people are watching, and they know full well what we're up to. A topless girl being led in among the rocks by her boyfriend – what else could it be but sex? I can feel their gazes on my naked breasts, some staring in disapproval, others wishing it was they who were about to place their erect penises in my cleavage and rub themselves off.

By the time we reach the shelter of the rocks I'm desperate to be taken. But it's not as private as we thought. There are still people about, shy sunbathers and a few peering into rock pools. We press on, first on flat sand between huge boulders, then on open wave-worn rock. The headland itself is completely exposed, but there are more boulders beyond, enormous ones, resting where they've tumbled down from the cliff. One group is close together, forming a little triangular space of smooth warm rock, ideal for me to kneel to my task.

I go down immediately, taking my breasts in my hands and holding them up to make a slide for Connor's cock. He's grinning down at me, squeezing the crotch of his shorts, which already looks impressively full. His fingers go to his flies, undoing one button, then a second. Out comes his cock and balls, big and heavy in the sunlight, the very essence of obscenity, as I've always been taught, yet so desirable. I take him in my mouth, sucking gently as I play with my nipples, my eyes closed in bliss.

As I so often do, I imagine myself surrounded by the nuns from St Mary's, each and every one of them staring in horror as I suck on a big ugly penis, making my man grow in my mouth in willing dirty lust. Now it's stronger than ever, because I've been parading myself near-nude on a public beach, and I'm still outdoors, clad in nothing but the skimpiest imaginable bikini pants and a pair of sandals. My breasts are bare in my hands, achingly sensitive, and are about to be wrapped around the cock now rapidly growing stiff in my mouth.

I don't stop sucking until Connor is fully erect, his cock sprouting out from his shorts above the heavy wrinkled sac of his balls. His penis is thick and slightly curved, its head glossy with pressure, a thing at once threatening and utterly desirable. Kneeling up a little, I offer my breasts, allowing him to settle himself in my cleavage – an awkward position, but he doesn't seem to mind. His hands come down to hold my breasts, clutching them in his passion and rolling them together around his cock.

My own hands are free and I know what I'm going to do. I can't help it any more. One hand goes straight down into my bikini pants and I'm playing with myself, stroking and teasing my soaking quim. My other hand is on Connor's balls as he fucks my breasts and I am lost in ecstasy as it all comes together in my head.

This is perfect. My triumph is complete. I have stripped in public, paraded myself near-naked. Pictures of my bottom and breasts will be on computers and in albums all over the country, and in Germany too. Not just in my bikini either, but bare, my breasts bare, bare for hundreds of people to see, for hundreds of men to enjoy. I've been taken by the hand and led away topless to have my breasts fucked, to be given a titty-fucking, something so rude, so wonderfully rude.

It won't be the last time, either. I'm going to do it again, in the same tiny bikini, only with bigger crowds, maybe on the seafront, maybe in town. I'm going to go in for wet T-shirt contests and show them how I look in nothing but knickers and a sodden top. I'm going to go into strip bars too, and do it for free, all the way to naked, showing off what I've got to dozens of lecherous men. I'm going to be proud and free and wanton, enjoying my body as I should, for ever. But right now it's about time I came to the orgasm that I need so badly.

I'm wishing I was doing it in front of the nuns, their expressions set in horror as Connor's big cock pumps in my cleavage and I tease my sex down my pants. How they'd hate it to see their star pupil, their innocent little Sarah, the one they thought they'd moulded so well, down on her knees among the rocks as she's given a titty-fucking. How they'd tut and mutter, how they'd remonstrate with me. But I'd take no notice, masturbating myself until I'd come, and so had Connor.

Which he does, all over my breasts and in my face, which is too much. I'm coming myself, my fingers rubbing furiously at my honeypot as I clutch at his balls while jet after jet of thick white semen spurts from the tip of his cock, splashing my neck, spattering my face, and going into my open mouth. But best of all it pours all over my huge, naked titties as I snatch at myself and come, and come, and come.

# Being Busty

Pippa is blonde and buxom and distinctly upper-class. She is also highly intelligent, educated at two girls' public schools and Oxford, where she read chemistry. At very nearly six feet tall and with a 40DD chest, she often finds that men are intimidated by her. Ironically, her body image doesn't reflect her true sexuality at all. Her fantasies are exclusively submissive and often extreme, involving bondage and worse.

'I like to imagine myself being rescued by a knight,' she tells me. 'Only after killing the dragon he doesn't release me but takes advantage of me instead. I'm chained to a post, in just a shift or something, and he comes up to me full of good intentions – until he sees the size of my breasts. He thinks for a bit, struggling with his conscience as I beg him to release me, but lust wins. He rips my shift open down the front, then spends ages having fun with my breasts, pulling my nipples and scratching my skin, that sort of stuff, whipping them too. I can't help but enjoy it, and he soon has me moaning and pushing them out at him, at which he loses control completely, lifts up my legs and fucks me then and there against the post.

Sometimes I imagine him pushing me down the post until I'm on my knees so that he can make me suck him, or so that he can come all over my breasts, after which he just leaves me there. If I'm in a really dirty mood I like to imagine him peeing on me too, once he's finished with me – all over my breasts – and leaving me like that for somebody else to find. Unfortunately, all the men I meet seem to want *me* to dominate *them*, which isn't my thing at all.'

### Pippa's Confession

'It's hard to know what to pick, as my real sex life has been so at odds with what I really want. If half the things I'd imagined had come true I could provide you with lots of good stuff, like my knight fantasy, or having my breasts roped through the bed end in the dorm and whipped in front of the other girls.

'I did have one boyfriend with a dirty habit, even if he always did get apologetic about it afterwards. He used to like me to kneel down and hold my breasts out so that he could put his cock between them and in my mouth, then come all over them. I used to wish he'd tie me up first and just do it, then leave me there with all his stuff dripping down me, with a mouthful of it too. I wish I'd had the courage to ask.

'I suppose the best time was when he did it to me at a country house – I'd better not say which one. It was risky because there were a lot of people about, but we managed to nip away from the guide and find this little alcove, just outside the public area. We could see the lawns, with people walking on them, but he made me do it anyway, sitting in the window seat with him facing me. First I had to pull my top and bra up and play with myself, especially with my nipples, while he watched – he always liked to watch

87

me play with my nipples. I was scared and was sure somebody would catch us, but that was almost as arousing as being bare in front of him.

'He put his cock in my mouth and told me to suck him, which I did, with all sorts of dirty thoughts going through my head. We had to be quick because there was a very real chance of being caught. But he didn't seem to care, feeling my breasts and putting his cock between them, making me hold them and jiggle them around his cock, popping it in and out of my mouth again and again. Soon I wanted to come myself, but I didn't dare get my jeans down.

'When he did it he made me hold my breasts out and stood so that he was really close, to let his balls rub between them. Because of that, most of his stuff went in my face and hair, which made a real mess. Still, it felt lovely. I was still cleaning up when somebody came into the room. We were out of sight and they didn't actually catch us, but it got my heart going like anything. He started to apologise as soon as we were safely back in the public part of the house, which he always did, however much I told him that I didn't mind.

'I was still very aroused, and the feeling wouldn't go away, so I was really naughty. After a bit I nipped off to the loos, which were truly old-fashioned, completely enclosed, so once I'd locked the door I was safe. I stripped off completely and knelt on the floor with my eyes closed, playing with my breasts until I was ready, then rubbing myself between my legs as well. At first I just thought of what I'd done, until kneeling on the loo floor started to get to me. The floor was tiled, very cold and hard too, so I began to imagine how it would have felt if I'd been the daughter of the house when the family lived there, and I'd been blackmailed into sucking off the footman.

'In my fantasy he really used me, making me strip and forcing me to polish his boots when I was nude, then smearing the boot polish all over my breasts and bottom to humiliate me. I imagined how slippery it would feel, with my breasts covered in it and my nipples sticking up all black and shiny, and how he'd put his cock between them and fuck in my dirty cleavage, until he was filthy with it. Then he'd put his dirty cock in my mouth to make me taste it and he'd wipe it in my face before coming all over me, especially over my breasts, laughing at me as I lost control and rubbed the whole sticky, filthy mess over my skin.

'I came like that, imagining myself being made to kneel on the cold, hard floor while he took advantage of me, and especially imagining having to hold my breasts together, black and slippery with boot polish, my face dirty too, and my mouth full of it, his stuff and the boot polish, and picturing how my breasts would look, big and black and shiny and smeared with a man's come.'

# Tales from the Boys – Alice, the Pirate and the Owl

'She's the best, the one in the pirate outfit.'

'Nah,' Jim answers. 'She's cute, sure, but Alice is cuter.'

He does have a point, and they're certainly the two best-looking girls at the party. We don't know either of them, although I'm determined that's going to change. Alice probably isn't called that at all, but she is dressed as Alice in Wonderland, only in a grown-up way – very grown-up indeed. She's blonde, as she should be, with long thick hair hanging down almost to her bum. Her dress is blue, with a white pinafore and lots of frilly white underskirts, and it's short, so short that she's showing a hint of her panties underneath. Better still, the bodice is low, and she is big, rather too big for the dress, so that she's showing several inches of soft pink cleavage and the full swell of what have to be two of the plumpest, roundest tits I've ever seen. She's with a man in a gorilla suit, and he's making her laugh by scratching under his armpits and making apelike noises. Maybe he's thinking the same as I am: that if she laughs just that little bit louder, then those two lovely round boobies are going to pop right out of her dress so that everyone can see.

I still say the pirate girl is cuter. She's dark-haired and slim, but just as busty as Alice. Her feet and calves are encased in suede boots, turned down at the knee to show red and black striped tights which cover her legs all the way up to a pair of tiny leather shorts worn snug over a round little bum and so tight that they're pulled up a little way between her pussy lips. Her top matches her tights and it is so well filled that it takes my breath away. Every contour of her tits shows through, and the horizontal red and black bands make them seem bigger still, while it's quite obvious that she has no bra on, with both her nipples making tempting little bumps in the fabric. She's having a serious conversation with an earnest man in spectacles, her pretty face set in a frown as she concentrates on what he has to say.

'You going to give it a go, or what?' Jim asks.

'I'm going to try,' I tell him. 'As it goes, I reckon I can have both sets of titties out of their tops before the night's over.'

'You wish!' he jokes.

'I do,' I tell him.

'Ten quid says you don't make it.'

'OK, ten quid to have both Alice and the pirate with their titties out before we go.'

Jim sticks his hand out and I shake it. I'm probably going to end up ten quid down, but I have to try. Just thinking of having those two pairs of lovely golden-skinned breasts bare is enough to get my cock hard, never mind what else I could do with them. But first I have to get them out, together, and that means putting the girls in the right mood.

It's no good trying to chat just one of them up, because if I succeed with one then I'll have no chance with the other. Maybe that would be best. It's what any sensible guy would do, but I'm a greedy bastard and a risk-taker. I want both pairs of titties on show, and I reckon I know how to do it.

First things first. I talk to the host and hostess, telling them what a great party it is and what a good idea it was to make it fancy dress. I only know them vaguely, but I do know they're just getting into hang-gliding. I've done a bit myself and I can talk the talk, so I'm soon well in. I know they've only been engaged a little while too, so I congratulate them and admit that I don't have a partner myself. As planned, the hostess immediately goes into matchmaker mode, pointing out which of the girls are single and suggesting who might make an appropriate partner for me.

Alice is single, but the hostess does not think that she would be good for me. Apparently she has a bad reputation for using men. That's just fine by me, just so long as while she's using me I get to fuck her and play with her titties. The pirate is with a boyfriend, not the intellectual type she's talking to but a bloke who's getting steadily drunk in the corner. The two girls know each other and were at college together, studying art and photography respectively.

Time for my next move. I start to circulate, introducing myself and talking to each little group in turn, including the ones that Alice and the pirate are with. I don't push it, just making sure they know who I am and swapping a bit of friendly banter. Being dressed as Darth Vader helps, because they can appreciate my well-toned body but they can't see my ugly mug. Jim's wandered off and is talking to a girl with long red hair in a cutesy little Robin Hood-style outfit. She hasn't got enough tit for my taste but she looks like fun, which fits in nicely with my evil scheme.

The party's going fine, with the level in the punch bowl well down, which gives me an opportunity to be public-spirited and mix some more. OK, so maybe the original recipe had a bit more lemonade and fruit juice and not quite as much vodka or rum or strong red wine, but I prefer my version. I even take a tray round to make sure that everybody's got plenty, particularly Alice and the pirate, who's called Jane by the way, though I'm finding it hard to think of her that way.

Next comes setting up the action, which has to be done carefully so that everything's just right but nobody can figure it's all been fixed in advance. I find the right place with no problem: a spare bedroom, nice and cosy. There are already some quite interesting prints on the wall, but not half as interesting as the weird stuff in the bathroom, which I move. The other accessories aren't too hard to find either, as my host and hostess are into that sort of thing and have a special table. I even get a choice, including some fruity ones – just what I need.

Move Five is a tricky one, getting the right people in the right place and the wrong people elsewhere. I wait until midnight, hoping that nobody important is going to go home early and spoil the fun. A few have already drifted off, couples mainly, leaving the serious drinkers and the ones who're up for fun, with luck. I know who I want: Alice and the pirate, obviously, Jim, and Miss Robin. The one I *don't* want is the pirate's boyfriend, who is now in the kitchen having a loud and drunken conversation about politics.

Alice and the pirate are talking together with another girl, a fat little thing with big glasses that make her look like an owl and tits bigger than both of the others' put together. She's got a sense of humour, though, because she not only looks like an owl naturally, she's dressed as one. I move in close.

'Have you seen Jan and Robert's original Beardsleys?' I ask, all innocent and arty.

'No,' Alice replies. 'Where are they?'

'I have,' the owl chips in. 'She got them in a junk shop in Cardiff for a few quid each. The owner obviously had no idea what he'd got. They're upstairs, in the bathroom.'

'I think they're in the spare room,' I tell her. 'Maybe they moved them.'

'The original Bons Mots must be worth a fortune,' says the owl.

I no longer know what she's talking about, but she's good for my cause. So is Alice, coming along like a bee to a honeypot.

'Do you think they'd mind if we had a look?' she asks.

'I'm sure they wouldn't,' I say quickly before the owl can suggest asking her. The owl looks far too sensible, which may be a problem.

They make for the stairs and I excuse myself on the pretext of getting another drink. Not a pretext exactly, because I grab a couple of bottles of red wine from the kitchen before tracking Jim down. He's in the front room, still talking to Miss Robin. I duck down next to them.

'There's something good going on upstairs in a few minutes,' I tell them. 'Don't tell anyone else, just come up.'

'Oh yes?' Miss Robin demands, and I can tell that Jim's caught a live one just from the tone of her voice.

'You'll see,' I tell her.

They're going to come, no question. I just hope that I can deliver on my promise.

All three girls are upstairs, admiring the picture of a guy with the biggest cock you ever saw which I'd found in the bathroom. It has to get them thinking, surely, and I swear I catch Alice licking her lips as I come in. I fall in with the conversation but there's not really much to do except listen, because the owl seems to be an expert on the subject. Or maybe she's just into monster cocks.

Move Five is complete apart from the presence of the owl, which is making a smooth transition to Move Six difficult. I'm going to try for a not-so-smooth transition when Jim and Miss Robin come in, both looking around to see what's on offer. Nothing is, even though Miss Robin is well into monster cocks, giggling like she's demented when she sees the one on the wall. She thinks that's what I asked them up for, which is just as well, but she's drunk too, and I think she's horny.

I play it carefully, letting the conversation drift until we're in two groups, Alice, the owl and Miss Robin in one, Jim, me and the pirate in the other. One bottle gets shared out and I open the other, which gives me a chance to give Jim a prod and a thumbs-up. He has no idea what I'm doing, but when I pretend to find the set of dirty playing cards in a drawer he suggests a game without even having to be prompted.

Miss Robin's well up for it, and the pirate as well. We settle down on the floor, and pretty soon Alice has joined in too, and the owl. That's two guys and four girls, but I'm not complaining. All I need to do is lose.

That's easy, and I even manage to do it without looking like a complete prat. I get two pairs, threes and sevens. Alice takes the pot with three jacks and it's time for the final move, the crucial one.

'What are the stakes, then?' I ask, digging my hand in under my robe.

'Can't we just play for fun?' Miss Robin complains.

'No, we've got to have stakes,' Jim answers her.

'I've got no money on me,' the pirate points out.

'I've only got a few quid myself,' I tell her. 'Oh, what the fuck, here goes.'

I take off my gloves, and that's it, pure and simple. We're playing strip poker and I'm the only who's losing my clothes, so none of the girls is complaining.

Jim may be in danger of losing a tenner, but he'd give a lot more than that to see what the girls have got, and it's odds-on that if he gets Miss Robin out of her knickers he'll be taking her home afterwards. He plays along, making sure that he loses the next hand and taking off his cloak. The owl wants to know what the rules are and I can see she's nervous, so I tell her. Anyone can throw in and they're safe, but, if you want to play and you lose, one article has to come off. It's good, because that way if she wants to watch but doesn't want to risk it she just has to keep throwing in.

I'm not home yet, because any of the girls could chicken out. But they're as bold as I'd hoped. They're also jammy as hell, because other than the pirate losing her boots, all four of them are still fully clothed by the time I've lost my cape, my own boots and my socks. I hadn't really bargained for stripping off in front of them while they've still got their gear on, but it looks like I'm going to have to. Jim's not doing so well, either. The next hand I throw in, but on the one after I've got aces and eights, and Alice wants to play.

'Who's in?' she asks.

'I am,' I tell her, and Miss Robin gives a nod.

We lay down our cards: my aces and eights, queens and fives from Miss Robin, and a full house from Alice, tens on twos. Miss Robin giggles and takes off her hat like she's doing a striptease. For me, it's not so easy. All I've got is my top, my helmet, my trousers and my briefs. I go for my trousers, with the girls laughing and clapping as I peel off.

'Deal the cards, Jane,' says Alice, and I'd be a lot happier about the enthusiasm in her voice if she was in just her knickers and a top.

This time my luck is in: three kings straight off. I ask for two cards and I'm the one with the full house. Now for some serious action.

'Who's in?' Alice asks, just like before.

'Me,' I tell her.

'Me too,' Jim adds, and Miss Robin confirms that she's in again with her nervous little nod.

'I'll raise,' I tell them. 'Two articles, or you can chuck in and just take one off.'

I'm half expecting Alice to protest, but she just shrugs. Then she speaks up. 'I'll raise you again, then, double.'

'Hang on, I quit,' Miss Robin chirps up, and she takes off her boots.

Jim throws in too, and he's in trouble, because all he's got is his one-piece bat suit. Off it comes, and I'm trying not to laugh as he shows off his skinny frame and his bright-red boxers. Not that Miss Robin seems to mind, cuddling up next to him as he sits down.

'So?' I ask Alice, and I can already see those big round titties being hauled out of her bra.

She puts down her cards. Four fours.

'Shit!'

All four girls are laughing at me, even the owl. I've only got three articles, and they know it. If I chicken out it's going to spoil the whole game, and I'll have no chance. There's nothing for it but to strip off and hope they don't mind me being such an ugly bastard. Not that I'm completely devoid of masculine qualities, and I let my briefs go first, giving them something to ogle and taking their attention off my face.

They're loving it. All four girls are bright-eyed as my briefs come down, and once I'm naked there's a new tension in the air. We're going to go the distance, I'm sure, just so long as I get a little luck.

The pirate deals. My hand is useless and it doesn't get better, so I throw in. With Jim and me stripped down the girls aren't being so cautious any more. Nor's Jim. All five of them stay in. The pirate raises. Jim chucks in and off come his boxers. The owl doubles and I reckon we're going to see some titty. Miss Robin folds and she has to lose two articles. That's her tights for one, leaving her with bare legs, then she hesitates, starts to undo the little green jerkin thing she's wearing, changes her mind and whips off her knickers underneath it. They're green too, which suggests she was planning on somebody getting to see them. That somebody would appear to be Jim, but not just yet. When she sits down she's careful not to flash any pussy.

'Anyone else?' the owl asks, and she is sounding confident.

Alice hesitates, perhaps counting up how many articles of clothing she has on. The pirate just nods.

'Beat that,' the owl says, and lays down a full house of aces on kings.

Now it's getting good, and if I thought she was maybe going to be a pain I was wrong. She's well into it, and she's watching the two of them with a smile on her face, a wicked smile, as they stand up. It's four items each, and Alice is hesitating about what she's going to lose, which makes it all the sweeter to watch. Her shoes come off, that's two, and her legs are bare, so it's the frilly underskirt she's wearing, then it's her knickers or her dress.

Off comes the underskirt and she's hesitating a lot more, blushing too, but we're all waiting and nobody's standing any nonsense, not now. Alice's hands go behind her back and my heart skips a beat as she starts to pull down her zip. I watch as her dress goes loose at the front, letting her titties fall forward a little, but not free, because she has a little strapless bra on underneath. Not that it covers much, just cupping each breast. She is lovely, with two good handfuls of soft pink flesh, each topped by a perky nipple showing clearly through her bra. Her panties match her bra, small and made of thin cotton, so she's very nearly naked as she sits down. Me, I'm stark naked, and my cock has started to rise, which is embarrassing but nice in a way. Maybe I can persuade one of them to give me a hand, or something more?

The pirate has started her own strip as Alice sits down. We can all count, we know she's going down to her panties, and so does she. Her boots are already off, and her leather shorts are over her tights, so those have to go next. She's cheeky, turning around and pushing out her bum as she takes her shorts down, and now my blood's really pumping. Her tights come next, and she gives us the same treat, easing them down to show off a pair of tiny black knickers beneath.

Now for the real treat. She is no innocent, watching us as she slowly pulls her top up, inch by inch, showing off her belly, the slight rise of her ribcage, the undersides of her boobs, and at last all of it: two lovely round breasts bare in front of me, each topped by a dark-brown nipple, both of which are hard.

All I need to do is get Alice out of her bra and I've won my bet, but I really don't care about that any more. My cock is hard, sticking up between my legs like a flagpole and making Alice embarrassed. But the pirate gives me an appraising glance, with luck wondering how it would fit in up her neat little pussy, which is only covered by her flimsy panty crotch as she sits cross-legged. The owl doesn't seem to care. Her stare is fixed on the girls, making me wonder exactly what she's into.

'I'm going to get you,' the pirate tells the owl as she deals out the cards.

I take mine, wondering what I can bet with if I want to stay in. Not that it matters this time, because I've got rubbish again and I throw in. So do Alice and the pirate, hastily, and Jim, leaving Miss Robin and the owl: two birds, one slim, one plump, both about to be plucked nude with any luck.

'I'll raise you,' Miss Robin says.

The owl just nods. All Miss Robin has on is her jerkin and maybe a bra. The owl doesn't need to double.

'Aces and kings,' says the owl, laying out her cards.

'A flush,' Miss Robin answers, putting down a line of five spades.

My tension, and my cock, drop a little as the owl takes off her silly bird feet. Again the pirate deals out, and now it's serious: unless they all chuck in, a girl is going to get naked once the hand has been played out. I want my luck to change. I want four aces and I want the others to have strong hands too, so that I can get all four of them in the nude together. I don't get my aces, but after exchanging three cards I've got a full house, jacks on fours, which has to be worth a punt when I've got nothing to lose.

'I'm in,' I tell them.

Jim and the owl chuck in, then Miss Robin. The pirate hesitates, then says she's in. Alice is looking confident, but I want that bra off so badly.

'I'm in,' she says, 'and I'll raise you.'

'Suits me,' I tell her.

Nobody seems to mind that I've got nothing to take off.

'I'm chucking in,' the pirate says.

Just as cool as you please she stands up and slips off her panties, to show us a nicely shaved little cunt with a ring through her clitty hood. My cock nearly pops on the spot.

I lay down my hand, grinning at Alice but with my stare fixed on those barely contained knockers, which I'm sure I'm about to get an eyeful of. She cocks her head to one side, pulls a silly face and puts down her cards, queens on fours.

'Shame,' I say, 'so, er, what do you want me to take off, girls?'

I'm laughing, until the owl speaks up. 'You'll have to pay a forfeit. One of you spank his bum for him, will you?'

'That's not part of the rules!' I protest.

'Oh yes, it is,' the owl tells me, and the other girls agree in chorus. Jim just shrugs.

'I'll do it,' the pirate offers. 'On your knees, boy.'

I am not feeling happy, but just to look at her makes me want to melt, with those big round breasts bare. Maybe if I let her spank me she'll go further. There's no way I can back out, either, not with Alice still in her bra. I do as I'm told, kneeling with my arse stuck out towards the pirate. I'm still hard, and I know how I must look to her, with my balls dangling down and my cock sticking out fit to bust. Maybe she'll touch me up. Maybe she'll toss me off, and if she does I'm not going to resist.

She just laughs and comes forward a little, on all fours so that her gorgeous boobs are dangling under her chest. I watch them swing and bounce as she smacks me, ten times and quite hard, but I bite my lip to stop myself crying out. The girls laugh anyway,

Miss Robin even clapping her hands with pleasure at seeing me get it.

Spanked now and feeling a bit more cautious, I go back as the pirate deals out again. They're excited, all of them, and nobody wants to stop. My hand's crap, and I throw in, although there's a part of me that wants the pirate to spank me again, or maybe Alice. Both stay in the game, and Miss Robin. Jim's being a chicken.

'I'll raise,' says the owl, and she's looking right at Alice's tits.

Alice hesitates, then gives an uncertain nod.

The pirate folds. 'I suppose I have to be spanked now,' she says, and she doesn't seem to mind.

I go for it. I have to. After all, she's just done me. 'Let me have a feel of your titties and we'll call it quits,' I suggest.

'You didn't beat me,' she points out.

'Hang on,' the owl cuts in, and lays her cards down.

She has three nines. Alice has three eights, and it's time her knockers came out to play. I want to take hold of my cock as she stands up with her face set in the cutest little grimace you can imagine. Her hands go behind her back, she opens her catch and I nearly come as her tits loll forward under their own weight. One cup drops off, the other she pulls away, and she's showing two of the roundest, pinkest titties you ever saw. Now I take hold of my cock. I can't help it.

'Dirty pig!' Alice tells me, but that doesn't stop her pushing her panties down – and she's nude.

'Stop wanking, you!' the pirate demands, and she's climbing around on her knees.

She sticks her bum out towards us, stuck right up with her cute little cunt peeping out between her thighs and her bumhole showing. Now I'm glad the owl's a lezzie, because she takes a moment to admire the view before planting six firm smacks to the pirate's quivering meat. I'm still wanking, whatever she said, and I'd be there with a couple more jerks, but I force myself to stop. The way things are going it would be a waste.

'Now I'm *really* going to get you,' the pirate tells the owl, rubbing at her bum as she sits down again.

The owl just smiles, looking thoroughly smug. She's showing less than anybody and I'm starting to agree with the pirate. What the little bitch needs is her panties pulled down and her fat arse smacked in front of everybody, then maybe she should have my cock thrust between her monster tits.

I take my cards. If the winners are going to dish out the forfeits I'm determined to get my share, whatever it costs. I've got a pair of twos, but when I chuck three in I'm dealt the remaining two. Now they're in trouble, real trouble, but I try to look doubtful as I speak.

'I'm in, I suppose.'

'Me too,' Miss Robin says, and Jim chucks in again.

Both Alice and the pirate throw in too, adding to my frustration. But the owl stays with the game. I glance at her, trying to figure out what she's wearing under her costume. Knickers, presumably, and with knockers that size she has to have a bra. I need four to get her stripped and hopefully cop a feel of her giant titties.

'Raise you,' I say.

She just nods, but to my delight Miss Robin chirps up. 'Double.'

Now the owl's going down, for sure. She shakes her head and chucks in.

'Two items,' the pirate says gleefully.

The owl doesn't answer. But she stands up, looking as if she's some sort of martyr as she unzips her costume and peels it off. Underneath she's in big white panties and a plain, badly straining bra. Her tits are *huge*, bigger even than I'd been imagining them, as round as balls and fleshy too, real melons, with hardly any sag despite the fact that she's a bit of a dumpling. Her bra is coming off too, and when it does I feel my cock twitch at the sheer awesome size of her.

I'm wondering if the owl does men as well as girls and how it would feel to bury my face in her cleavage. I have to shake my head to get my mind clear enough to concentrate on my cards. It's just Miss Robin and me, and she's down to two items at most, so if I win she's in trouble. I lay down my cards. 'Four twos.'

Her hand goes to her mouth. 'Oops!'

She has a full house, fours on threes, and it's not enough. We're all watching as she peels off her jerkin. Underneath she's nude, with a pair of perky tits decorating her slender body and a nicely rounded little bum. I'm licking my lips, contemplating what I'm going to do to her, but Jim gives me a warning look.

'You're on, mate,' I tell him – and he immediately takes her down across his knees.

The little slut is sticking her bottom up and purring, and as he spanks her she sticks it up higher and purrs all the more. His smacks aren't hard, just playful, but they still leave her cheeks pink, and the moment she's been done they're in each other's arms. They climb up onto the bed, out of the game, and I'm wondering if it isn't time I made a move on Alice. But the pirate is dealing again. With three of us nude and the owl in just her knickers, whatever happens has got to be good.

My cards are crap, which is just fine by me because if I chuck in it means some sort of lezzie show, with luck, and the owl seems to be well up for it. I could never have imagined that she was such a dirty bitch. The pirate folds. Alice and the owl stay in. Alice wins and off come the owl's panties, exposing a big white bottom and a furry cunt, more than a little wet.

The pirate deals again, her fingers shaking, and I pick up. I have a pair of nines, and after I've swapped I have a pair of tens as well. Win or lose, I'm going to go for it. So is everyone else. Alice raises, the owl doubles and I redouble. Only then does the pirate chuck in, but she asks to have her forfeit held back until we know who's won. Alice doubles again, but the owl and I are sticking with it. I speak up.

'OK, whoever wins gets to do whatever they like.'

'Except for fucking – you're not fucking me,' the owl responds, her voice a weak croak.

I nod, hoping that the prohibition doesn't include fucking between her mammoth tits. Alice looks worried and glances from one to the other of us, but she nods and lays down her cards. She too has two pairs, sevens and fours. I'm going to feel her up. I'm going to make her suck my cock. I'm going to fuck her titties and spunk all over them.

I put down my cards. Alice looks at them and her eyes go wide. Her lower lip is trembling a little and her nipples are hard. I nod to her, just as the owl speaks up. 'Three kings.'

Both of us turn to look at the owl. Now I'm worried. The spanking I got from her hurt and I reckon she doesn't like men very much. Yet I've got to have Alice, if it takes all night.

The pirate gets it first, kneeling across the owl's legs with her bum stuck up as she's spanked, which makes her titties wobble and leaves her with glowing pink cheeks and a wet cunt. This time she makes no threats, and as she climbs off she kisses the owl who gives her a final smack and beckons to Alice.

Alice is not too sure about getting it from another girl. But she crawls across to the owl and gets into the same position, bum up and titties swinging. I can see everything – the full spread of her bare bottom with a tight pink bumhole showing between her cheeks and every crease and fold of a very wet cunt. The owl's enjoying it too, and she's in no hurry, stroking Alice's titties and bottom. When a finger goes up Alice's cunt I think my blonde beauty is going to protest, but all she does is make a little whimpering noise.

I've got hold of my cock because I can't stop myself. The pirate calls me a dirty little boy, but she's no better, with her nipples rock hard and one hand on her belly as we watch the owl deal with Alice, finger-fucking her and groping her tits, until Alice is gasping and moaning. I have to make a move or I'm going to spunk in my hand, so I crawl quickly across to the pirate.

'What do you think you're *doing*?' she asks as I take her hand, guiding it to my cock.

She doesn't mean it because she takes hold, wanking me, and as I reach out to touch her breasts there's only a moment of resistance. They feel every bit as wonderful as they look: full and firm, heavy and smooth. I begin to tease her nipples and she pulls harder on my cock, while across from us Alice's face is working in a weird mixture of ecstasy and consternation as the owl molests her, groping her tits, spanking her bottom and fingering and rubbing at her cunt.

I'm going to come. But Alice gets there first, closing her eyes and crying out as the owl brings her off. As she hits her peak I reach out and take hold of one dangling titty, just to help the owl make her come. Now there's no resistance at all, and I have them, both of those beautiful girls, one luscious, heavy titty in each hand, with the pirate wanking hard on my cock. I kiss her and she responds, her mouth opening under mine, and Alice is crawling over to us.

Then both of them are in my arms, my hands exploring as I please, cupping and stroking their breasts, with my erection poking up between us as they grope at me, squeezing and stroking my balls, jerking at my shaft, and all three of us kissing together, our mouths open and our tongues entwined. Even the owl is getting in on the act, masturbating as she watches us and fondling Alice's bottom.

The owl comes first, and the pirate is playing with herself too, sticky fingers pushed deep into her slit as she tugs on me. I start to kiss Alice and the pirate's tits, licking at all four fat globes in turn, sucking their nipples too. It's too much. I rock back, rising to my knees as I toss myself off in front of Alice.

'Me too,' the pirate sighs. 'Do it on me.'

'All three of you, please,' I gasp as the pirate moves in close.

To my surprise and delight, the owl moves in too, the three of them pressed close together, titties lifted for me to grope even as I jerk frantically at my cock shaft. Now *this* is heaven: three chesty girls side by side, tits held up for me to spunk over, and the best of the three actually rubbing at her cunt so that she can come as I do it.

Behind us Jim and Miss Robin have finished, and they're watching, the girl giggling as I let go and jet after jet of spunk erupts over Alice's tits, and the other girls' breasts too as I do my best to give each one her fair share. The owl gets it next, my jism spattering over both huge knockers and in her face too. The pirate has her mouth open, and some spunk goes in, the last drops, then my cock. She's sucking on me as she comes, squirming in ecstasy with her hand working between her thighs, her titties jiggling madly, her bottom stuck right out, cheeks wide apart, showing off her busy fingers and her twitching bumhole to her boyfriend and to our host and hostess as they all come through the door.

# Being Busty

Bronwen is a Welsh lass with a spectacular chest and one of the most extrovert personalities I have ever encountered. She plays rugby and goes in for women's wrestling, so despite her size she is remarkably firm. She is also remarkably uninhibited and regards her abundant chest as a positive asset to be flaunted if and when she feels so inclined. I have actually known her to hold a man down and shake her breasts in his face after he'd made a cheeky remark about her chest, a reaction that shocked him deeply, and she has provided the inspiration for the 'Modern Amazons' story that follows her confession.

She is full of entertaining tales but one of her best comes from an evening in a pub shortly after the Wonderbra was launched. Some girls were seated at a nearby table, all fairly drunk, with one of them proudly showing off her enhanced endowments by leaning forward to let the others see down her top. Bronwen happened to be passing their table on the way to the loo, and seeing this display she said, 'Those aren't tits. *These* are tits' – and flashed her 40EE chest to the girls and the rest of the pub, rendering everyone briefly speechless.

### Bronwen's Confession

'I have nothing to confess. I am completely innocent. Sure.

'I like to shock men, I do, and I get really pissed off that because I'm big I'm supposed to be this timid mousy thing who's ashamed of her body. Fuck that. I've got ten times what any skinny bitch has, and it's all natural too. I'm proud of my body, but it takes a real man to be my lover, not some wimp.

'Getting my tits out at rugby matches and stuff is no big deal. How about streaking? That's a laugh, but I suppose *you* want something good and dirty. There was a guy once who tried to stop me and the girls from coming into some shitty club in Nottingham. We sat on him and took turns to put our tits and arses in his face, right in the street. A lot of guys like that. A lot of guys would pay good money for that.

'There was one guy, when I was about eighteen. He was well into my tits, but he just wasn't my type at all, too weedy. I tried to turn him down gently, but he just got more and more persistent, sending me flowers and chocolates and that, and asking me out again and again. In the end I gave in and let him take me out. I made it plain that he shouldn't expect anything, but you know what that sort of guy is like. He just assumed that because I'd let him take me to a restaurant it meant we were an item, and when I told him no he got in a right state.

'I was going off to uni in a couple of days but he didn't know that, so after he'd been begging and pleading for ages I just grabbed his head and stuck it up under my top, hoping that would satisfy him. It didn't. The little bastard clung on like a leech, slobbering all over my tits while he tried to get his cock out. I let him do it in his hand, just to shut him up, although the way he was pushing his face down my cleavage I'm surprised he didn't suffocate himself.'

# Tales from the Boys – Modern Amazons

'That's the deal,' the guy in the yellow shirt tells me. 'You beat her and she blows you – right there in the ring.'

'Are you going to try?'

'What, get my dick out in front of a couple of hundred blokes? No way!'

I answer with a shrug and turn to where an impromptu ring has been set up in the middle of the bar. In the ring stands the girl who has made the use of her mouth the prize for any man who can force a submission from her. Barbarella, the posters say she's called, and something tells me that Barbarella does *not* expect to be sucking cock tonight.

She stands maybe six foot, maybe a little more, with a proud Latin face and a mass of jet-black hair tumbling down her back. Beneath the smooth feminine contours of her body she seems to be solid muscle, most of which is showing. Her legs are exceptionally long, rounded and well formed, yet as she paces from side to side of the ring, taunting the audience as she goes, her footfalls send just a faint tremor through her flesh. Her hips are big, her bottom a heavy rounded ball of muscle within her skintight leather shorts. Her midriff is bare, and I've seen male bodybuilders with less well-defined six-packs. Her arms match her legs, long and feminine yet decidedly muscular. Most impressive of all is her chest. Her breasts are huge and extraordinarily firm, each massive orb perfectly encased in the same black leather as her shorts. OK, so that's not going to help her wrestle – but it's sent the blood pumping straight to my cock.

It's not surprising that my companion at the bar doesn't want to fight her. No doubt he'd be more than happy to have his cock sucked in front of an audience, but he knows it's not going to happen. He's shorter than her for one thing, and probably lighter. He's also sober, relatively. If he fights he's going to lose – and he knows it.

Me, I'm not so sure. She's a lot younger than me and a lot fitter, but I must have at least eight stone on her in weight and my greying hair and tailored suit make me look like the well-heeled oil analyst I am and not the roustabout I once was. Maybe I can take her.

Maybe. If not, what do I care? My ego's not so fragile that I can't laugh it off when I get beaten by a woman, and I'm not going to be the only one either. In fact, I don't mind the idea of having her pin me down, perhaps with those massive breasts right in my face. I'd rather win, and if I do I'm going to make her drain me dry, because I need that blow job really badly.

Six weeks in Alaska taking samples of crude oil in some of the most godforsaken wilderness on earth. Six weeks of biting, cock-shrinking cold and not so much as a tatty old porno mag for relief. Six weeks without so much as a *sight* of a woman, let alone any sex. Yes, maybe I can take her.

Not yet. First I want to size Barbarella up. She's strong for a woman, obviously, and my bet is that she's skilled too, or she wouldn't be up there whipping up the audience to pay their money and climb into the ring with her. It's fifty dollars a go, which may be a bit steep for some of the local rednecks, but I've lit cigars with bigger bills.

I order a beer, watching her as I drink it. Now she's really getting into her act, calling out to men in the audience and calling them cowards and weaklings. A lot of them are already drunk and it can only be a matter of time before one rises to the challenge, especially when Barbarella suddenly jerks down the zip at the front of her top and wrenches it wide open, showing off her bare breasts.

They really are impressive, great heavy bumpers of flesh topped by long dark nipples, both of which are hard. She's firm too, amazingly firm for such a chesty girl, with no more than a couple of inches of sag from inside a leather wrestling top to bare. I want to suck those tits, rub my face between them, pull her nipples until she moans, fuck in her cleavage and come all over them – all that, and more.

Finally somebody rises to the bait. He's one of a group of men, locals, all pushing him forward, no doubt in the hope that she's going to make a fool of him. It looks pretty likely. He's tall but skinny, with sandy hair and protruding teeth above a weak jaw, a real hayseed. And he's drunk, his face red and his blue check shirt open to the waist to show a pigeon chest thinly covered with gingerish hair.

Barbarella does her top up while the man pays his money. He climbs into the ring, braying like an ass and calling out remarks to his mates who are cheering him on and making obscene suggestions about what he should do with her. She takes no notice but sinks into a crouch, her arms spread, her dark eyes fixed on his body. She reminds me of a stalking cat, absolutely poised and purposeful, full of energy and tension.

He comes on, crouched low like she is and beckoning to entice her into a move. She is not to be drawn, merely moving slowly sideways to stop him getting at her flank. One of his friends calls out, reminding him that he's said he'll give her a spunk facial. He turns his head, just a little, and she moves.

She's on him before he can even react, his arm caught and twisted up into the small of his back, her weight on him, and then he's flat on his face and pinned to the mat. I don't know what the move is called but it's pretty effective. She has him helpless and furious, thumping his one free fist on the canvas and bleating pitifully that it's not fair and he wasn't ready. Her response is to catch his other arm, turn him slightly to the side and lean forward to shake her breasts in his face, slapping the heavy leather-covered globes against his cheeks.

His friends are going wild, clapping and catcalling and suggesting that she should give him a spanking. Barbarella threatens to do it but he gets into such a state that she lets him go, laughing at him and asking if there are any real men in the audience as he scrambles hastily from the ring. She's well pleased with herself, raising her arms in victory as she makes a lap of the ring before once more beginning to call for challengers.

I'm still not sure. The skinny fellow was a pushover, true, but she was frighteningly fast and skilled. I didn't realise that losers risked serious humiliation, either, and I suspect that she won't let the next one get off so lightly. That is, if there's going to be a next one – the men in the audience seem pretty wary of her.

Not all of them. A man steps out from the shadows at the back of the bar. He's young, lean but well muscled, and his shirt is already off in readiness. There are tattoos on his arms, a snake curled around one and a pattern of death's-heads on the other. He has a strong, serious face beneath a mop of tawny hair and from the way he carries himself he seems to know what he is doing.

I immediately wonder if it's a fix. He doesn't look the type, and nobody else seems to know him. Then again, nobody knows me either, and what man wouldn't like his cock sucked by a beautiful girl? Plenty, is the answer to that, if it has to be done in public and after beating her in the wrestling ring. This guy, I'm not so sure. He looks like he stepped out of a Hollywood movie studio, and the way he flicks out five ten-dollar bills onto the table looks like showmanship to me.

Barbarella is waiting for him, and both of them crouch down as soon as he's in the ring. He's wary, and his attention's not going to be distracted by anyone, so she comes straight in. Their limbs tangle as each of them tries to get a grip on the other and they disengage. She jumps back in a way that makes her breasts bounce while he staggers away and clutches at the ropes for balance.

He's not a local and the crowd don't want him to win, jeering at him and making suggestions to Barbarella about what ought to be done when she has him helpless. Neither of them takes any notice, circling warily before suddenly joining battle again. He manages to jerk her top up this time, spilling out her breasts. Either it's part of the act or he's done it to distract her so that he can get a proper hold. But if so it doesn't work. Instead of pausing to cover herself up as any normal woman would do, Barbarella uses the moment to get him in an armlock, from which he escapes only with a frantic lurch.

They break apart again and the crowd are cheering and whistling with delight at the sight of Barbarella's naked breasts. Once again I feel my cock stir and I know that I'm going to have to take my turn, whatever happens to the man who's now in the ring. Again they close, and this time he goes for her shorts. Immediately she slaps her hands down to stop herself getting stripped, but his move is only a feint, and before she can react her arms are pinned to her sides in a bear hug.

Barbarella's still fighting and they go down together, landing hard on the canvas, which seems to knock the breath out of her. He has her pinned in an instant. After just a moment of wild struggling with her face set in frustrated rage that may or may not be real she gives in. The crowd is cheering immediately, their allegiance changed to the winner on the instant and with no sympathy for Barbarella whatsoever. They call for her victorious opponent to take his cock out and get her sucking, to fuck her breasts and make her do his balls, to stick it to her so that she gags on his knob, and to spunk in her face.

He just smiles and looks around the room as he rises. Barbarella stays on her knees, gasping for breath, defeated, looking up at him as he eases down his fly's zip and pulls out a thick dun-brown cock. He's right in the middle of the ring and she is forced to crawl to him on her hands and knees, with her leather-clad bottom sticking out at most of the audience and her heavy breasts swinging beneath her chest in plain view.

The crowd have begun to chant 'Blow job, blow job, blow job', and he is standing with his hands on his hips and his cock and balls hanging out, looking down on Barbarella as she crawls over to him. She tries to rearrange her leather top but he shakes his head and she stops, leaving her breasts naked as she kneels at his feet. He reaches out to grip her by the hair, takes hold of his cock in his other hand and feeds it into her mouth. Her cheeks pull in and she is doing it – she's sucking cock in public.

Part of me wants to feel sorry for her, because surely she has to be ashamed of what she's doing? Yet she doesn't show it, sucking and licking at the young guy's cock and balls with every evidence of skill and long practice. I wonder if that may be what gets her off – being defeated and made to perform sex acts in public – because if it isn't then she ought to be an actress.

He's looking down at her as she sucks, betraying nothing of his feelings as his cock grows to erection, even when he's hard and she's sucking vigorously on the head of his prick and tickling him under his balls. Only when she starts to wank him into her mouth as well does it become too much. He grunts, and then he's come, full in her mouth with his hand locked in her hair so that she's forced to swallow his spunk.

The crowd are well pleased, cheering him to the echo, and suddenly there's no shortage of challengers. Men are queuing up and I join the line. But my stare is still fixed on the guy who beat Barbarella, and as he climbs out of the ring I swear that he winks at her. So it *was* a fix. But I still reckon I can take her, especially after she's had five or six bouts. In fact, with the number of people who want to fight her she's going to be exhausted. She'd be better off if she just climbed down to the queue and got sucking. Or so I reckon.

What I don't realise is that Barbarella's not the only wrestler on the programme. She takes the next two guys down, one easily, the second not so smoothly, but he's sporting and doesn't make too much of a fuss when she sits on his back and spanks his bare arse. The crowd now know that she can be beaten and that she sucks for real so they're still well up for it – even when Barbarella says goodnight and climbs down from the ring, making way for another girl.

This one's called Stomper – and I can see why. She is huge: not as tall as Barbarella, maybe, but a lot wider and a lot heavier. Older, too. Her thighs are like tree trunks, and her backside wouldn't look out of place on a carthorse. As for her tits, if I thought Barbarella was busty then I didn't know the meaning of the word. Stompers's bazoomas are gigantic, like those earth-mother figures that ancient peoples used to carve, only there is nothing motherly about her. She looks downright evil.

I'm not at all sure if I want to face her, and I'm not all that sure if I want a blow job off her either. Then again, it doesn't really matter if I want it or not. *Nobody* is going to be getting his cock sucked by Stomper. A sumo wrestler might be able to take her down, but no one from this bunch of drunken townies and farm boys could. Certainly the guy who's next up won't be enjoying the pleasures of Stomper's mouth because he's rooted to the spot and his face is working in fear as he stares at her. She grins and pulls him up into the ring, one-handed.

He gets taken down – no surprise. Stomper doesn't have much in the way of technique, just brute force. He tries to run, but she's faster than she looks and he's caught in seconds. The entire crowd are staring in fascination and horror as she tucks him under one brawny arm, pulls down his trousers and the under-pants beneath and spanks him until he howls. Unlike Barbarella, she's not big on mercy.

The next guy goes down just as easily and gets his backside smacked. Next comes a big fellow, over six foot and solidly built, but he doesn't have the moves. After ten minutes of grunting and straining they call it a day and he leaves the ring with his pride intact. Now I know Stomper does have skill too, and I'm hoping she changes over before it's my turn to go in.

My card is numbered, and there are five more guys to go before I'm on. The first one chickens out, trying to make a joke of it and asking for his fifty dollars back. He doesn't get it, and the jeers and boos are louder than if he'd taken his medicine. The next one puts up a fight. Stomper gets him in the end but lets him keep his jeans up as she slaps him, and I know she's getting tired.

The third guy's just a clown, trying to get a rise out of Stomper by imitating her. He succeeds – and he also succeeds in getting his head sat on during his spanking. The sight of his face disappearing beneath Stomper's monstrous bottom is highly comical, or at least it would be if I wasn't up myself so soon. She pulls his legs up for his spanking, his arse bare, his cock and balls flopping around while he's done. He starts to get hard, which the crowd thinks is hilarious, and he's not so full of himself when he finally leaves the ring.

Two to go. But to my immense relief Stomper takes her applause for the night after vanquishing the next man and retires. I can feel my tension growing as I wait to see who'll replace her, but whoever it is she has to be easier, surely? 'She' is a tall athletic blonde who calls herself Lightning. She's impressive in her way, but she doesn't even have Barbarella's weight, never mind Stomper's. I can see that she's younger, too, and she doesn't quite have their confidence. Maybe it shouldn't, but that turns me on.

Lightning looks good, very pretty, and she's in cut-down jeans and a short top that's tight over full breasts, high and well rounded, the way I like them best. Now I'm really getting hard, because being sucked by her is going to be quite something, and I promise myself that I'll do my best to get her tits out before the end. First I have to beat her, and to judge by the way she's handling the man who's just climbed up into the ring that's not going to be so easy. She's fast, really fast, with some good moves too, and she's making him look like an idiot. He never even manages to catch her. The bell's gone before they've even really come to grips and she's laughing at him as he climbs out of the ring.

I'm on, and I walk down. Like the other men that the locals don't know I get booed and they're calling out for Lightning to win. I hardly hear them, concentrating on her as she crouches down, as lithe and as poised as a big cat. She's watching my eyes, ready to react to whatever move I make. I can't catch her, I know that: she's too fast, too slippery. But I have to make a move and I come forward slowly. She waits until I'm close, darts off to the side, swings back around me and before I can react she's given me a kick in the backside. The crowd loves that – they're hooting with laughter as Lightning and I face off again.

This time I meet her stare, my mouth set in a firm line. Then it suddenly goes slack as I clutch at my chest and sag down onto the canvas. My face twists in pain as I look up at her. She's coming forward, worried about me, and I've got her before she realises that she's been tricked. My weight is on top of her, her shoulders are pressed hard against the canvas. She's still wriggling, but it really only makes her tits quiver. I've won.

The first thing I do is pull up her halter top and spill out those fine big breasts. Lightning protests, but I've still got her pinned and they're soon out, two full mounds of firm pink flesh on her chest, each topped by a conical nipple just a couple of shades darker than the surrounding skin.

'If they stay out,' I offer, 'I promise I won't make you gag. I won't even make you swallow.'

Lightning's response is a dirty look but after a moment she nods. I let go and stand up, raising my hands in victory. The crowd don't really like it, but they sure want to see her suck and the dirtier spirits among them are already clapping. The few women in the hall are either calling me names or demanding that I get my cock out. Some are doing both.

Lightning comes up to her knees, grovelling prettily for the sake of the show, although she does not look happy about what she now has to do. Again there's that hint of vulnerability, and again it turns me on. I've promised that I won't make too much of a pig of myself, but looking down on her I realise that it's not going to be easy. She's kneeling at my feet, a defeated girl ready to suck my cock and with her top pulled up to show her firm, heavy titties, the conical nipples now sticking up and a little apart.

I reach down to tickle them. She tries to pull away, but I've caught hold and I spend a moment fondling one plump globe, feeling its weight and texture and running my thumb over the nipple, until at last it begins to grow stiff, the bud popping out under my touch. At that Lightning gives a shiver, and a low moan comes from deep in her throat. She's quite helpless. I squat down and take hold of her other breast as well, exploring the pair of them with the blood already pumping into my cock.

So long without a woman and now I have her, to amuse myself with as I please, and her tits are far, far too good to be wasted. I stand up and unzip, pulling out my cock. The audience are as noisy as ever, but I'm barely aware of them as I snap my fingers at Lightning and point to my prick. I've stepped back a couple of paces and she's forced to crawl to me, her titties swinging and bobbing beneath her chest. This time there's no dirty look, only downcast eyes as she comes up fully onto her knees and takes my already erect cock into her mouth.

I put my hands on my hips, showing off a bit as she sucks. It feels good to have so many people watching as such a beautiful girl is forced to go down on me. I take her hair, pulling her head back a little to make her suck on my knob as I start to wank myself down her throat. With that her big blue eyes turn up to look accusingly at me and remind me of my promise. She's right. A few more hard tugs and she'd be getting a mouthful, while the temptation to jam my prick down her throat and spunk in it as she gags on my knob is hard to resist. I manage to hold back, though, because I have a better game plan.

My cock is rock hard as I pull it out of her mouth. Lightning looks up, surprised, but as I squat down she realises what I'm going to do. Briefly she protests, but I've already wrapped those meaty titties around my cock and I'm fucking her cleavage. She calls me a bastard but then she takes over, holding her breasts up to squeeze them around my cock and jiggle them. I'm looking down, watching the head of my cock pop up and down between those soft meaty pillows as the expression on her face moves between pleasure and resentment while her breasts are used.

It looks good, too good, and Lightning's expression changes to one of shock as several weeks' worth

123

of spunk erupts full in her face. Some of it goes in her mouth and over her nose, a little trickles into one eye, but most of it splashes back down over her tits, and for one perfect moment I'm fucking in the well-lubricated valley of her cleavage, made superbly slick with my own sperm. She gives a little sob, maybe of excitement, maybe of disgust, but I'm too high to care as I finish off by popping my cock into her mouth to be sucked clean, with her still holding up her spunk-smeared breasts.

I'm done, perfectly content, and so is she, giving way to Stomper once more in the ring. The crowd are with me, well pleased to see Lightning so well used. Men I've never met before slap me on the back and offer to buy me beers. I accept a few, propping myself against the bar as I settle down to watch the rest of the fun. Not that there's much, because the crowd is getting rowdy after my performance with Lightning and they want to see Stomper made to suck cock. She's no fool and quits while she's ahead. The three female wrestlers retreat to jeers and offers of money for sex.

With my sexual tension gone and the show over, I settle down to some serious drinking, joking with the men around me as we sink rounds of Bud. It's good, but by about one in the morning the long journey that I've had is starting to catch up with me. I'm also getting randy again, wishing I'd taken longer over Lightning and wondering if there's another girl to be found. Not in the bar there isn't, or at least nobody to compare with her, and I decide to call it a night and content myself with a porno and the use of my right hand back in the hotel.

By the time I get there I'm ready to drop, with just about enough energy to strip off and shower, then stick a DVD on as I towel myself down. The film's nothing special, just your usual American industry stuff, full of girls with dyed blonde hair and more silicone than there is in the valley. I watch anyway, sipping a beer from the mini-bar, and after a while I lie back on the bed, my towel over my middle and one hand on my cock. On the screen a girl who looks more like Jessica Rabbit than a normal human being is riding a man, her colossal, impossibly firm tits bouncing to a rhythm that is as soporific as it is arousing. I'm drifting towards sleep, and I'm almost there when there's a knock on the door and a female voice calls out.

'Room service.'

I'm fairly sure that room service doesn't include what I want. But when I tell her to go away she knocks again, and speaks once more. This time there is something unmistakably sultry in her voice, and familiar. Surprised and a little hopeful, I walk to the door and open it a crack. Outside is Lightning, now in a long coat and shades, over the top of which she is looking at me with those same big blue eyes I remember from when her tits were wrapped around my cock. I open the door to let her in but before I can close it I realise she's not alone. Stomper and Barbarella push in behind her.

'Hey, I –'

I stop. Somehow I don't think they're in the mood for reasonable discussion. As Stomper steps forward and pushes me back onto the bed with a single well-placed shove I'm seriously considering calling for help. Only the fact that she has let her coat fall open stops me. She is almost naked underneath, her massive breasts and the solid bulge of her belly showing. I decide to wait a little.

'You weren't too nice to my girl, were you?' she drawls, her voice coarse, its accent from somewhere in the South.

'It was the deal,' I point out. 'You set it up yourselves – nobody made you.'

'Yeah, that's right,' she replies. 'But you cheated, mister, and where me and my girls come from we don't like cheats.'

'It was a fair move,' I protest. But I know I'm lying.

What I don't know is what they're up to, because Stomper has come close to the bed and is standing over me with her chest on show and just a pair of knickers to cover her sex. I'm torn between fear and lust, because while she may not be all that prepossessing it looks like both Lightning and Barbarella are dressed the same way.

'What are you going to do with me?' I demand. 'I can call the staff.'

'You yellow?' Barbarella asks.

As she speaks she opens her own coat. Like Stomper she has very little on underneath – nothing, in fact, except her knee-length leather boots, so that the richly furred swell of her pubic mound and her massive breasts are bare. I find myself swallowing, just as they turn to look at the TV on which the girl with the pneumatic chest is now being fucked from behind, with the camera focused on her face and her swinging breasts.

'Hey, girls!' Lightning laughs. 'He was jacking off!'

Barbarella laughs too. Stomper grabs my towel and before I can stop her it's been jerked away, leaving me stark naked with my half-stiff cock lying on my thighs. All three of the girls grin as they crowd closer, and again I feel that flush of mingled fear and anticipation. I move back a little, still very uncertain despite their obviously sexual intent. After all, just because they're having fun with all this needn't mean that I'm going to enjoy it.

'What are you going to do with me?' I repeat.

'You got a straight choice, boy,' Stomper drawls. 'You say sorry to my girl or we're going to tie you up like a hog for market and dump you a couple of miles down the highway.'

That's an easy choice.

'I'm sorry, Lightning,' I say. 'It was wrong of me to trick you like that.'

'Damn right!' she answers. 'And what's with fucking my tits? That was no part of the deal.'

'I just like them,' I say, shrugging. 'Like I said, I'm sorry.'

'That ain't much of an apology,' Stomper tells me. Now she has begun to remove her coat.

Part of me wants to scream for the staff, another wants to see what's going to happen, which is why I don't react as she pushes me all the way down on the bed and straddles my body, pinning my arms. Her monstrous breasts loll forward into my face as she lowers her weight onto me and as they squash out over my eyes and nose and mouth I'm helpless, unable to see, hardly able to breathe, smothered in fat pungent breast-flesh with my legs kicking feebly and my cock and balls fully exposed to Lightning and Barbarella.

'Suck on this, baby boy,' Stomper drawls as she feeds a nipple into my mouth.

I try to resist, but one of the other girls closes a hand on my balls, her nails digging in under my sac. With no choice in the matter I start to suck, making Stomper laugh.

'He's suckling me, girls,' she says, 'suckling just like a piglet. Now you girls have your fun, and you, boy, you keep your mouth busy at what you're at, and don't say a word. Got it?'

I try to nod, not that she can see me with my face completely enveloped in her breasts, but she can certainly feel. Her nipple is huge, filling most of my mouth, and for all her bulk there's no denying her femininity. Worse are the two other girls who have my cock and balls completely at their mercy. I'm genuinely scared, but I know I can scream if I have to, and I try to just let it happen, even as my legs are pulled up and apart, because I can feel my cock stiffening again.

Now I'm really spread out, and the girls can't help but notice.

'Look at baby boy – he's getting a hard-on again!' Barbarella calls out. 'Hey, Mom, look what you're doing to him!'

Stomper just laughs and pushes her teat more firmly into my mouth. But the others grab hold of my cock and balls, wanking me hard and squeezing my sac until I'm wriggling beneath their mother's weight. I'm completely helpless and the knowledge that Stomper and the younger women are a mother and her two daughters is making me more aroused than ever, causing the girls to squeal in sadistic delight as my cock grows in their hands.

They're right up against my raised legs, their breasts pressing against the flesh of my thighs and helping to hold them up. I can feel their nipples, and I'm sucking not just willingly but eagerly. Lightning laughs and I feel something wet on my balls: one of them has spat on me, and again, lower down. Something hard and round presses against my anus. I don't know what it is but all I can do is relax as I am penetrated. Both girls dissolve in hoots of laughter as they watch until Barbarella calls out: 'Hey, Mom, we've stuck a bottle up his ass!'

'You do that, baby,' Stomper grunts. 'Fuck it good. How'd you like it, mister – how'd you like getting fucked?'

I don't answer. I can't. I'm writhing beneath her weight as her daughters start to bugger me, feeding the beer bottle I'd been drinking from in and out of my anus. I'm barely able to breathe, unable to see, and yet my cock is in a state of raging erection, as stiff as I've ever been and ready to spunk. The girls press still closer, squashing their breasts against my legs and around my balls, rubbing my cock on their nipples even as they jerk at me and thrust at my anus. Helpless, smothered in breast-flesh and well and truly buggered, I can hold back no longer. I come all over the girls' breasts as I feed on their mother's teat, a long moment of blinding, jerking ecstasy that leaves me weak.

When I'm done they *really* get to work. I'm made to lick up my own come from the girl's breasts. I'm made to kiss Lightning's anus to say sorry for what I did earlier. I'm made to crawl to each of them in turn and lick them to orgasm, but I no longer care. For this night at least they have made me their grateful slave.

# Being Busty

Angela is over-endowed, by her own standards and by those of any but the most fanatical of large-breast devotees. Her measurements make a mockery of the conventional scale, obtaining bras has become a nightmare for her, and in hot weather her breasts become so uncomfortable that she is seriously considering surgery to have them reduced to a more manageable size. Despite all this, in the right circumstances, with the right men, her abundance of flesh can be powerfully sexual.

She says, 'It's as if men want to *drown* themselves in my chest. They just can't get enough. OK, it's only some guys, but I'm a big girl all round, and the way the mags and the TV go on you'd think I wouldn't get any male attention at all. The truth is that my worst problem with sex is guys who come off in their hands while they're still paying attention to my boobs, or who want to fuck them instead of my pussy.'

### Angela's Confession
'It's not easy when you're my size. Everyone stares at my breasts, and most of the time it's as if being big

makes me some kind of idiot – and as if it's my own fault. Blokes stare all the time, most of them with a sort of horrified fascination, some with a guilty look, like you know they want it but wouldn't dare try. Then there's the few, the ones who are genuinely obsessed with big breasts and don't give a damn what other people think.

'I know this sounds pathetic but I always gave in easily, just because it was so nice to feel appreciated for once. Before I came down to London my sex life was a string of rude encounters followed by getting dumped the moment a possible boyfriend's mates found out and started to laugh at him. I turned to Net dating in the hope of finding somebody better, which led to me moving down south, but was a mistake. Jacob wasn't really into big girls at all, he was just so insecure that he wanted a partner he felt nobody else would find attractive – which, believe me, is less than flattering.

'We didn't last, hardly surprisingly. But by then I'd started to go to this club especially for big girls and that was where I found my niche. With the first black guy who approached me I thought he was taking the piss, which I'd had men do to me before. He was six foot, in his mid-twenties, and absolutely gorgeous. I couldn't believe he'd be interested, but he was genuine, and a really nice guy as well. He wasn't the only one, either.

'I really let myself go, making up for years of lost time. One time, I remember, at that same club, I took four guys into the loos. All of the men were black, and each one of them was far better-looking than any of the blokes I'd been out with before. It felt amazing, after a lifetime of rejection, to have four men all over me. I let them strip me naked, and they stood round me as I sucked them and played with them. I wished

I had four hands and four mouths and a big black cock in every single one. All four of them came for me, in my mouth and over my tits, and I was so high that I was rubbing the spunk from one into my nipples while I sucked the next, and playing with myself too. I must have come five or six times, and since then I've never looked back.'

# Tales from the Boys – Tom

Her blouse is going to rip. It has to. There is no way a few pieces of thread can hold in a pair of tits like hers. They are fucking huge, the size of footballs, easy, and just as round. She shouldn't be allowed out like that, not even in her own garden. It's an incitement to crime, and she's got Long Max so hard that my balls are starting to turn blue.

She's pretty, with blonde hair down to her shoulders – real blonde, I reckon – and her nose turned up in the air, a bit like a pig, a nice cuddly pig, but, fuck me, those tits. Her blouse is putting up a fight, but it's not going to win. It can't. If she bends down to pick one more weed out of that flowerbed of hers it's going to go. Out they'll come, two great big love-balls, all pink and soft, just nice to stick eight inches of dick between.

'She's got to come out sometime,' Bodrum Mick says, for maybe the thousandth time, breaking in on my plans for Miss Titties down in the garden below.

He's talking about Jacqueline Desmond, the one we're staking out for pics, but when it comes to looking Miss Titties is the better deal. He's a Turk, Bodrum, and a right pig with the girls. Likes 'em with plenty of everything, he does, so Miss Titties is right up his street.

'Bollocks to Jackie D,' I tell him. 'Take a gander at this.'

He swings his lens round, aiming down the same way as mine, takes a while to focus, then nods real slow, like a butcher sizing up a prime piece of meat – which is exactly what he is doing. After a bit he moves his prick in his jeans and gives his verdict. 'Jesus, you won't get many of them to the pound.'

'You won't get *any* of them to the pound, Bodrum my son,' I tell him. 'I reckon she's got ten pound of titty flesh in each holder there, easy.'

'Ten pounds?' Gorgeous Gussie chips in, zooming in on her himself. 'I wouldn't think so, although she is certainly well endowed. Consider, she weighs perhaps ten stone, of which her breasts cannot possibly represent more than five per cent, so –'

'Shut up, Gorgeous,' I tell him. 'What do you know? You're a bum man, you.'

He is and all. Comes of going to public school, where they're so used to sticking it up each other's poop chutes that when they get out they like to do the same thing to girls. Dirty bastards. Gussie is, anyway, for all that he looks like he's been modelling for Moss Bros or something. He's our face man, 'cause the tarts'll always talk to him on account of how he looks so nice. They may think different once he's had them up the shitter but it don't matter by then, 'cause the pics are in the can. Even the marks slow down for him, sometimes.

That's the two sorts of women you get in my business: tarts and marks. Now your tart, she wants to show off, and she'll let you get a picture easy, maybe take her tits out if you ask nice. But your mark, now she's already made it, and she's going to give you a hard time, 'cause once they've got a few quid in the bank they always think they're so fucking superior. I mean, they make you laugh, yeah? Just 'cause they're getting knobbed by some footballer they think they're Princess fucking Diana.

Jacqueline Desmond, she's a mark, big time. It's like this. We're on this hill, the usual boys, five experienced paps. That's myself, Bodrum Mick, Gorgeous, Mick the Sleaze, and Rattigan. On one side of the hill there's Phil Desmond's place, which is the dog's bollocks: big garden full of statues and shit, swimming pool, the works, all packed away behind fuck-off big gates, a security fence and a pair of Rottweilers who'd have your nads for lunch soon as sniff your arse. Phil, he's just been signed by United, seventy-five grand a week, and he's an all-right bloke. Jackie, now she's a stuck-up bitch, but the punters, they love a bit of that. Ten grand for a good shot of Jackie, easy. Get her with her tits out and you're on more than her old man. Not for me, 'cause I'm in-house. But I still get a nice fat bonus.

Stupid really, 'cause she ain't got much up top at all, and what she *has* got is mostly silicone. Who wants to see that? I like 'em real, big and round and bouncy, with fuck-off big nipples on the top, sticking up like wine corks. Which is why, after waiting all fucking day for Jackie D to come out of her house, I've turned my lens the other way, down the other side of the hill, where my busty little cracker is doing the weeding.

She is better than looking at some rich bird's empty garden, far and away better. Every time she moves I'm sure that blouse is going to break and it's all going to come tumbling out, or maybe she'll fancy a bit of sunbathing and strip off. Now that *would* make a peep show, no error. I could probably even sell the pics to one of the mags for a few quid, and bollocks to the Sexual Offences Act. Who's going to know she wasn't posing? Fake up a release and you've got it. Better still, make it legal.

'D'you reckon she'd go for it?' Mick the Sleaze asks, his filthy little mind following the same track as mine.

It's his job, Mick's, getting the dirty pics for the rags, celebs with their tits out on the beach, pissed It girls showing their knickers and that. He's good at it too, skinny and a short-arse, so they never see him coming till his camera's halfway up their twats.

'Could be,' I answer him.

'You've got to be fucking joking,' Rattigan says. 'What, go for a couple of hundred with her when you could get ten large for Jackie D? You're fucking losing it, the pair of you.'

Now Rattigan, he's a wicked bastard. Do anything for money he would, and he's got about the same amount of conscience as a shark. He's got about the same taste in women as a shark, too – always goes for their legs.

'Ten large for you, maybe,' I tell him. 'Not for me.'

That's the thing, you see. Everything I take, it goes straight to the boss, Ed – Mr Crawshaw he likes us to call him, only he's no different from the rest of us, just older, that's all. He was taking snaps of girls with their tits out back in the 1960s, and his eyes still haven't gone back in his head properly. Most of his hair's gone, too, from all the wanking. Ugly bastard.

Ed'll take anything of Jackie D, and I get my bonus, but *Good Morning* only want shots of celebs, 'cause that way they can show pics of girls with their tits out and claim it's in the public interest and all that crap. Now Miss Titties, she's just your ordinary girl next door, and *Good Morning* won't want anything of her, even tits out. That means I can sell where I like, and it's getting tempting.

She's quit with the weeding, and is unfolding a sun lounger, with all twenty pound of titty meat jiggling in her blouse as she tries to get the lounger open. I'm zoomed right in and just for a second I can see right down her front, with all that gorgeous meat just hanging there, pink and soft and ripe for the fucking.

'Nice,' Bodrum drawls, only to pull his camera back around real fast as Rattigan gives a warning grunt.

Jackie's door's opened, just a crack, but Rattigan's clicking away like he's got a pair of A-list movie stars in his sights, stark naked and with their tongues up each other's jacksie. I don't bother, 'cause I seen it all before. She knows we're there, and she's taking the piss. Odds on she won't come out all day. Sod her. I'm going to give Miss Titties a go, see if I can't talk her out of her bra for a pony.

'I'm off,' I tell them as the door shuts again.

'To do what?' Rattigan demands.

'Her, with any luck,' I tell him.

'You're fucking mental, you know that?'

I don't bother to answer him, and start off down the slope. Miss Titties's house is one of a terrace, all the same, with little square back gardens lined up at the bottom of the hill. Soon I'm down there, and she's looking surprised to see a bloke leaning on her garden fence with eighteen inches of monster lens in his hand. I give her the spiel: how I couldn't help noticing her, how she's amazingly beautiful, how I'd love to take some photos of her, the works.

Close up, she looks even better. She's maybe twenty-two, maybe younger, and she's still got a bit of puppy fat on her. I say a bit. Down her blouse she's got enough for a litter of St Bernards, lovely skin too, like cream, and she *is* a real blonde. She's chatty, friendly like, and soon I'm in the garden.

'Who do you work for, then?' she asks when I've given her my card.

'*Good Morning*,' I tell her.

She reads *Good Morning*.

'Do you suppose I've seen anything of yours?' she asks.

'Sure you have,' I tell her.

She has, plenty.

'I suppose you're after the Desmonds?' she asks.

'That's right,' I admit.

She's a bit doubtful, but I give her the old sensitive bit, explaining how I don't really like that part of my job but it pays the bills. I prefer more artistic work, I tell her, but there's not much market for it. She asks a few more questions, the usual stuff: do I know many celebs, do I do the royals, what do I think of the whole Princess Di thing? I give her the usual answers.

All the time this is going on, yours truly is trying very hard not to stare at those bounteous titties. It is not easy, 'cause she's got more breast meat than a Christmas turkey, and the old titty rod won't go down. I reckon she's noticed too, 'cause she's trying not to look, just like I am. She's not running away, either.

I give her a bit more spiel and take a few shots, arty stuff and no use to anybody really, 'cause pretty girls with their clothes on are ten a penny. As I take them I give her plenty of flannel, telling her how wonderful she is and all. When I say I'd rather be looking at her than Jackie D she giggles, like we both know it's impossible. It's not, it's the plain truth, and I tell her so. She's flattered, I can tell, and it's odds-on that those big fat titties are going to be coming out before too long. I decide to go for it.

138

'How about a few teasing ones?' I ask. 'Maybe with your blouse a bit down or something?'

She takes a glance either side, checking to see if any of the neighbourhood gossips are about, and cool as you please she undoes the top button of her blouse, showing a good three inches of deep pink cleavage. I nearly come in my boxers and then it gets better. She gives a little shrug and her blouse is down off her shoulders, showing her bra straps. I've got a good line for that.

'Nice,' I tell her. 'But your straps don't look good like that. Would you mind tugging them down so they don't show?'

She wouldn't mind, and down they come, showing off more flesh – pale, smooth, creamy flesh. Once again her eyes flick down a little, and I'm beginning to think I may be in for more than I bargained for. I know the lads'll be looking, and I want to make the bastards green. Miss Titties makes the adjustments and her shoulders are bare, and more, 'cause the highest button of her blouse that's still done up is now under serious strain and there's a fair bit of tit bulging out at the top.

'Beautiful,' I tell her, and I mean it. 'A little more, perhaps?'

I don't say a little more of what – I leave that to her. What she does is to look me right in the eye and unsnap another button. Now I can see right down her cleavage, with those two big pink love-balls pushed together to make what just has to be the most darling cock-slide in existence. She knows it too, and I'm wondering where she gets all her confidence when she bends down and lets 'em loll forward. Now there's twice as much cleavage on show.

'Gorgeous, just fucking gorgeous,' I tell her and that's the end of the pretence.

139

Her fingers go down to the next button and I'm clicking away like crazy, catching every movement as she lets it all out, opening her blouse to leave the pair of them straining out of the gap, pushed together so she's got plenty of cock-slide on show, which is well inviting. Her bra is pink, and it's big, 'cause no small one's ever going to hold her. But it's nice, with plenty of lace, and her nipples show through, good and hard.

'Do you think we should go indoors?' I suggest, 'cause the boys'll be looking and even if she doesn't care who sees I'm not having pictures of me giving her one in every office from Wapping to Outer Mongolia.

She knows what's going to happen if she lets me in, and she hesitates, just for a second. Then she's reaching out her hand and I've taken it, letting her lead me indoors. Inside, it's all very smart, nice new kitchen and a main room with a big glass table and black leather furniture. That's where she takes me, and she's giving me a peep show before I've had a chance to set the tripod up again.

The last three buttons go and her blouse is right open, and off. Now I can really see her figure. She's got a neat little waist, which makes those titties look even bigger, and she's all soft and rounded, not an ounce too much, not an ounce too little, not on her tummy and hips, which are half showing out of her low-rise jeans. Up top it's a different matter. She's got more than any one woman has a right to have but, boy, am I glad of it. I can't take my eyes off them.

'Would you like me to take my bra off?' she asks.

'Yeah, that would be good,' I tell her. The understatement of the fucking year.

Now I'm all eyes, watching her as her arms go behind her back to get at her catch. She looks a little bit shy, which is nice, and a little bit excited too, which is even nicer. There must be three or four hooks there, just to hold it all in, so it's giving her a bit of trouble, making her titties jiggle. Then it's open, and they've flopped forward, not much at all, 'cause she's wonderfully firm, but still forward, making them look bigger and rounder than ever.

Her cups are loose, and I can see down one, to a rosy-coloured curve at the top of one nipple. She gives a little giggle, probably 'cause I'm drooling down my chin for her, and takes them in hand, still holding her cups on as she sticks them out at me, teasing. I'm still taking pictures, but I've got the camera on LCD so I can watch those titties in the flesh, waiting for the moment when she reveals all.

And she does, peeling one lacy pink cup off and then the other, all the time with a little smile on her face like butter wouldn't melt in her mouth. They're gorgeous, better even than I'd imagined, so big that she's having trouble holding them up in her little hands, and pale, and real smooth. Her nipples are big, and lipstick pink, and hard, just as I'd imagined, like a pair of little corks sticking up in the air.

'You like my boobs, don't you?' she asks, all cool and innocent, like she wants to know if I like the colour of the wallpaper.

I don't really manage an answer, just a sort of gurgling noise. She giggles again and makes quick work of peeling off her bra, then starts to jiggle them about and bounce them in her hands. That's too much for yours truly, far too much. I come forward and grab them. She gives a little squeak of surprise, but she doesn't back off, and they're in my hands, those beautiful titties, ten pounds each, easy, and so firm. I stick my head between 'em, rubbing 'em against my face. I squash 'em together and lick right up her cleavage. I suck her nipples, squashing those great big titty-pillows together so that I can get both of her nips in my mouth at the same time.

All the time she's giggling, and she's backed up against the wall, but once I've been sucking for a bit she gives a little moan. I suck harder and she moans again, deeper, getting well into it. And so am I: my cock feels fit to burst, and when I finally come up for air she notices immediately, looking down at the bulge in my trousers.

'You look like you could use a little help with that,' she purrs, and her hand is on my crotch.

*She* doesn't need any help, none at all, pulling down my zipper and burrowing in with what feels like long practice. I'm still feeling her up, squeezing those monster titties and tickling her nipples, 'cause that's what I'm after, just like she's after what she now has in her hand.

'I suppose you'd like me to take you upstairs?' she purrs.

'The way I feel right now, you can take me out in the garden,' I tell her, and she gives her little giggle again.

I couldn't get any harder, and the way she's wanking me I'm going to come on her tummy, which is where I'm pointed right now. She stops, which is just as well, only she doesn't let go but leads me by my cock, out the room and upstairs. Her bedroom's well girlie, no sign of a man at all, which makes life a lot easier. I strip off, knowing I won't have to do a runner, and so does she.

Nude she's an absolute doll, with a bouncy little arse and just the sweetest little cunt peeping out from between her thighs, a real blonde bush too. A bit of a kiss and cuddle, just to be a gentleman, and I lie down on the bed, 'cause I know how I want her. It is definitely not her first time, 'cause she knows exactly what to do, climbing on top and guiding me into her.

I reach out and take hold, feeling 'em bounce in my hands as she rides me. Her eyes are shut and there's a look of bliss on her face, lovely, but it's those titties I'm thinking of. They're just so big, so heavy, so good. I can't get enough. It wouldn't matter if I was up her for ever, I still couldn't get enough. I just need her. I need her huge tits, in my hands and in my face and around my cock, for ever.

Almost too late I stop myself, or I'd have given her a cream filling in under a minute and she wouldn't have got hers. Always let 'em get their kicks: that way they'll come back for more. I want more of Miss Titties, a lot more, so I try and take it easy, closing my eyes to shut out the sight of all that gorgeous jiggling meat and trying to think about something else, like Bodrum's face when I tell him I've been up to my balls in dolly bird.

That helps, 'cause there's nothing more likely to put you off sex than Bodrum's face, but I'm still sheathed in tight slippery cunt, and I've still got two of the finest titties I've ever had the pleasure of in my hands, and it is not easy. She's started wiggling her arse too, like she's trying to rub herself on me, and that's almost too much. Only now she's there, wriggling her cunt on my dick and screaming her head off, and at the last second she snatches her titties out of my hands, squeezing at 'em and pinching her nipples as she comes.

I let her finish, but I'm not taking any bullshit about what happens after. As soon as she's climbed off I've got her in position, sitting with her back to the wall and me straddled across her front. She's a good girl and holds 'em up for her titty-fuck, with her own cunt cream making her cock-slide nice and

143

slippery. It is heaven, with those great fat pillows of titty-flesh wrapped around my shaft, and my balls slapping on her hot skin, and her rock-hard nips rubbing on me, and her gasping and giggling and telling me she's glad I like her boobies.

That's what does it for me. She's getting off on her own titties, and I love that. Some girls just don't seem to get it, but not this little darling. She loves 'em, rubbing 'em round my cock and laughing 'cause I'm so into them. I think of how she showed 'em to me, loving every minute of it, and how she had a good feel when she was coming. That's too much, and I'm creaming all over 'em.

She takes it well, still holding 'em while she gets her pearl necklace and giving me a nice kiss to finish off. I stick it in her mouth, just to say I've done it, really, 'cause I'm already coming down, but she seems to like to suck, and I leave it there till she's finished. Now, up until this point I've not really been paying a lot of attention to my surroundings. Who would? It's only as I'm waiting for her to finish with my prick that I take a look, and I'm a bit surprised.

It's a girlie room, like I said, but I hadn't realised just how girlie. There's a poster of Beat Boys up on the wall, and another one of Martin Steele. There's dollies too, and teddies, and OK, so that's not so unusual for a girl, but there's loads of them, and they're mostly pink. That don't fit with the smart new kitchen and the leather décor. First I'd had her down as a bored housewife; married young and up for a bit 'cause she's pissed off with being stuck at home all day. Once her titties were out she could have turned out to be a Martian for all I'd have cared, but now I see the truth. It's her parents' gaff. Now she's no jailbait, not with a pair like hers, but I have to ask. 'How old are you, darling?'

'Eighteen,' she says, cool as a cucumber, and this while she's wiping my spunk off her tits – with her knickers if you please.

I don't rightly know whether to feel ashamed of myself or well chuffed. But I've done the dirty deed and she seems happy enough, so what's to do? She's very cultivated about it too, offering me a cup of tea when we're dressed and asking if I take sugar. There's two sorts of biscuit and all, Rich Tea and those with the little bits of chocolate in, very nice. I'm just on my second cup when her dad comes in.

Now he's a big bastard, with tats all down both arms and oil on his hands, so it looks a bit iffy at first, but I've soon charmed him round and we're sitting down at the table cosy as you please. He's a Spurs fan and all. Talking footie with a bloke when you've just spunked all over his daughter's tits takes a bit of getting used to. But it's all sweet, at least till the daft cow goes to put her dirty knickers in the wash basket, right on top, with the arse piece looking like she's just mopped up a broken gold top.

# Being Busty

My own dear wife is by no means under-endowed – how else would it be? – and has kindly provided a few insights into being busty from the female point of view. Like most well-endowed women she finds that male attention tends to be directed to her chest, which can be a good or a bad thing, depending on circumstances. Being bisexual, she has also found that her breasts provide a good way of finding out whether or not other girls have similar inclinations, as those with a lesbian streak are also invariably drawn to her chest.

She takes particular pleasure in smothering her partners' faces – men's or women's – against her chest, and also in being suckled, but not in being clamped or tormented as she is too sensitive. When being titty-fucked she enjoys the friction against her nipples as much as or more than the feel of a cock between her breasts, and the sense of holding herself for it to be done to her. Another thing that she enjoys, perhaps not immediately apparent from a male perspective, is the feel of the weight of her breasts, particularly when she is in a kneeling position for sex, when they've just been exposed. Best of all, she relishes when she has been put across the knee for a spanking and her chest has been exposed to add to her humiliation.

### Penny's Confession

'So many confessions, so little space. Where do I start?

'How about going dogging in the car parks below Alexandra Palace? That could be great fun, although it could be risky too. Long before we were married we used to go up there with my friend Yvonne and get up to all sorts of things, generally with an audience. I love the buzz of knowing that there are people out there in the dark and yet only glimpsing the occasional movement or a hint of somebody's face.

'We'd always bring a few beers or a bottle or cider so that Yvonne and I could screw our courage up a little, but it didn't take long. The first thing was always to lift our tops, just to show our bras first, then all the way, so we'd be sitting there, our tits bare as we showed off and touched ourselves – and each other. Yvonne always made a point of stressing that she wasn't a lesbian, but that didn't stop her playing with me, or letting me play with her. Sometimes we'd even suck each other's nipples hard.

'Sometimes we'd leave it at that, or just sit topless while we took it in turns to toss off my boyfriend. Sometimes it would go further, and our knickers would come down so that we could be spanked while leaning across the back seat. Or we'd take it in turns to do each other. That was always my boyfriend's favourite thing, and he'd sometimes make us pose like that while he tossed himself off, with our bare bottoms stuck up and our tits dangling underneath us, so that anyone out in the bushes would get a fine view.

'Yvonne had quite small tits, what my other half calls apples, but with quite big pointed nipples. She was exceptionally slim, so she always gave the impression of being a lot bustier than she really was. I'm rather bigger, and fuller. I like to think that between us we gave a great many men a happy evening.

'This was all some time ago, before dogging had really caught on, although there was no shortage of dirty old men in the bushes. What we never managed to do was involve another threesome and the only time we tried to it ended up in a car chase. I still don't understand the man's objection, unless it was that the two girls who were with him weren't actually willing to play and he was simply jealous.

'We've always liked sharing a girl, particularly a busty girl. One memory that stands out is our half-Japanese friend Micki, who has lovely big breasts and adores having attention paid to them. Her favourite thing is to have as many people attending to her as possible, or being passed around at a party to have her breasts felt, her nipples suckled or even put in clamps. But my own favourite thing was to have her sit between us, with one lovely round breast each to be kissed and licked and suckled while she masturbated, after which she would always be more than willing to go down on her knees for me.'

# Tales from the Boys – Tom in the Ladies

Why does everybody think blokes like me are complete bastards, just because we take pics of celebs? We're just doing our job, that's all. I take the pic. A magazine buys the pic. You buy the magazine. Simple. You think we killed Diana? Bollocks. *You* did.

Another thing. These celebs need to realise who makes 'em. We do. So they ought to show a bit of fucking gratitude, you'd think? Fat chance. They're supposed to be role models too, specially for young people, so if they get up to naughties it's our job to inform the public, yeah? So you see, when I catch Catherine Whitefern in the Ladies' bog at Club Sophisticat, snorting coke up her pert little nose from off of her mate's titties, my duty to you is to get the pics and sell 'em.

OK, so what I do is take a couple of pics, then ask if I can join in. She tells me to go fuck myself, so now I'm going to publish the pics. A bit of gratitude, maybe a tits-out blow job from the pair of them, and I'd keep my gob shut and nobody else would see the pics. OK, maybe not, 'cause if Ed 'Mr' Crawshaw doesn't want them for *Good Morning* then I am going to make a mint from the sleaze mags.

It's not an easy job, either. I have to fight to get out with my camera, with three fuck-off big bouncers on me. I make it, but one of them catches me a shiner and a half, so bad that the quacks have to put a stitch in above one eye. It fucking hurts and all, but it's worth it. I can see the headlines already: 'Catty Cathy in Lezzie Coke Romp' maybe, if it's in *Good Morning*, or more like 'Blowing Bazookas!' if it's in a rag.

Ms Whitefern's going to wish she'd blown me, she really is. Now she's in shit, and I don't give a fuck. In my job you can't afford to be compassionate. You don't think about all the sponsors who're going to go ape shit or how she's going to keep herself in Prada and Gucci when she's had all her contracts cancelled. You take the snaps, pocket the dosh and leave the hacks to fit the moral bullshit to the pictures.

So that's the way it stands. I take the pics in to Ed and he is well pleased. He wants exclusive, no time limit, but a bit of bargaining and I make him see the error of his ways. We agree on two days' exclusive before I can put the pics on the open market. It makes sense. His way I get my bonus, he gets a pat on the back from the Big Boss. My way, I get my bonus and the freelance money, he gets his pat on the back and a percentage of the bonus. The Big Boss, he'll be too happy looking at his circulation figures to worry about it.

I make for the coffee machine, and who should be there but Katie from accounts. Now Katie, she's the office hottie, well posh, and with the best tits in the place. Not the biggest, maybe, but the best. If rumour is to be believed, she's well dirty too. Ragi, from down in the mail room, says she sucked his cock and he's not known for bullshit. Me, I've wanted her out of her bra since the first day I saw her.

Unfortunately Katie seems to have a blind spot for me, or maybe she's only into black cock, 'cause so far she's knocked me back every time. That doesn't stop me thinking about it, 'cause she *is* fucking gorgeous, nice and slim, with a little round arse and those gorgeous tits. She's pretty too, and friendly, but with that snotty way posh girls have, which makes you want to bend them over forwards and fuck them up the arse with a titty in each hand while you do it.

Today she's wearing a sweater, cream-coloured cashmere, which makes her titties look bigger than ever, and sort of mysterious, like you want to see more. I *definitely* want to see more, but she's a bit wary of me these days 'cause she knows I fancy her and maybe doesn't want to admit to herself that she feels the same way towards me. But like I say, she's a nice girl, and very sympathetic, so when she sees my shiner she comes straight over to me.

'Oh, Tom, your poor eye!' Katie says. 'Are you OK?'

'Yeah, it's nothing,' I answer, touching my eye like it hurts ten times worse than it really does, 'cause if there's one thing I know it's that you never can tell where a bit of female sympathy will lead. They love it, all that injured-warrior stuff.

'No, it's not,' she assures me. 'Here, let me look. Oh dear, that is terrible. Have you been to see the nurse?'

'I dropped in on Casualty at St Mark's,' I tell her, 'and there's only the one stitch.'

'Oh, you poor thing! What happened?'

I've sat down on the chair next to the coffee machine, and Katie's making lovely soft cooing noises as she examines my eye. Those lovely titties swinging in her jumper are just a few inches away. This is not the time to tell her the truth, 'cause she's sure to side with the girls – not all the truth, anyway.

'Goes with the job,' I tell her, real casual. 'Some people don't like their photos taken, and a lot of 'em employ bodyguards.'

Katie gives a little tut of disapproval, clearly aimed at whatever bastard took a swing at me. I wince as she touches the cut, always a good move, although in this case it's not a fake one.

'They want you well enough when they're trying to make it,' I go on. 'But they soon change their tune once they've got there.'

She gives a shake of her head, which makes her tits wobble and increases my heart rate by about double.

'It wasn't even a sneaky shot,' I lie. 'I asked and everything.'

Again she shakes her head, and again her titties do a little dance in her sweater. If she keeps this up I'm going to burst a blood vessel, but I can't resist it.

'Lost his temper right off, the bodyguard did,' I tell her.

I'm waiting for the head-shake shimmy, but she stands up. 'Maybe a dab of TCP,' she suggests. 'I've got some in my desk.'

Amazing the things women keep in their desks. Useful, though.

Katie trots off, her neat little arse wiggling under her office skirt. I'm a bit on the hard side, what with thinking all morning about what I saw in Club Sophisticat and then Katie wobbling her knockers in my face, and I wonder if I might not push it a bit. She's well posh, like I said, and she turned me down flat at the Christmas party, but Ragi got his and there's nothing like having been in the wars to get a woman going. It's got to be worth a go, and when she comes back with the TCP I give her a line. 'This is a bit embarrassing, Katie.'

'Oh, don't be silly.'

'I don't mind you doing it, but maybe in the loos or something? I wouldn't ask, only he gave me a couple of nasty kicks and all.'

'Whereabouts?'

'My legs, mostly. Split the skin, he did.'

'Ouch! You poor thing – but I can't go into the Gents', Tom.'

'The Ladies', then.'

'You can't go into the Ladies'.'

'On the third floor, I can. There's only blokes up there.'

Katie knows that's not strictly true, and she's still not sure about it. But she's a natural mum and after a bit more argy-bargy she goes for it. Either that or she's after the same thing I am only she doesn't want to look easy. So it's up the lift and off to the Ladies' loo, only just as we're about to go in who should be coming out but Philippa Mellors, the old bag who writes the morality column. She notices my black eye and the look she gives me is anything but sympathetic. But she doesn't say anything and as soon as she's gone we nip inside.

Katie's still playing Little Miss Nurse and it takes me a bit more persuasion, and the suggestion that Philippa Mellors might have seen us go in and will come back, before she'll go into a cubicle. When she does I lock the door behind us and drop my kecks to show her my bruises – and something else besides, 'cause Long Max is doing his best to get out of my boxers. She has to notice, but she plays it cool, dabbing a piece of cotton wool where my skin's cut, but she's going to have to go lower, 'cause the bruise is right down my thigh. I think I'm going to burst as she takes the hem of my boxers and tugs them down a little, dab dab dab with the TCP, and a little further down, and dab dab dab with the TCP, and a little further, which is too much for Long Max, who's just popped out to have a look round.

'Tom, *really*!' Katie says.

'Sorry, love, can't help it,' I admit. 'You turn me on.'

'Well, put it away,' she says, all very understanding but firm too.

'You wouldn't, would you?' I ask.

'Wouldn't what?' she asks back, as if she didn't know.

'Toss me off,' I suggest. 'Come on, darling, I can't go back out in the office like this – look what you've done to me.'

'I haven't done *anything* to you, Tom King!'

She has, though, and the evidence is right there in front of her face, all eight inches of it. I take hold and give him a little tug, like I just can't help myself. She bites her lip.

'You do it, then,' she says suddenly, 'but *really*!'

I nod, trying to look apologetic, and push down my boxers as I take my seat. Katie stands back, trying to look like she's pissed off with me, but it's not working. Her eyes are big and round for one thing, and they're staring straight at me. Soon she's biting her lip again, then suddenly she's sat down on my knee and she's got me in hand.

'Honestly, Tom, what would my boyfriend think?' she asks, wanking away for England.

She's still trying to sound like she's only doing me a favour. If that's the game she wants to play, then fair enough.

'Don't tell him,' I suggest. 'Thanks, Katie, love, I need this bad.'

She makes that little tutting noise again, but this

154

time there's some sympathy. I let my hand stray to her bum – just testing the water. All she does is wank harder, maybe keen to get me off before I get out of control. Maybe keen to get me off before *she* gets out of control. I'm going to come if I don't watch it, but I try to hold out, sure that she's getting horny. Thinking of Ed Crawshaw's face does the trick, and now she's stroking my nuts and running her thumb up over my helmet, nice dirty tricks every girl should know.

'You're lovely,' I tell her. 'Really lovely. I've got to see you.'

As I speak I've started to pull up her jumper, real urgent, like I'm about to come. Katie squeaks, but there's no real fight in her and up it comes, over a nice lacy bra, white, with those two lovely round titties sitting in their cups like a pair of puppies in a nest, their little noses poking through the material.

'Beautiful,' I tell her, and before she can stop me I've caught underneath her cups and pulled 'em up, flopping out those darling boobies right into my eager little hands.

'Tom, no!' she yelps. But I'm already rubbing my thumbs over her nipples and she gives a sort of choking sob.

Boy, she looks good, her face and neck all flushed now, with excitement and embarrassment too, I reckon, her nice creamy-coloured jumper and her bra pulled up, and those gorgeous titties bare and jiggling from the motion where she's wanking me. I just keep groping, doing my best to get her going properly, although if I spunk in her hand right now I'm still going to be well chuffed.

She's given in, pushing out her tits and making little moaning noises in her throat as I feel her, and she's not wanking as hard, more having fun with my cock than trying to get a dirty job done quick. I'm happy with that, just as long as those darling titties are out, and when I take one in my mouth there's no resistance at all, just a low moan. She's stroking my hair as I feed on her tit, real mumsy, but she's wriggling her bum on my leg too, which ain't.

'Would you like to climb on?' I offer, 'cause it's getting to look like Katie wants her own.

'Oh, God, I'm going to do it. I'm going to fuck you, Tom,' she says.

Now she's let go of me, and she's in a right state, trying to get her tights and knickers off at the same time before she's even bothered to take off her shoes. She gets it right in the end, though, and up comes her skirt, showing off a neat little cunt, all shaved 'cept for a tiny triangle of fuzz right over her slit.

'Very smart,' I tell her. But she's not listening any more.

Katie climbs onto my lap, facing me with her legs across my body so that I can guide Max into her cunt. I oblige, and she's well juicy, taking him nice and easy as she sighs in pleasure. Her arms come around my neck and she's riding me, bouncing up and down on my cock, which is just heaven, 'cause, the way she's stuck on, it puts her titties right in my face. I grip her under her bum and bury my head between 'em, licking and kissing them, sucking her nips and making 'em slap in my face.

That is good, real good. I'm lost in Katie's titties as we fuck, with her little round arse in my hands and her hair flying everywhere. I'm going to blow, I have to, and I've done it, right up her cunt with my face buried deep between those heavenly titties. She's nearly there too, wriggling on my cock like she's demented and saying the dirtiest things. Well, you have to oblige the ladies, so I stick a finger up her arsehole like she wants and go back to titty-sucking as she brings herself off on my cock.

I remembered that she said she had a boyfriend, just before I spunked in her, so it's no big deal. Any problems, and he can carry the can – although you've got to watch it a bit nowadays, what with genetic testing and that. She doesn't seem to care anyway, just acting a bit shy as we clean up and making me promise never to tell anyone. I give her my word, telling myself I might actually keep it and all, 'cause she's far too posh for the likes of Bodrum and Mick the Sleaze to perve over. She's tells me it has to be a one-off too and I agree, only I'm not so happy about that.

As I come out of the loo I am feeling well pleased with myself, too well pleased to really watch what I'm doing. And what do you know? There's Philippa Mellors standing by the sinks, arms folded under her saggy little tits, looking at me like I've just twanged her knicker elastic.

'I suppose you realise that I am going to have to report this?' she says – and, boy, is she loving it.

'There's nothing to get worked up over,' I tell her. 'Katie was just giving me a couple of dabs of TCP to help with my cuts.'

'No, she was *not*. You were having *sex*.'

The way she says 'sex' it's like she's accusing us of cannibalism at the very least. Probably 'cause she doesn't get enough herself and, frankly, who'd give her one? She's always been like that, though, and I know it's no use arguing. So far as she's concerned, when it comes to sacking offences, having a quick shag in the staff bog is well up there with flogging stuff to the competition, telling the proprietor where he can stick his head and maybe even setting fire to the print shop. Our only chance is to bullshit our way out.

'No, we were not,' I answer her, all offended. 'As I said, Katie was very kindly attending to my cuts, that's all.'

'Why didn't you go to the nurse?' she demands.

Well, the nurse hasn't got a pair of D-cup knockers for a start – on account of being a bloke, mainly – but this is not the time for funnies.

Katie comes out of the cubicle behind us. She has a brain, and has smartened herself up properly and disposed of all incriminating evidence. She also has the bottle of TCP. When she speaks her voice is straight out of the freezer. 'Are you accusing me of improper conduct, Miss Mellors?' she wants to know.

'Frankly, yes,' comes the answer. 'I heard you, and I know what I heard. You were having sex.'

'That's insulting!' Katie answers. Which is when they really start in, hammer and tongs, the way only women can, 'cause any two blokes would come to blows in no time.

Katie's an ace, all cold and formal, like you'd never think she'd been riding on my dick and telling me to finger her bumhole just a few minutes before. Unfortunately, when it comes to being a haughty bitch Philippa's got twenty years of experience. She knows she's in the right, too, 'cause she must have heard everything. Finally it comes down to brass tacks.

'We'll see what Mr Crawshaw has to say about it, shall we?' Philippa says, smug and nasty.

'Very well,' Katie answers, and off we go.

When we tell him what's going on Ed Crawshaw puts his sensible face on, the one he wears when he's on the BBC. Makes him look fair and equitable, it does, when the truth is that he's a mercenary bastard like the rest of us. He's got Philippa saying we did and Katie saying we didn't. There's no separating them, but here's the bottom line. Philippa, she's a big name, been doing her column for donkey's years and gets a bigger postbag than the problems page. Katie, she does her job OK but Crawshaw can get another accounts clerk any time he wants. Me, I've had more formal warnings than any of them have had hot dinners, but I'm good, and he knows it. I also have an ace up my sleeve. On the other hand he's been itching to make an example of somebody for months, on account of him reckoning we old hands don't give him enough respect.

So it may well be that he wants Katie or me for the chop. Make it Katie, and he's going to have her union on his case, screaming sexual discrimination and unfair dismissal. Make it me and, well, I've worked it out even before he's given us his first portion of bollocks-speak.

'The situation is this,' he says. 'First, may I say that I appreciate your concerns, Miss Mellors, and that you were correct within the scope of company guidelines on male/female staff relationships to bring this matter to me, particularly with respect to issues of, er, respect. However, as I am no doubt sure you will appreciate, I cannot accept your statement in the face of Miss Chesham's flat denial. Therefore, insofar as you are concerned, Miss Chesham, I am asking you to accept a purely informal warning and return to your desk.'

Katie's off the hook, and she looks well relieved. But Philippa bloody Mellors won't leave it.

'I cannot accept that as a decision, Mr Crawshaw,' she says. 'Disciplinary procedures are absolutely clear in stating that we operate a zero-tolerance policy with regard to sexual discrimination, and so far as I, and no doubt every other woman in this building, is concerned, Miss Chesham's act in permitting Mr King to enter the Ladies' toilet represents an intolerable affront to women's rights to privacy and respect for that privacy, and is therefore in gross breach . . .'

Philippa Mellors goes on a bit, but I can see Crawshaw wilting. If there's one thing that the Big Boss is hot on it's women's issues, and Ed's wondering if he wouldn't rather handle the union. At last she shuts up – and, sure enough, he's changed his mind.

'Well, yes,' he says, 'you are of course correct, Miss Mellors, and therefore . . .'

Now Philippa is looking well smug, and Katie looks like she's going to be sick as Ed goes on. But she doesn't have to worry. I stop the flow and ask for a chance to speak to Ed alone. Philippa gives it a bit of strop at that, but she reckons she's won and in the end she goes. Katie gets told to wait outside in the corridor, like she was a naughty schoolgirl.

'Best leave it, Ed,' I advise as the door clicks shut.

'I'm afraid that's out of the question, Tom,' he starts, all mock friendliness.

'No, no, you don't see it, do you?' I tell him. 'How many times have I cut you a percentage for allowing me to sell out of house?'

Suddenly he's not looking so happy, for real. 'That's blackmail, Tom – you can't.'

'Try me.'

We go on a bit, but the upshot is I get another formal warning and Katie gets off free – well, *almost* free, 'cause now those nice big titties are going to be coming out of her bra again, and soon. OK, so I am a complete bastard. But that's just me.

# Being Busty

Miriam is a Londoner who subsidises her normal income with a little domination. Her speciality is body worship, for which she is admirably equipped. At around five foot eight, with a womanly yet elegant figure and a 38DD bust, she has found that she tends to overawe many men, which by good fortune is entirely in keeping with her own natural sexuality. I myself was not a little impressed with the sense of presence and command that she projects, and although it is not usually my thing I could well imagine myself grovelling in adoration of her magnificent chest.

Miriam seldom allows physical contact, and any man who wishes even to see her chest fully naked must beg very earnestly indeed. A few in fact prefer her to remain clothed, often while they themselves are naked: they simply want to gaze at the twin objects of their adoration, covered though they are, as she moves about the house. More frequently, she will dress in one of her collection of beautifully made corsets or something else from what seems to be a never-ending supply of lingerie and simply pose while the man concerned kneels naked on the floor to masturbate. Occasionally she will go bare for some lucky or privileged male. But actual contact is something that she reserves for a few favoured lovers, preferring to keep her 'slaves' at a respectful distance.

Whatever the case, Miriam's own pleasure comes from the power of having a man at her feet, so lost in awe at her breasts that he is driven first to beg for what she could give so easily, then to masturbate, completely surrendering his dignity in his need. As she says – 'It's wonderful to think that men get so excited over me. My breasts are simply part of me, something I have all the time and can conceal or reveal at will, play with when I please, adorn how I please, while to them they are objects of worship. What better than to see the craving in a man's eyes as he masturbates over something that to me is so everyday? It makes me feel like a goddess.'

### Miriam's Confession

'I keep firm control over my relationships, and only ever get involved with men who will follow my personal rules and accept punishment from me if they break them. The trouble is, a lot of them *like* to be punished and will deliberately break the rules in the hope that I'll administer it. Sometimes that goes too far, like the man who wanted to do my washing-up in nothing but a frilly apron, then broke half my dishes in the hope that I'd beat him for it. I didn't. I just made him pay for the crockery, then threw him out.

'Usually they're not that bad, but I do like to play a little game in which they do get punished but not in the way that they want. Most of them want to be spanked, preferably on their bare buttocks and over my knee so that they can try to rub their cocks against my thighs. I won't have that, so I make them touch their toes or kneel on a chair instead. There was one man I really made to suffer.

'He wanted to worship my breasts, but he was incredibly fussy over the details. I had to be in black boots with at least four inches of heel, leather trousers and a leather waspie, also long leather gloves and a veil, so that only my chest was exposed. He then wanted me to stand over him while he masturbated, so that he could look up to my breasts. As you can imagine, that sort of gear doesn't come cheap. But I said I'd do it if he paid for everything. He didn't like that, but was willing to do it as long as he took the clothes away afterwards so that nobody else could ever appreciate me in them. I told him not to be ridiculous, and finally we agreed to pay half each and that I'd keep the clothes.

'The first couple of times he came it was OK, although he was so demanding that I wasn't getting much out of it myself. I had to stand in exactly the right position, looking down with my chest stuck out and my hands on my hips, and stay like that until he'd finished himself off, which used to take ages. He wanted to touch me too, and for me to come down over him and lower my breasts into his face so that he could suck on me as he came.

'I wouldn't have that, but he got increasingly desperate and demanding until eventually I agreed that he could – as long as it was on my terms. By that time I was really fed up with him, and I'd discovered that he was quite homophobic too. So what I did was to invite this gay friend of mine round, Rick, a huge fat guy with an enormous beard, what's called a bear. Rick got himself ready in my bedroom over a gay-bondage magazine, and when the client was fit to burst he came in. I was sitting in a chair, with the client kneeling in front of me, pulling at his cock as he waited for my permission to suck my nipples, and Rick simply walked up to me, spunked all over my breasts and then told the guy to get licking. He was still trying to get his pants up as he went out of the front door.'

# Tales from the Strange Ones on the Outside – Buying Bras

I know I shouldn't do it, but I can't help it, and I'm
not really hurting anyone, am I? I just like bras, that's
all – and more than that, I like women's breasts. I like
them so much that I can barely say the words. Am I
worthy to say the words? Probably not, but when I
do it sends a shiver right through my body and my
cock starts to grow. I can't help it.

To me, a nicely presented lingerie catalogue is
far more alluring than any crude pornographic magazine. I could stare for hours at all those pretty
girls in their pretty bras: everything from sweet
little A cups up to the magnificence of the double
letters, the FFs and GGs, designed to hold in
real women, big women, powerful women. White
is nice, pure and virginal, the colour of the proper,
the untouchable woman. Red makes me scared,
the colour of the woman at play, the lively, the
aggressive woman, who always makes me feel so
weak. Pink is feminine, something I worship, something I aspire to so much but can never attain,
any more than I could be a god. Green is for
the army and that scares me more than red; a

six-foot fifteen-stone woman in a khaki uniform, with a mid-green GG holding in her bounties, it makes me feel faint. Blue is free and beautiful as only a woman can be. Yellow is mischievous and hints at what might be done to me for the thoughts in my head and what I dare to do. Black – black is best, the colour of the dominant woman, the woman who understands the goddess within herself and will take no nonsense from mere men. I love them all, though, and I'm not worthy of even the least. But that doesn't stop me going out shopping on a Saturday. I can't help it.

I don't remember when I started to like bras. I think it's always been a part of me. I remember the first time I went shopping. I had a girlfriend at the time, Naomi: Naomi of the beautiful dark hair; Naomi of the tight sweaters; Naomi of the perfect B cups that she permitted me to see one chilly autumn afternoon on Hampstead Heath. She was so lovely, Naomi, full of life and health, and her breasts, so perfect, high and proud and firm, her nipples pointing just a little above the horizontal and each of them a perfect circle of rose-tinted flesh.

That day I remember as if it was yesterday, walking hand in hand in the chill air, Naomi talking of this and that, me wondering if I dared to suggest that she invite me closer to the objects of my worship. I kissed her in the woods, and she didn't seem to mind. I kissed her again and dared to let a hand steal to her chest, to touch the outline of one divine breast beneath her sweater, and she let me. I asked if she would, just maybe, lift up her sweater for me and show me her bra. She did, and more, laughing at me for my eagerness as she tugged up that soft black sweater to show a pretty white bra, no seams, with just a tiny frill along the top of each cup. Another swift tug and she had lifted those cups, baring her beautiful, wonderful chest to put me in thrall to her for ever.

Are they not so far above us? They give or not, as they please, these beautiful creatures we call women, whom mere males can only worship in awe. She held me so easily, Naomi, making me her eternal slave simply by showing me what she possessed, what she could touch as she pleased, what to her was simply a part of her being, but to me was the sangreal, nirvana, my heaven and my Shangri-La. The quacks say it is because I have no sisters. What do they know, the fools? Man was born to worship at the altar of a woman's breasts. How else could it be?

I wanted to buy Naomi a bra. Those that she had were pretty, in a simple way, but they utterly failed to do her justice. She needed black, a silk half-cup with a border of broad lace to set off her beautiful upturned nipples. I determined that I would buy her one, and to this end I went into the West End, to London's most famous emporium, because for the object of my worship only the best would do, regardless of expense.

To be a man in a women's lingerie department is to be deeply conscious of one's physical inferiority. All around one are delicate scraps of clothing: silk and satin, cotton and lace, elastic, nylon, straps and catches, all designed to adorn the female form. And to think that those little scraps will one day press against female flesh, taut against legs and bellies and bottoms, but most of all against breasts, breasts, breasts, breasts.

Just to walk among such displays makes me weak, and very conscious that I am committing an outrage just by being there. For what woman wants to see some lumpen maladroit male loitering between the aisles when she is buying her most intimate garments?

Of this I was acutely aware, red-faced with embarrassment and fighting the urge to run away somewhere and rid myself of the awful excitement building up within me.

I made myself do it, determined to honour my goddess. But I had no idea how I should go about it. Oh, I knew what size she was, because I had held each article she owned against my face and read each tiny detail of every single label. My difficulty was that I did not dare touch, let alone go through the displays to find the perfect article among so many.

My problem was resolved by an assistant, so typically unaware of my emotional turmoil as she asked if she could help. I remember her vividly. She was quite tall, and slim, with that cool, detached way some women have about them. She had brown hair, worn in the full style fashionable at the time and a crisp blouse loose over a lacy white A-cup, the side of which I could just glimpse between two buttons.

To this calm, aloof goddess I had to describe my girlfriend's chest, a process that made my face go beetroot and turned my cock to a rigid bar in my trousers. I was sure she would notice, and I nearly fled. But she had me mesmerised, asking if I knew Naomi's cup size and suggesting that a matching set of bra and knickers might make a more suitable present than a bra on its own.

I think I answered, but I doubt that my reply was coherent. The assistant's response was to lead me to a stand, hung with matching sets of knickers and bras, black silk and red silk, black lace and red lace, small and medium and large, designed for the most delicate and angelic of women, for staid matrons too. Yet each item was the colour of sex and the colour of authority. It was all I could do to answer her questions as she held up one article after another, each one a fantasy for me and the bar of my cock now aching with need. And then, then this –

'I may be a little smaller than your girlfriend, but I think this is pretty,' the assistant said. And she held a lacy black bra across her chest.

She smiled as she said it, her head cocked a little to one side, and pushed out her own exquisite little breasts to fill the cups. It was as if she had taken hold of my balls and cock and wrenched them. Her simple, easy gesture was far, far too much for my weak male body. I came in my pants, an orgasm of shattering intensity that left me mumbling and incapable, with a stain spreading rapidly across the front of my trousers. I fled, defeated.

Sadly, my relationship with Naomi came to an end when she caught me masturbating into the cups of one of her bras. Rightly, too, did she dismiss me, for it was a disgusting and utterly unworthy thing to have done, but I simply could not help myself. I never did buy her that special bra, yet that episode in the lingerie department made an indelible impression on me.

I wanted to go back, badly, but I knew it was wrong, a gross invasion of women's privacy. For months I tried to fight the urge, but it only grew stronger. I could remember every detail, every word that the cool, slender assistant had said, and above all, that awful, wonderful wrenching sensation of coming and being completely unable to stop myself coming. Even the agonising shame I'd felt afterwards was desirable, and absolutely appropriate for my crime, which excited me in turn.

Many, many nights I lay in my bed, wanking pathetically at my cock as I played the scene over in my head again and again. Sometimes I would elaborate, daring to think yet more inappropriate thoughts: of how I might have begged to show her my penis in one of the cubicles, of how she might have taken pity on me and cleaned me up, but most often of how she might have taken me behind one of those tantalising little curtains and tried the bra on for me.

My surrender was inevitable, my male mind far too weak to resist the demands of my sexuality. I went again, this time to a different store but one with a lingerie department no less large – and no less alluring. This time, though, it was harder still. I had no girlfriend, and my mind was swimming with guilt as I examined the treasures on display. Had nobody paid me any attention I think I would have run, but after maybe fifteen minutes an assistant asked me if I needed help.

She was small, blonde and compact, full of feminine delicacy and grace: a nymph. I do not think I could have faced the great stern goddess who ruled over the department, but while I was certainly in awe of the nymph she was the gentlest of sisters, full of sympathy and grace. To say that I felt like a worm as I pretended to her that I had a girlfriend of roughly her size and build would be an insult to the worm. I knew that beside her I was nothing, utterly worthless, and that what I was doing made me more worthless still. Yet I did it, because it was making my cock hard and I have no strength.

I was sure that she would realise. Maybe she did, but she still took pity on me. Nymphs are like that sometimes, forgiving in a way that is beyond male understanding. Maybe she did realise but it amused her to tease me even so. I would like to think that, although to be teased by such a one as her is a privilege I could never aspire to. Maybe she did realise, but felt it best that I should suffer the full consequences of my behaviour, because the greater the pleasure the worse the self-recrimination. Always.

Whatever the case, the petite blonde girl brought my torment to a peak more exquisite even than on the previous occasion, showing me bra after bra and talking casually of support and of lift, of catches and of lace panels, things that no man really has the right to hear. I stayed hard, painfully so, but it was not enough to provide that final shock. In the end I had to ask if she could hold one against herself, with guilt and the humiliation burning in my throat as I said the words.

But she did it, as coolly and as casually as her sister of the time before, pushing out her little breasts and holding the bra that I'd chosen across them as she looked down at her chest with an expression of faint criticism on her face, as if she could ever be anything less than perfect. I should have come at that. One tug at my cock and I would have done, but before I had been taken by surprise. Now I had forced the issue.

I bought the bra and retreated in confusion to the nearest lavatory, where I brought myself to climax in a welter of guilt and ecstasy. That was the second time. On the third I lost my nerve, overawed by the stately buxom giantess who came to serve me. On the fourth I was even less lucky: the assistant immediately divined my true intent and threatened to call security if I didn't leave.

That incident should have stopped me, and it did in fact put me off for a while. But I was back within a year, crawling out from under my stone like the worm that I am. Had the same thing happened again I think my nerve might have failed completely and permanently. But as chance would have it the assistant who chose me was another nymph, dark-haired and pert, full of joy and blessed with a beautiful round pair of D cups for which I ached the moment I set eyes on her.

I went through what was becoming a routine: my confession of ignorance and embarrassment, my description of my fictitious girlfriend's bust and the comparison with that of the dark-haired assistant, my polite and deferential request for help. She helped – oh, how she helped. When I'd made my selection, a pretty pink confection of lace and bows, and made my sneaky request, she immediately gave a crisp little nod and started off towards the changing cubicles.

And she changed into the bra and showed me how it looked on her. Oh, but it is so easy to say that, so hard to bring across the sheer power of that, for her, simple act. I stood rooted to the spot as she entered the cubicle, one of those with wooden doors that allow the head and the feet of the occupant to show. I watched with open mouth and bulging eyes as she took off her top and bra and hung them on a peg. I gaped like the miserable, guilt-ridden, happy fool I am as she slipped into that lacy pink bra.

She beckoned, just a little gesture of her hand, and I came stumbling forward. She smiled at me, a calm professional smile to put me at my ease. She opened the doors and struck a coquettish pose, displaying her bounties to perfection, round and soft in their beds of lace and ribbon, so utterly, agonisingly desirable. I came, with that same wrenching feeling, as if far more than just my tepid seed were being pulled from my body. From that moment on I was addicted beyond any hope of recall.

So began my career path, one that many men must know: a yearning, too strong to be resisted, for the object of our desire drives us inexorably on, despite the sure knowledge that our actions are immoral, reprehensible and above all the grossest of insults to the very thing we crave the most. How wretched I felt – and how ecstatic. How reliant I became on my dirty little game, quite unable to raise an erection without the stimulus of a woman's bra. How pathetic was my lot, reduced to ever more frenzied masturbation as each act made me ever less worthy of a real relationship.

Now, four years on, my dirty little habit has become the driving force of my life. I have done well enough, I suppose, by conventional standards, achieving a not inadequate income in my chosen career of accountancy. My colleagues think of me as a good fellow, perhaps a little austere and not easy to get close to. This is not an accurate picture of me. I am in truth the most degraded creature who ever lived, quite unfit for company, especially for female company.

Yet I must maintain the mask, even instructing my secretary and my female juniors when I should be grovelling naked at their feet. No, not naked, because why would such divine creatures wish to look at my body? Yet I certainly have no right to the dignity of clothing in their presence. Maybe a box would be best for me, a box made of cardboard in which I could be kept in the cellar and let out only to perform the simplest of domestic chores during the hours of darkness, naked but unseen.

Yes, I wear the mask of conformity, but each weekend finds me up to my dirty little tricks, ever further afield as I seek out new stores where I will not be recognised. I have been to Birmingham, Manchester, Leeds, Bristol and further afield still, while presently I plan to treat myself to a trip to Paris, or New York, or perhaps Warsaw, where I might be lucky enough to enjoy the charms of a Polish girl: they are so often marvellously busty.

For the time being I have chosen a location closer to home, northern Islington, where a new shopping mall has just been opened complete with many of the most promising chains. One in particular has caught my eye, specialising as it does in lingerie for more generously endowed women, the true goddesses. It takes all my courage even to address such beings, and yet they represent the holy of holies. My dream, and my favourite fantasy, is that one day such a woman might try on a bra for me.

She should be tall, six foot for preference. Not fat, but full-figured and firm, with long, shapely legs and womanly hips, a heavy, muscular bottom, a well-marked waist, good shoulders and an abundance of thick brown hair, all this to help set off a magnificent chest, large and round and firm, each glorious breast as big as my head, a true earth mother, a goddess.

I am smartly dressed as always, for despite my degraded nature I have no wish to present myself in slovenly attire and earn even more disgust than is my natural due. A quiet suit and an appropriate tie, in keeping with the reserved and polite image that I wish to project, and which I have found gives the best chance of one of those moments of exquisite agony for which I have come to live.

Always wary of a potentially disastrous confrontation with the police, I have parked some distance away and I carry no identification whatsoever, only my keys and a little money. In the event of my arrest it has always been my plan to deny everything and refuse to co-operate at all, in which case they must eventually let me go. The sad reality is that I would soon confess, certainly if I were to be confronted by a female police officer.

As always, I am nervous as I approach my target. As always, I am trying to find an excuse to put the event off, telling myself that I am being watched, that for whatever reason it is not a good day for my adventure. As always, I continue, stopping only when

I reach a shop in which the window display immediately draws my attention.

There are a number of mannequins, elegant exaggerations of the female form, all of them in equally elegant poses. What few clothes they have on are in black or red, made of rubber or leather, the stuff of the sex trade, deeply sordid and suggestive of an attitude towards women that I could never countenance, for all the undoubted allure of the black rubber bra adorning the bustiest and most central of the five mannequins.

I make to move on. But at that moment a panel opens in the screen behind the mannequins and an assistant steps into the window space. This is not the sleazy, furtive male employee of my imagination, but a woman. She is perhaps five foot eight in height, thirty or so, well built, with a fine pair of breasts that I guess as an E despite the loose black crop-top worn over them. Her legs are magnificent, long and powerful, big yet shapely, her bottom a glory of heavy female flesh encased within leather shorts. Her midriff is bare, her belly fecund yet firm, her navel pierced. Her hair is dyed black and falls in abundant curls to the small of her back. There is nothing sleazy about her, nor furtive. To the contrary, she radiates self-possession and certainty.

For a moment I watch as she fits a studded belt around the waist of one of the mannequins, paying no attention whatsoever to me even though I am immediately on the other side of the glass. Clearly to her I am utterly inconsequential, which is exactly how it should be. Here surely is my goddess, a woman as close to the image of my fantasies as any I have seen. And the shop sells bras.

I am going to do it. I have to. The chain curtain that closes off the door chinks slightly as I pass through and I am inside. My first impression is the scent: leather and rubber and incense and female perfume all rolled together to produce a heady effect, as if I had walked into a temple to womanhood – open, sexual womanhood. All around me are mannequins like those in the window, displaying clothing made exclusively for women and exclusively designed with sexual display in mind. There are also racks of dresses, of skirts, of tops, of stockings, and of bras: bras made of leather and bras made of rubber, bras trimmed with feathers and with abundant lace, bras set with sequins and metal.

My knees are weak, my mind is reeling with the heady incense and with *her* presence, because *she* is now there, looking at me, her face not unkind but full of force. She knows, she must do – I can see it in her eyes. She knows what I do and what I think about. She knows that I am dirty, a grovelling worm utterly unfit for her company. She knows that my cock is already growing hard in my pants and that she is the cause of my excitement.

I start to apologise, mumbling as I turn to flee. But she calms me with a smile, a smile of complicity or understanding. As I hesitate another woman comes out from the back of the shop, also dressed in black, also big, but with a great mass of chestnut hair piled up on her head. Her fingers, her ears, her arms are all heavy with jewellery, and like her companion she has on a simple black top covering full, heavy breasts. Like her companion she smiles a welcome, and I am trapped.

'May we help at all?' the first of them asks.

It is the same question to which I must have responded a hundred times, until my answers come automatically. But now I'm tripping over my own words as I respond. 'Please, yes. I was hoping to buy a bra for my girlfriend, or perhaps ... perhaps a matching set?'

'Anything particular in mind?'

It's a common reply, to my relief, and as I answer I am beginning to fall in with the familiar routine. 'Um. No, not really. I am afraid that I must confess to not really knowing a great deal about this sort of thing, only that she particularly wants something, er, exotic in the way of lingerie.'

'Exotic we can do. Do you know her size?'

It is going to plan, after all, and although the guilt is raging through me I still have the suspicion that this woman knows exactly what I'm up to and is simply playing my game. I give my disarming smile, allowing my embarrassment to show as I answer. 'Oddly enough, she's about your size.'

'That's convenient.'

She says it casually, with just a touch of laughter in her voice. Is she really playing along? Does she understand me and yet not hate me?

'Does she like girlie things, or something with a hard edge?' her chestnut-haired friend asks. 'I'm guessing a hard edge?'

She is looking right through me, as if she's reading my soul. Yes, I want a hard edge. I want her in a leather bra, lifting her magnificent breasts into frightening prominence as I grovel at her dainty feet.

'Perhaps something like that,' I answer, choking now on my own passion.

Her response is to step out from behind the counter and walk to a rack at the other end of the room. I follow, the dark woman behind me as if she is my warder. The rack holds bras made of soft, supple leather, black and bright lipstick red. I can only stare dully as the chestnut-haired girl flicks through them with her strong fingers, each one heavy with rings and tipped with a black-painted talon. She takes up a bra, a huge thing with straps over an inch wide and great rounded cups. I manage a weak nod, imagining it encasing her immense breasts.

'How about this style?' she asks. 'Or this?'

She has moved to the next rack and chosen another bra, this one in deep-crimson velvet, something I've never seen before. I already feel I want to come, but I'm trying hard to hold off, hoping for more. They're teasing me, I'm certain, and, with women so bold, who knows how far it might go?

'Yes, very nice, but it's hard to be sure of the exact fit,' I mumble.

'That's the trouble when you're big,' the dark woman says, her last words sending a jolt to my cock.

How can she say that so casually, referring to the size of her breasts in front of a mere man, drawing attention to how large they are?

'Who is your girlfriend closer to?' the chestnut-haired woman asks. 'Donna or me?'

Donna – it is the perfect name for the dark woman; full of motherly authority. And I am being asked to look at her breasts. I do, my lust swelling close to breaking point as I glance between them, taking in those rounded, heavy orbs beneath the black cotton, so lost in my desire that I can barely manage to equate the question with what I am doing. Maybe whoever I choose will try a bra on?

The chestnut-haired girl is bigger – she's magnificent, in fact – but Donna's breasts have an aggressive thrust to them that speaks straight to my degraded soul. I cannot decide.

'I'm not really sure,' I venture. 'In between, I think.'

'I think this would fit me,' Donna says, taking the velvet bra from her friend and holding it to her chest.

I try to speak but all that comes out is a little choking sound. For an instant there is a hint of a knowing smile on Donna's mouth and her eyes flick down to my crotch. She's noticed, and suddenly I'm terrified, unable to speak, unable to act.

'I think we've got a live one, Ella.' Donna laughs, and turns to me. 'What, do you want to see me try it on? Do you?'

It is the question I've wanted a woman to ask me so often, and yet I cannot answer, rooted to the spot in sheer awe of her, and of her friend. She just laughs, as if handling grubby little perverts like myself is not only everyday, but faintly amusing. Not exciting, not in any way important, just amusing.

'Dirty boy,' Ella remarks as she too glances down at my crotch.

I am looking from one to the other, completely unable to cope with the sheer power of their femininity.

Ella makes a face, dismissive, contemptuous. 'He doesn't look like he's got much, does he? But he *is* very excited. So, what d'you reckon then? Do you want us to put the bras on?'

I know she's tormenting me. I know she'd never do it, but I can't help my answer. 'Yes. Please,' I say, my voice so weak that I can barely hear it myself.

'Oh?' Donna asks. 'And what would your girl-friend say if she knew you were getting horny over us?'

'I don't have a girlfriend,' I admit in a feeble whisper.

'A voyeur, huh?' Ella accuses. 'And you thought you'd get away with it?'

'No,' I lie, shaking my head.

Now I realise I could never have got away with it, not with them. They're different to the other women

179

I've taken advantage of, in that they have no innocence to abuse.

'I'm sorry,' I say, hanging my head. 'Please don't report me.'

'We wouldn't do that,' Donna assures me. 'But I do think you ought to buy a bra.'

'Of course, yes,' I reply. 'Happily. I'm so sorry to have wasted your time, and for my behaviour.'

'So you should be,' Ella tells me. 'And just to make you think a bit, you're not only going to buy a bra, you're going to wear it home.'

Donna laughs, and I am horror-struck. I can't be made to wear a bra. It's wrong, wrong in every way. I don't have the right. I'm just a man. Yes, I'm just a man, and I can no more resist them than rise above the limitations of my body.

'This one should do,' Ella says, selecting a bra from the rack.

It's a pink A cup with a broad fitting, made of nylon, a tacky thing, quite unsuitable to hold a woman's breasts. But for me, yes. I realise that she is even wiser than I had imagined.

'In the back,' Donna orders. 'That's where we deal with creatures like you.'

I go through a heavy curtain of black beads into a large fitting room, painted red, with a huge mirror on one wall and two chairs.

'Put it on,' Ella orders, and she hands me the bra.

My fingers are trembling so hard that I can barely manage and my cock is threatening to burst with every movement that I make. The two women watch, amused, disdainful, as my upper clothes come off. I am near to tears as I stretch the tiny pink bra across my chest, but they are as much tears of ecstasy as of shame. It doesn't fit, because I have nothing to fill the tiny cups, let alone anything of the right shape. Both the women laugh at me, and as I struggle to raise my gaze to meet theirs Donna speaks. 'I think I know what he needs.'

She pulls out a chair, smiling. Ella laughs and takes the other chair, placing it opposite the first. I have no idea what they are doing, not even when they sit down, facing each other, so close that their knees are interlocked. Only then do they speak again. 'Get over our knees, you filthy pervert,' Donna orders. 'We're going to give you a good spanking.'

Her words cut into me like knives. I am going to be punished, spanked. I cannot resist, not for a moment, and deep down I know this is what I need, what I have needed from the first: to be punished for what I do, for my filthy habit, for what I am, a grovelling, perverted little worm. Now it's going to happen, meted out from two true goddesses. I go down, laying myself across their laps, feeling the shape and texture of their legs against my body, their bellies too as they take hold of me, and their breasts, full and heavy on my back, touching me, weighing me down, those magnificent breasts on my back, a sensation that has me close to orgasm, and they have begun to undo my trousers.

My trousers come open and are tugged down. I am taken firmly in the women's grip and I am spanked. It hurts so much, but even in my pain I am more aware of their bodies than of anything else and most of all of their breasts, moving on my back, slapping on my flesh just as their hands are slapping on the seat of my underpants. I can't hold myself. My cock has wormed its way out of my fly, rubbing on Donna's leg. I hear her tut of disgust as she feels it, but she doesn't stop spanking.

She spanks harder, and so does Ella, to set up a rhythm on my buttocks, stinging me, and making their breasts bounce on my back, which is more than I can possibly handle. My cock jerks and I come, all down Donna's leg, and her immediate cry of disgust only serves to provoke a second ejaculation. I'm pulled off their legs immediately, the spunk still dribbling from my cock-head as I'm put on my knees.

'You filthy little shit!' Donna snaps. 'You've spunked on me!'

I can hardly deny it. The evidence of my crime is right before my eyes, running thick and sticky over the fishnet encasing her magnificent thigh. I look up, mumbling an apology, but Ella cuts me off. 'Make him eat it!'

'Yes,' Donna answers. 'That would be appropriate.'

'No, please,' I start to say, my mind flooded with the guilt that is always so strong after orgasm.

Ella is taking no nonsense from me. She squats down beside me and takes hold of my head. She pushes me forward, and I simply don't have the strength to resist because her breasts are pressed against my body, firm and bulky beneath her top. I can feel her bra, something full with strong seams, strong enough to accommodate her. Curbed like that, I do it. I lick my own mess off Donna's leg – man's mess, thick and salty and slimy, utterly disgusting. But as I do it I realise that I should have been made to do it long ago, to punish me for being what I am, to make me eat the filth I produce from my sordid, degraded arousal. As my mouth fills with the horrible taste and I struggle to swallow it down my ill feelings start to fade and soon I am in heaven once again.

I am as I should be, grovelling near-naked at a woman's feet, punished for one disgusting crime and again for a second offence provoked by the first. As Ella forces my head onto Donna's leg, rubbing my face in the spunk, I am whimpering with ecstasy. She is holding me so close that I can feel every contour of her huge breasts, and I can't stop myself. I've grabbed at my cock, tugging furiously at the half-stiff shaft.

'The dirty pig!' Ella laughs. 'He's wanking himself!'

'Let me, please,' I beg. 'You are so wonderful, so beautiful – you're goddesses. Let me do it, I beg you, and hold me, hold me to your breasts.'

I'd never dare say such a thing, not normally, but it's a call of desperate need, if not one I expect to be answered. To my amazement, it is.

'OK,' Donna says. 'But you *are* a pathetic little specimen, aren't you?'

'Yes,' I tell her. 'Yes, I am, utterly pathetic, utterly unworthy. You were right to spank me. You were right.'

'Sh!' she says, her voice now soothing and matronly, and she has taken hold of me.

I'm in their arms, held by the two of them, and Donna is pulling her top up, lifting it to display two magnificent breasts held in the confines of a black underwired bra, an E at least, or more. My head is under her top, my face is pressed against her breasts, between them, and now she's tugged up her cups as well. They are bare, two full, womanly breasts pressed bare to my face and I am in an ecstasy far beyond anything I've ever known. I nuzzle, I kiss, I suck, whimpering in ecstasy as I masturbate, determined to come again.

'Let me take your little willy,' Ella says softly. 'You can play with my boobs too, if you like.'

As she speaks she has pulled them out. Now she takes my cock in her hand, tugging at me, something no woman has ever done before, condescending to touch my weedy, pathetic little penis. Donna lifts her top, Ella closes in and I am smothered in breast-flesh, so big, so full, so firm, so much of it. I wish I could suck on all four. I wish I could be there for ever. I wish I could drown in their bosoms.

I can touch, they're letting me. I can feel their curves and the weight of them, the material of their lifted bras, satin and lace, their stiff nipples, wet from my mouth and with my come, a hideous imposition on my part. But they don't seem to mind. Ella is pulling at my cock, and Donna has my balls, squeezing them gently. They're rubbing their breasts in my face, deliberately, two glorious goddesses deliberately rubbing their breasts in my face as they masturbate me, and I've come again, a feeble orgasm all over Ella's hand, which she immediately pushes to my mouth to make me lick up the spunk.

Afterwards they kick me out into the street, still in my pink A cup beneath my shirt and with both the bras they were wearing in a bag, all paid for. They have made it very clear that I shouldn't make too much of what has happened, and that if I make a nuisance of myself I won't be welcome. They have also made it clear that I can come back another time, and if I'm very lucky, maybe, just maybe, they'll take pity on me again. As I walk back towards my car I am in heaven.

# Being Busty

Paulette is a shining example of just how weird and wonderful female sexuality can be. I grow very tired of the limited range of what is permissible as dictated to us by *Cosmopolitan* magazine and its ilk, but girls like Paulette help to restore my faith in the glorious variety, not to say perversity, of womankind. She also took me completely by surprise, because I met her on a game show hosted by that gay man with the irritating voice who seems to get everywhere. She was a contestant, I was part of the show, and it was only when talking to her afterwards that I discovered that there was more to her than mere looks.

Born in Jamaica and sharing that country's wonderful attitude to the female figure, she is proud of her 'boobies and bumper' and has no illusions that she has what men really like: an abundance of full firm female flesh. Her bottom is magnificent, her breasts more so, astonishingly big and round with jet-black nipples each larger than the end joint of my thumb – and I have tested that. Her warm brown skin is also highly desirable, but all this beauty is secondary to her real achievement. She keeps herself in milk.

She says – 'I suppose I'm a natural, because when I was pregnant my milk started much earlier than for most women. My hubby has always loved to suckle my boobies, and when he found he was getting milk he loved it even more. Then when Josh was born I had ten times what he needed, and those nipple pad things are a pain, so I let hubby keep on feeding, and he's never stopped. Then there's the other guys, but I'll confess to that. I express, too, and if I try I can squeeze out maybe half a pint at a go – and we are well bad, because we keep it in the fridge: sometimes when guests come around they get boobie milk in their coffee instead of cow's milk!'

### Paulette's Confession

'In the sex game I'm what you call a milkmaid. I don't milk cows, nothing like that. I milk myself, or let guys suck on my boobies for the milk. A lot of people are going to think that's weird, but a lot of guys are into it, and a lot of guys who'd never thought about it all but just like big boobs, they get into it and all. That's all I do. No sex, but if they want to wank their little cock while they're having a suck, that's fine by me. Sometimes I do it for them but that's the limit.

'I got into it after I'd been feeding hubby for a couple of years. He's been crazy about my boobies since the day I met him, and me giving him milk sends him straight to heaven. It's good for me too, don't get me wrong, and with hubby, when he's had his feed and both my boobies have been sucked dry, then I am always up for sex. He likes it best between my titties, the way a lot of guys do.

'Thing is, when you're milky your nips leak, and even with hubby I'd sometimes get stains on my top. Now I'm sitting on a train one time, middle of the day when hubby's at work, feeling so heavy I just can't wait to get home and squeeze a little out into a cup, and this guy is looking at me. When you're as big as me men stare anyway, but I knew what he was looking at, and when I left the station he starts to follow me.

'One street and I'm thinking maybe it's just chance. Two streets and I'm not so sure. Three streets and I'm ready to knock him into next week – which, believe me, I can do. Only when I turn around he comes out with it, just like you or me would ask for the time – will I let him suckle on me for two hundred pounds?

'I gave him such a clout on the side of his phiz he must have been seeing stars for a week, but then I got to thinking. Two hundred pounds, just for letting a guy suckle on my boobies? That's good money and, like I say, I can take care of myself, so I'm not worried about having men around the house. Hubby, his favourite fantasy, other than my boobies, is being made to watch while some well-hung brother gives me sex, so he's OK with it. Two months later I put an ad on the Net.

'The first guy, he was a really sweet old gentleman. All he wanted was to be cradled in my arms while I fed him, just that, and he was so polite all the time. Most of my men are, bringing me presents and all sorts. Most of them like to talk before we do it and all, which helps them relax. Then I go on my nursing chair, open my blouse, take out a boobie for them and feed it into their mouth while I hold them. Most often they just lie like that, maybe take out their cocks and pull off while they suck. Sometimes, with my regulars or with guys I like, I'll pull them off myself. But what they all like, and what they all get, is big milky boobies.'

# Tales from the Strange Ones on the Outside – In Milk

'Emily?'

'Rosanna! You look beautiful.'

We hug and I enter the house. Rosanna *does* look beautiful, and in the ten years since we parted at the college gates she hardly seems to have changed. Her hair is the same pale blonde that I remember, and longer than ever, falling all the way down her back to her bottom. True, her figure is a little fuller, her bottom rounder and heavier, her breasts fuller – much fuller, in fact. But then, she has just become a mother. All in all, she looks more like a Norse goddess than ever, and as always she makes me feel tiny.

For an hour we just talk, catching up on old times. I meet baby, a miniature version of Rosanna, pale-haired and sturdy, which brings us to the painful bit of the conversation, her ex. I listen with sympathy as we eat, although I already know most of the story. They'd been together for four years when she got pregnant. A natural mother, she assumed that it would cement their relationship, maybe even lead to marriage. He'd wanted her to have an abortion, and after a blazing row he'd left. That was nearly a year ago and she's beginning to get over it, but she still has a tear in her eye as she finishes the story. I hug her again, aiming to comfort her, but her size and the softness of her body as she hugs me back bring on very different feelings, and memories I've never been able to shake.

We open a second bottle of wine and continue to talk, but my mind is drifting back, ten years back, to college and how we sat together in just the same way in her room, both drunk after somebody's party and getting gradually drunker, with the level in a bottle of cheap vodka already below the halfway point and still falling. I remember watching *The Rocky Horror Show* on Rosanna's portable TV, leaning against her. I remember the sense of feeling warm and comforted yet a little frightened all at the same time as the way she was touching me grew gradually more intimate. I remember her kissing me and holding me tight against her chest. I remember tumbling together into her bed for a night of dirty, drunken sex. And I remember details: me straddled naked on her body, giggling as I suckled at her breasts; her telling me I was a naughty girl and holding me down to smack my bottom; the taste of her sex as I went down between her thighs to lick her to heaven.

Three times more it happened after that. We were never open about it – both of us had boyfriends – but we weren't ashamed, either. It was our delightful little secret, that Rosanna would let me play with her beautiful big breasts in return for putting me across her knee and smacking my bottom, in each case just helping the other with needs our boyfriends were unable to meet. The spankings hurt, quite a lot, but I came to enjoy it, while she had quickly come to appreciate the pleasure of holding me in her lap and letting me bury my face in her naked breasts, kiss her adorable flesh, lick her nipples stiff and, best of all, suck on them as she masturbated me.

Now, getting slowly drunk once again, I'm growing ever more conscious of the way Rosanna's breasts swell out beneath her top, bigger even than before, and that on the crown of one nipple there is a small tell-tale wet patch. She is in milk, and it is impossible not to imagine suckling from her, a thought that sends a stab of guilty shame through me at the same time as it gets my pussy tight with desire. I wonder if her thoughts are all that different, if she's wondering if I'd let her pull down my tight jeans and the panties beneath to smack my bottom the way she liked to. It would be a fair trade, and I'm willing, but would she be? Dare I ask?

Maybe it's time for a little confession.

'Do you remember the endless rows about who was pinching other people's stuff from the fridge?'

'Yes! And we never did find out who it was.'

I just smile. Rosanna looks at me with genuine disapproval.

'Emily! You didn't?'

'I did. I could never see what the big deal was, and then when you all started to put your names on things I just couldn't resist it.'

'What, so was it you who switched all the name tags around that time?'

'Yes, so you and Marian had that big row about whose coffee jar was whose. I was trying so hard not to laugh.'

'Emily! That was an awful thing to do.'

Rosanna really does disapprove, which is making my tummy flutter a little, but I'm not sure if I haven't pushed it too far. I still have to try.

'I'm sorry,' I tell her. 'It was just that . . .' I stop.

'Just that what?' she asks after a pause.

'Just that, that I . . .' Again I stop. And now I'm blushing, for real, with my stomach tying itself in knots. I tell myself that I haven't seen her in years. If she throws me out now it won't really make much difference. But if she doesn't, if she takes me down across her knee and smacks my bottom – well, once she's smacked my bottom she's bound to let me have a suckle, surely? It's a risk worth taking.

'That I wanted your attention,' I go on. 'That I, that I hoped you'd do what, what you used to like to do, only for real.'

I'm blushing furiously now, and lying, because while I did occasionally pinch milk or coffee or spread, and I did swap a few of their silly labels, it never occurred to me that it might be a way of getting her to spank me. That was always something I permitted so that she'd let me suck her, however much I came to enjoy it later.

Rosanna looks at me, the implication of what I'm saying sinking in. My face must be red as a beetroot – surely she's going to realise what I'm getting at? I want it. I want it now, nice and hard on my bare bottom before I'm put to her breast with my trousers and panties still down and allowed to suckle her as she takes me to orgasm.

'You only had to ask,' she says.

'It wouldn't have been the same,' I tell her. 'I wanted you to punish me for real. Maybe, maybe you still should. Now. Please?'

There, I've said it, and my heart is beating fast and so hard. My hands are shaking, my teeth are pressed hard against my sucked-in lip. She has to do it, or I'm going to run and not stop running until I'm miles and miles away from the awful mixture of embarrassment and desire now flooding through me.

'I . . .' she says. 'I don't know.'

'Please?' I repeat, and now I'm begging. 'Please, Rosanna? It used to feel so good, the way you used to take me down over your knee, and tell me I was naughty, and pull down my knickers for me, and . . . and the way you used to hold me afterwards.'

'You used to shiver all over,' she says, and there's a catch in her voice at the memory.

'It felt so good,' I tell her, 'with my bottom all warm and bare and you cuddling me, and touching me. Please do it, Rosanna, just the way you used to. Please?'

'But I'm feeding,' she says, glancing down at her chest. 'Oh dear, I'm leaking again. I'd better express.'

'No, no, don't,' I say quickly, and the words are tumbling out before I can stop myself. 'I'll do it. I'll suckle you.'

She's looking at me as if I'm mad and I'm feeling sick with embarrassment and shame for what I have just asked.

'Please?' I say again, feeling utterly pathetic and with the tears starting in my eyes.

Rosanna sees that I'm about to cry. She bites her lip, and then she's beckoning to me, not speaking, unable to meet my stare but pushing her chair back from the table to make her lap accessible. I stand up, drain my wineglass and walk around the table, shaking hard. She's in jeans, her legs together, offering a broad blue surface for me to lie over and receive my spanking. I undo the buttons of my own jeans and go down, draping myself across her lap.

Just to lie there bottom up across her lap fills me with a sense of deep relief, so strong that my tears burst free even as Rosanna begins to pull down my clothes. I am completely hers, helpless in her grip, ready to have my naughty bottom smacked – and it feels so good. Down come my jeans and panties, all together, and my bottom is bare, bare and trembling, my cheeks a little parted, my bottom-hole showing to her, just the way she always liked to have me.

Rosanna's hand touches my bottom, lifts, comes down again with a firm swat – and my spanking has begun. The tears are streaming down my face as I'm punished, and she never says a word, simply dealing with my naughty bottom as I sob my emotions out over her lap. After a while her spare arm comes around my waist, holding me in so that I can feel the bulk of her breasts against my body, so big, so firm, while I feel so tiny and helpless in her arms.

Soon I'm getting hot between my thighs, the pain fading to pleasure as my bottom warms, until I'm sticking it up to meet the smacks and squirming against Rosanna's knees. She continues to spank me, no doubt taking out ten years' worth of need on my wriggling bottom, and all the while my own need rises until I can barely control myself.

Finally the spanking stops, leaving my bottom a hot glowing ball behind me. I leave my jeans and panties down, rolling myself over on Rosanna's lap so that my face is pressed against her chest. Just the touch of those heavy matronly breasts against my face sends a jolt of pleasure through me, not so very far from orgasm, and as I take hold I am lost in bliss. My hands aren't big enough to hold her properly, and I'm too urgent as well, groping clumsily at her and rubbing my face against her top.

Rosanna smells of milk, human milk, which drives me into a wriggling, squirming frenzy, my mouth questing for her nipple. As always, the spanking has robbed me of every last scrap of dignity, allowing me to behave as I really want to, with completely unrestrained lust. Rosanna, though, is calm and purposeful, and she knows what needs to be done. Taking me gently but firmly by my hair, she pulls me back from her chest, allowing her to tug her top free of her jeans.

My mouth is still wide with need, and I'm making involuntary little sucking motions with my lips as she exposes herself, just one breast, as if she really were about to feed her baby. She is in a feeding bra, a huge thing with poppers at one side so that it can be opened easily. I'm staring as she pulls it wide to spill out one huge breast. The pad she's put in to soak up the spare milk falls to the floor as she reveals herself, and her nipple is bare, big and dark, the huge teat spotted with tiny drops of milk.

Rosanna pulls me in, my mouth fills and I'm sucking, my face pressed firmly to her breast-flesh, my lips tight on her engorged teat, sucking up the sweet-sharp milk as I wriggle in pleasure on her lap. My arms go around her, taking hold of her body, while her own arms enfold me and I am lost in ecstasy, needing only that final touch to bring me to completion. She knows what to do, curling my body onto her lap and slipping one big hand under my bottom.

It feels good to be bare, my hot bottom thrust out as she caresses me, soothing my cheeks and tickling between them, on my bumhole. I suck harder, my pleasure rising higher still, to a sublime ecstasy far beyond anything that any man could ever give me. I'm being fed at the breast, an intimate, private thing that no man could provide, and better, my bottom has been smacked first to bring me to that state of total abandonment that I can reach no other way.

Rosanna's finger is up my bottom, pushing gently but firmly into my slippery little bumhole, and she has begun to manipulate my pussy, using the palm of her hand and her thumb, burrowing between my sex lips to find the taut eager bud of my clitoris. As she begins to masturbate me I'm whimpering with pleasure against her breasts. My mouth is full of her milk and I gulp it down, immediately returning to sucking, harder than before.

I'm going to come, my ecstasy rising as I suckle and Rosanna rubs at my sex. As it starts I think of how we are: her so calm, so cool, so strong, a true earth mother, me wriggling on her lap, my spanked bottom naked and red, my bumhole penetrated, my pussy already contracting against her hand, my mouth wide on her breasts, suckling her, suckling my beautiful big Rosanna as the tears stream down my face. Suckling.

She holds me tight as I jerk and whimper my way through my orgasm, all the while stroking my hair and stroking my sex, to soothe me as she brings me off. Even when I'm done she still holds me, my body trembling violently in the aftershock of my climax, providing me with the cuddle I need almost as badly as I need the ecstasy.

Only when I am fully ready does Rosanna adjust herself, first to put me to her other breast and drain a little milk into my mouth to stop the leaking, then to rise and push down her own jeans and her panties too. By then I'm kneeling at her feet, smiling up at her as she spreads her thighs to show me her plump blonde-furred sex, moist and ready for my tongue, as she always used to be. And as I hope she will be many, many times in the future.

# Being Busty

Shelley is out and proud about her 34D chest, and has never had any difficulty in making the best of her assets. She has little sympathy with women who complain about being busty, and points out that it's a lot better to have them than not. At school she was the one having her breasts fondled behind the bike sheds when she should have been in class, and her first job was as a topless ice-cream girl in the south of France. Since then she has stripped off her top for the occasional magazine to draw attention to the various causes she supports, and has done the same thing many, many times for the sake of pure indulgence.

What's more, as if in reward for her open joy in herself, her breasts never seem to change, having remained full and firm for all the years I've known her. Some might put this down to exercise, a healthy lifestyle and sensible bras, but she has a different explanation. 'When I was seventeen,' she says, 'and all the boys were so into my tits, I made a pact with the devil: he could have my soul if I kept my figure all my life. He hasn't let me down so far.'

## Shelley's Confession

'Confessions, confessions. Let me see. There was the time I stripped off nude in the woods, got painted up like a zebra and was hunted down by men with nets, but that's probably too weird for your readers. You can see the pictures on the Net, though, if you know where to look.

'I'll tell you something else I did which was not nearly as weird but a lot naughtier. This band had hired the old horse hospital near Russell Square to launch their new video. It was pretty amateur stuff, but a good laugh and several of us went along to support them and take advantage of the free beer. I got really drunk – I mean really, *really* drunk. Afterwards, six of us went out to find somewhere to eat, me and my friend Rachel and four guys, one of whom was dressed as a priest. Somebody said there was this really good Italian restaurant and he knew a shortcut, which turned out to be an alley at the back of Corum's Fields.

'That was a major relief for me, because I was dying for a pee. We'd been talking about all sorts of naughty things too, and I was in the mood to show off a little. So I said they could watch, and I did it with my top pulled up to show my tits as well. The boys loved that and, I tell you, if they'd just had the guts to ask I'd have given them blow jobs all round, then and there. They didn't, which was probably just as well, because we weren't the only ones using the alley.

'So we went to the restaurant and had pasta and pizza and a couple of bottles of Chianti. But by the time we got out it was getting on for one in the morning. Rachel and I shared a cab, and she lives close so she came in for a coffee. After that it all gets a bit hazy, but I remember her joking about watching me pee, and asking if *I*'d like to watch *her*. Quite how we got from there to me kneeling in the bath and her squatting over me I don't know. But I *do* remember her pissing all over my tits, first on my top so it stuck to my flesh and my nipples showed through, then bare, with my wet top and bra pulled up. It felt lovely, and I was rubbing it in and playing with my wet nipples, and laughing all the time, because it wasn't just horny, it was real fun too. Before Rachel had even finished I was trying to kiss her pussy, and we did it right there in the bath, rubbing each other off with our tits pulled out and completely soaked in her pee. That's filthy, I know, but I still remember that orgasm.'

# Tales from the Strange Ones on the Outside – Red-letter Day

There is a big red circle around the number thirteen on my calendar, a big red circle and the single word *Paris*. I don't really need it, because I know perfectly well what day it is. How could I forget?

I take special care dressing: white stay-up stockings with a broad edge of lace, white lace panties and a bra to match, holding my breasts snug in the cups. A plain green summer dress goes on top, along with heels high enough to make walking a little awkward without actually appearing clumsy. I brush out my hair and tie it in a green ribbon, a girlish conceit that helps to keep me self-conscious as I walk down to the station.

Everything is as normal, the 7.43 a few minutes late, my fellow commuters grumbling and glancing at their watches or talking into mobile phones. I change at Finsbury Park as I do every other morning, taking the Victoria Line into the West End. As usual I get out at Warren Street and make my way towards the office, taking my customary shortcut through the mews.

There is a car badly parked, at an angle so that it blocks my way. It is an old blue Mercedes. As I edge past a man steps out from the back door of the nearby pub, right into my path. He is big and ugly, and he is grinning right at me. I hesitate, and turn at a sound. Another man is behind me, a man with a face like a rat's and eyes that glitter with cruelty. In his hands is a roll of black and yellow tape, and there is no doubting what he intends to do with it. Both men move forward. My mouth opens but no sound emerges. Their hands take hold of my body and I wriggle helplessly in their grip as the boot of the Mercedes is opened.

I'm bundled in. My arms are twisted cruelly behind my back and taped into place. My dress is ripped wide at the front, my breasts popped up out of my bra. My panties are pulled off, stuffed into my mouth and tied into place with my own hair ribbon and a length of tape for good measure. My ankles are lashed together. The boot lid slams down and I am alone in the dark, shivering with reaction. My dress is rucked so high that my bare bottom is showing, my breasts are bulging from the front of my torn dress, and my mouth is full of the taste of my own sex. My wrists and ankles are bound tight, far too tight to permit my escape. I feel utterly helpless, utterly vulnerable, but can only whimper out my feelings into my panties as I await my fate.

The car starts and pulls away. I'm wondering if anybody saw. If the police might already know. As we drive away I'm listening out for sirens. None comes, and soon I can feel us picking up speed. I try to work out where the car is going. We must be on the Westway, surely, heading out of the city, to somewhere quiet, somewhere they can use me at their leisure, somewhere nobody will be able to hear my screams.

And I *am* going to scream. I am going to scream my head off. I would already be screaming if my panties weren't tied into my mouth. Now I can't even talk. I can't beg for mercy or release. All I can do is take what's coming to me – and it will come, I know that with a cold certainty that has me wriggling and jerking in my bonds, close to real panic.

We drive. I don't know how far. I don't know for how long. Sometimes we're going fast, sometimes slowly, sometimes I'm still, sometimes my body is rolled from side to side as we take corners. Finally we stop. I'm shaking as I listen to the slam of the car's doors, then the men's voices, a joke, something about a mother-in-law, not about me at all. I don't matter.

The boot lid lifts and bright sunlight floods in. I find myself staring up into the men's faces from wide eyes and I'm more conscious than ever of my flaunted breasts. The ratlike man gives a dirty chuckle and reaches down to stroke one nipple, then pinch it hard enough to make me jerk and set my breasts quivering. Again he laughs and begins to toy with me, amusing himself with my breasts by tweaking and twisting my nipples until, despite myself, both teats have come out, hard between his rough fingers, and I'm squirming in my bonds. The big man looks on, amused, until his friend has had his fun. Then he reaches in and lifts me up as if I weigh nothing at all.

I'm thrown over his shoulder, my bare bottom stuck high in the air and my breasts dangling upside down from my chest, a sight that makes the rat laugh. He makes a rude remark about the way my sex shows from behind and smacks my bottom, leaving my cheeks tingling as I'm carried away from the car. We're outside a house, a big house, built of red brick and flint, with a high-arched front door. I'm carried in, across a hall and down a flight of stone steps into a gloomy room where I'm dumped on the floor, shivering.

The rat has followed and both men are standing over me in dark silhouette. My ordeal is about to begin, I think, but they merely take a moment to enjoy the sight of my helpless near-naked body and leave. As the door closes I am plunged into absolute darkness. The floor is stone, hard and cold, bringing on an urge I can do nothing to quell. As I lie there waiting for whatever is to be done to me I wet myself.

I don't know how long I lie there in my own urine, but eventually light floods in on me and I twist myself around, my stomach churning again as I see not two but three figures standing over me. The third is a woman, very tall, very thin, her brown hair drawn back into a tight bun, her face set in an amused smile that makes it no less harsh. Her dress is a sheath of golden silk, elegant and expensive, in utter contrast to my own torn and filthy garments.

'Look what we have here,' she sneers. 'If it isn't Robert's pretty little secretary. Not so smart now, are we, you cocksucking little bitch!'

She kicks me twice, hard, forcing me to roll over onto my back. I'm holding my legs tight together, trying to show as little as possible to the leering men, but it's not easy. My breasts are on plain show, and they feel huge and vulnerable the way they've been pulled out of my top, while my bottom is right in my puddle. The woman steps closer, standing over my legs.

'You don't look so smart now, do you, you little tart?' she says. 'Maybe I'll take photos for him. Then he won't think you're so fucking wonderful, I'll bet, not lying there in your own piss, you filthy little whore. Dave, get the camera.'

The big man backs away, leaving the rat to watch as the woman comes forward a little more to stand straddled over my body, her elegant black heels planted to either side of my waist. My own shoes are lost. I look up, biting my lip in apprehension as my gaze follows her stocking-clad calves to the hem of her dress, and higher, up to her slender hips and elegant waist, to the thrust of her breasts, high and proud above me.

I try to meet her gaze, to plead for mercy, but I can't. Her stare is too intense, too full of cruelty and malice. She's going to do what she wants with me and my begging will only amuse her. I start to panic again, wriggling in my pee, my breasts quivering, making the rat laugh. Dave comes back, now holding an obviously expensive digital camera.

'Video this,' the woman orders. 'As a souvenir for my husband, so he can remember what happened to his cheating little bitch-whore.'

Dave gives a dirty chuckle as he begins to adjust the camera. I can only wait, trembling, not knowing what is about to happen to me. But as Dave starts to film, the woman begins to talk.

'Look at her, Robert, look at your little bitch-whore. Look at those fat tits you like so much. I bet she likes to flaunt them at you, doesn't she? I bet she gets them out in the office and does the typing for you topless, the common little whore! Well, watch this, Robert, watch what I'm going to do to your whore of a secretary's fat breasts.'

She reaches down to tug up the hem of her dress, up her long, elegant legs, showing the tops of her stockings, the crotch of her panties, black and silky, tight over the pouting shaven lips of her sex. Her fingers find her gusset, pulling it aside as she grins down at me, her expression demented. I can see everything: the neat pink centre of her sex, the tiny bud of her clitoris within its hood, her pee-hole – which opens, spraying urine all over my breasts and into my face.

I'm writhing beneath her as I'm pissed on. It goes all over my breasts, soaking my bra and ruining my dress. It goes in my face, splashing into my eyes and soaking the material of my panties. It goes up my nose too, so that I'm soon blowing bubbles of yellowish snot as I struggle to breathe. My mouth is full of the taste of her. She's laughing as she does it, making the stream of her urine comes in pulses, splattering over my belly and over my breasts, which feel hot and wet. My skin glistens with pee, my nipples stick up high and hard. As she shakes out the last few drops she is smiling, her painted mouth twisted up with cruel glee at what she's done to me. She steps away and smoothes her skirt down over her legs.

'There we are, Robert.' She laughs. 'One pissed-on bitch whore.'

Dave stops filming and gives a pleased thumbs-up to the woman. She takes no notice and moves away, her face now set in an expression of fastidious disdain.

'Filthy little tramp,' she tells me. 'You stink. OK, you two, wash her down and string her up.'

She leaves the room, the gentle sway of her hips taunting me as she goes, her command absolute, her poise perfect, and me lying bound and helpless on the floor, sodden with her urine and my own, my breasts thrusting out fat and round from my ruined clothes, two men leering down on me. I really think they're going to piss on me too, but the rat quickly turns away, holding his nose and laughing. Dave joins in and together they leave the room, only to return almost immediately.

Both have buckets of water, which they throw over me. It's freezing cold, leaving me puffing and blowing through my nose and making my nipples harder than ever. I'm shivering too, with cold as well as apprehension, and they laugh to see the state I'm in as they reach down to grip my arms.

I'm pulled roughly to my feet and held tight while my wrists are released – but not to free me. Instead, I'm dragged writhing to where a great iron ring is set in the ceiling. A thick rope hangs from it, to which shackles are attached. My wrists are forced into the shackles and locked into place. Dave hauls on the other end of the rope and I'm lifted onto my toes.

Hung up by my hands I'm more helpless than before, unable to do anything except writhe in pathetic remonstration and whimper into my pee-soaked panties as they strip me, using a knife to cut away the remains of my dress and my pretty bra, even slitting my stockings and ripping them down to hang in tattered shreds around my still taped-up ankles. I'm nude, completely vulnerable, my breasts especially, now thrust out in front of me, glistening wet, my nipples still painfully stiff.

The woman comes back, now with a glass of brandy in one hand and an old-fashioned medical bag, heavy and black, in the other. My eyes turn to it by instinct and a lump rises in my throat. I start to shake harder than before, hard enough to set my breasts quivering, which amuses Dave. He begins to play with them, pulling out my nipples and flicking his fingernails against them until I'm wriggling with pain, which only encourages him.

'Shall we let her scream?' the woman suggests, her voice smug with satisfaction at the thought of my torment.

'Why not?' the rat answers. 'Nobody's going to hear her.'

He steps close, to jerk away the tape holding my panties in place and cut my pretty hair-ribbon. I spit out my panties, which fall onto my thrust-out breasts, slithering down my cleavage to leave a faintly yellow trail. The waistband catches one nipple and they hang there, a ludicrous sight that Dave finds particularly amusing, pointing it out to the rat. 'Look at her panties – what a laugh!'

The rat responds by pulling them off and rubbing them in my face, once more smearing me with the woman's pee.

I can't speak at all – I can only gasp for air and spit yellow dribble down my chin and onto my breasts as the woman speaks. 'Stop messing about, you two. You can have her later. For now, bind her and put her in clamps.'

'You got it,' Dave answers, and takes something from her, a coil of thin black rope and two small silver gadgets like miniature crocodile clips.

I wince as he comes back to me, because I know where those clips are going. It's hard not to beg for mercy as he takes hold of one of my breasts, his fingers loitering on my flesh as he binds me, wrapping the rope around me, first one breast, then the other, until both are standing swollen from my chest, red with pressure and feeling as if they're about to burst.

'Hold still, will you?' the rat demands as I begin to writhe in fear of the clip that he has lifted to my breast. 'Hold her, Dave.'

Dave takes hold of me, his arms around me and his hands on my breasts, squeezing them to make my nipples stick out further than ever. I can only whimper pitifully as the rat applies the clamp to one nipple but I cry out in pain when the jaws actually close on my flesh. They both laugh, and Dave immediately changes his grip, squashing out my other breast. As the second clip is applied it hurts no less than the first. I'm left hanging from the rope, whimpering with pain, my breasts bound and my stiff nipples clamped hard so that the tips are two rounded, protuberant buds of dark-red flesh.

Across the room the woman is setting out the contents of her medical bag: pieces of glittering chrome equipment, a vial of clear liquid, swabs and cloths, and two small black devices the sight of which makes my stomach go tight.

I find my voice. 'No,' I beg. 'Not that – please, no.'

She turns to me, her eyes glittering.

' "No"? Who the fuck are you to tell me "no", you little whore, you little piece of shit! If you didn't want it, you shouldn't have gone down on my husband's cock, should you?'

'He made me!' I whimper, but before I can say more the woman lashes out, slapping me hard across my face.

'Lying bitch!' she screams. 'How dare you! He didn't *make* you – you flaunted yourself at him, didn't you? Didn't you? Yes, you did, you flaunted your fat tits at him, you dirty whore, and went down on his cock, to try and take him away from me, didn't you? Yes, you did, you slut, you dirty, greedy little bitch-whore – and do you know what I'm going to do with you? Do you? Do you know what I'm going to do to those fat tits he liked so much?'

I nod feebly. I do know. I know exactly, in every detail. Robert loves my breasts. He loves them because they're full and round and perfect, un-blemished. Now she's going to ruin them, to make me into the sort of woman she sees me as, a slut and a whore. I cry out in anguish as she steps away, writhing now in my bonds despite knowing that I'm utterly helpless, despite knowing that nothing I can do will stop it happening. At the table she lifts one of the two black devices and depresses a trigger. I see the prongs emerge and I start to scream.

'Get her ready,' she orders. 'Dave, the camera.'

Both men obey. Dave begins to take photos, concentrating on my breasts as the rat takes the clear liquid and begins to swab me down, cleaning around my nipples and pinching each bud in soaked cotton wool until both teats are fully, achingly erect in their clamps. Only then does the woman step close, the horrid device in her hands.

'Do stop writhing,' she says casually. 'You'll only make it worse for yourself.'

I struggle to bring myself under control, but I can't help it. My breathing is hard and ragged, my muscles are jumping uncontrollably, the movements combining to make my breasts shiver and twitch. I'm sobbing badly too, despite myself, and shaking my head in pointless denial of what is about to be done to me. The woman is grinning as she comes close, extending one hand, now sheathed in a white latex glove, to take hold of my left breast, lift it and squash my flesh to make my nipples stick out further still, easing the hard teat between the jaws of the lancing gun, then pulling the trigger. I scream again as my nipple is pierced but somehow I force myself to stay still, knowing full well that the slightest movement could result in far worse pain.

Now there is a small silver rod though my nipple, ruining me, marking me as a slut and a bad girl. With that knowledge my resistance snaps, and I'm hanging limp in my bonds as the woman goes to my other breast, once more lifting and squeezing my flesh out to make my nipple as prominent as possible. I gasp and jerk as the jaws of the gun meet in my flesh, but that is all. She's marked me, and I hang from the rope helpless and defeated as she once more steps away.

Both my nipples are pierced by short silver rods, designed to hold the wounds open until something more appropriate can replace them: little bars shaped like tiny cocks, which I am to wear always so that everyone who sees my naked breasts will know of my disgrace. Yet even that doesn't mark me as a slut well enough, and the woman has gone back to the table to take up the other device, adjusting it with an experienced eye as the rat once more begins to pat down my skin with alcohol, this time over a wider area around each nipple.

My new piercings hurt and I'm shaking badly, both with pain and the anticipation of more agony to come. The woman gives a complacent, satisfied nod as she slots the ink cartridge into the tattoo gun she's holding – and it's going to happen, it's really going to happen. The men step back, both of them grinning and evil, their stares fixed on my naked quivering breasts and my newly pierced nipples. She takes their place, and I'm gulping air and twitching as she brings the gun close to my flesh, unable to control myself. But it's not fear of the pain that's the worst thing, it's the sure knowledge of what she is about to do to me – mark me, sully me, soil me, just as she did when she pissed on me. But this will be permanent.

She takes hold of my left breast, squeezing a little, lifting. I feel the cold touch of the tattoo gun, she presses the trigger home and I cry out in pain and anguish as the tiny needles bite into my distended flesh. Now it really *is* too late. My piercings would mend, but the tattoo will mark me for ever, mark me as what I am. I look down, unable not to, at my poor bare flesh, red with strain, but still fresh, still smooth, though no longer flawless. I'm marked, the little red letter taking shape beside my nipple: a 'B'.

I'm sobbing violently as I watch, so hard that the woman is having trouble keeping my breast steady. Still she works, her face set in concentration as she slowly picks out each of the five letters, the B, the I, the T, the C, and the H. Now I'm marked, my right nipple surrounded by neat red letters, quite big enough for anyone to see if I ever dare to go topless on a beach again, or at a sauna, anywhere. I'm marked as a bitch.

My whole body is shaking with my sobs as she stands back to admire her work, her face set in malign satisfaction at what she's done. I feel as if I'm going to go into some sort of fit, my muscles jerking and pulsing, my sex contracting to squirt little jets of urine onto the floor at my feet. She merely laughs at me, thoroughly enjoying herself as once more she steps forward, this time to take up my left breast. I give one heartfelt sob, but it is all that I can manage. Already it's too late. My breasts are ruined and she may as well do the job properly.

When the needles bite I gasp in pain, and I'm still sobbing as the vibration of the tattoo gun runs through my body, but not as hard as I was before. I watch as she picks the letters out, as slowly and carefully as before, each one just so, to make sure that everybody can read them, the W, the H, the O, the R, the E. It's done. I'm marked as a bitch and a whore, and with the realisation of exactly what that means a powerful shiver runs right through my body.

I'm ruined completely, marked for what I am, a bitch and a whore, a bitch-whore, fit only to be used for other people's amusement, to be stripped and beaten, made to suck cock and lick pussy, pissed on and spunked on, fucked at will and fucked up my bum when my pussy is too sloppy with sperm. I scream out for what I've lost, and she is pressing the gun to me once again, lower, between my thighs, not the point, but the top of the hard barrel burrowing in the wet fleshy slit of my sex, pressing to my clitty – and she's turned it on.

Immediately the vibrations hit me I'm screaming and jerking in my bonds. It's more than I can stand, far more. My whole body goes into orgasm immediately, my every muscle jerking uncontrollably, my cunt and anus in furious contraction, my breasts bouncing and quivering as she brings me off, laughing in my face as I go through my helpless orgasm. And all the time the truth of what she's done to me is raging in my mind.

My breasts are spoiled, ruined, my beautiful smooth, pale breasts, pierced as a slut and tattooed with those two awful words, the perfect words to mark me for what I am, a bitch and a whore, a bitch and a whore. Now they'll all know. They'll make me strip and make me suck. They'll fuck my tits and fuck my mouth. They'll fuck my cunt and fuck my arsehole. They'll whip me and piss on me and use me in every way. They'll string me up and whip my breasts and laugh at me as they read my tattoos – bitch and whore.

I scream as a new peak hits me, stronger even than before, so strong that my vision starts to cloud over red and I very nearly lose consciousness, but with those two words still running through my brain, over and over again, even as the woman removes the tattooing gun from my sex and my ecstasy slowly begins to fade. As I hang my head in exhaustion I see them on my breasts, as I will see them now every time I strip, every time people strip me – bitch and whore.

It takes them a while to get me down and sort me out so that I can speak clearly. When my nipples are unclipped and my breasts are unbound they hurt more than ever, but my mind is numb. As I sip the brandy that the woman brings in for me I'm still shaking badly, but with each sip of the fiery liquid I come a little closer to normality. Finally I can think clearly enough to sort myself out. Both Dave and Robert have gone off to get lunch ready, leaving me with Paris as she puts her equipment away. My bag is still in the boot of the car.

'How much?' I ask.

She gives a wave of her hand, dismissing my offer. 'I couldn't possibly charge you, darling. You're too much fun to play with.'

'Are you sure?'

'Of course.'

'Thanks. *You* were good, too.'

I smile and rise to kiss her.

# Being Busty

Micki is half English, half Japanese, and she grew up in Tokyo, only moving to the UK in her late teens. Physically, she has inherited more of the European than the Oriental, with curly brown hair, typically Western facial features, and an impressive 36E bust. As a child growing up in Japan being different made her feel ugly and insecure, although she is in fact strikingly pretty. Only when her breasts began to develop did she start to attract attention, even if it was mainly jealousy and spite from the other girls. From the boys it was pure lust, and thus as she developed she came to see her breasts as her greatest asset and the focus of her sexuality.

Now in her twenties, she craves attention to her bust and genuinely appreciates the sort of comments that many women would find annoying. She also appreciates physical attention, so much so that any man with sufficient social skill and the courage to ask is likely to be rewarded with a display of her mammary magnificence, quite bare. He may even be permitted to touch and suckle her nipples, which are dark and large. Boyfriends do better still, because even without her strong sex drive she enjoys the feeling of confidence and being admired that is provided by being asked to take a cock between her breasts.

## Micki's Confession

'I've always had this thing about attention to my breasts, even when I'm getting plenty of it. Maybe my ultimate fantasy is to have men so heavily into me that they're begging just to be allowed to *see* my breasts – they daren't even dream of touching them. I like to think of them trying to smooth-talk me out of my bra and growing increasingly desperate when I don't respond, maybe offering me money or to buy me things, sometimes even threatening me or trying to blackmail me.

'If they really tried it on with me I'd probably kick them in the balls, or run away screaming. But in my imagination I always give in, shyly taking my bra off down my sleeve and lifting my top to give them a flash. Inevitably they want more, and I end up having to suck cock while I'm felt up, or getting my tits fucked. If I'm in a *very* dirty mood I sometimes imagine them losing patience and just taking what they want, with me pinned to the ground and my top and bra lifted to let them see me and have a good feel before wanking all over my tits. That *is* dirty, isn't it?

'A favourite fantasy is to imagine myself as a Manga girl, a cartoon, with impossibly large tits. When I masturbate I hold them up with my arm and look down, so that they seem even bigger than they really are, and imagine myself getting into the sort of awkward situation Manga girls are shown in, like having my blouse ripped open and my tits licked, or tripping over my knickers in the street so that my tits burst out of a halter top.

'Only once has anything even vaguely similar to my fantasies happened to me in real life – except for with boyfriends, of course. But that's not really the same, is it? I'd come back from a walking weekend in the Pennines, straight off the moors and into the train, so that I turned up at Euston looking a right mess, with my rucksack and muddy clothes. I was starving too, so I bought a sandwich and a can of drink and sat down to eat them on the station forecourt.

'I hadn't been there five minutes before a man approached me. I thought he was a plain-clothes detective or something and was going to move me on, so I was really apologetic about it, until I realised he was actually trying to proposition me. He obviously thought I was homeless, because of the way I looked, and was hoping to get some cheap thrills out of me. What he offered, in this really guilty, grunty voice, was a fiver for a feel of my tits and to wank him off.

'A fiver! Can you imagine the insult? I'm a floor manager in one of the Japanese banks, by the way. It just didn't sink in for a moment, I was so taken aback by his sheer cheek, and before I could tell him to fuck off my dirty little mind had started to work. I was telling myself that I should do it, because if I didn't he'd only push some girl who was really in trouble into it instead, and that I would give the money to the first genuinely homeless person I saw. Amazing how we make excuses for our behaviour, isn't it?

'So I did it. I really did it. I let him take me around to some grubby little alley somewhere at the back of the station and I tossed him off with my top and bra up so that he could feel my tits. It felt so weird – and so horny. I can remember every moment of it too, from start to finish. As we walked together he kept glancing at me as if he was worried I'd run away, and

215

he asked really intimate questions, like what my bra size was and how early I'd started to get tits.

'Then there was the alley. God, that felt so horny. It wasn't even that well hidden, just a grimy little space behind where a wall stuck out a little. He made me go up against the wall. I will never forget the way his hands pulled at my top, getting it out of my trousers and lifting it up over my tummy, then my boobs, and the way he stared, his gaze riveted to my chest.

'I was in a sports bra, which I always wear when I go walking because it stops my boobs bouncing and they don't get so sore underneath. He didn't like that, muttering about how I ought to wear a proper bra, with plenty of lace, and how he would buy me one. That didn't stop him pulling it up, and the moment my boobs were out his fingers were all over them.

'That was so strong, and not at all like when my boyfriend does it. I felt I was genuinely being molested, and while a part of me wanted to scream and run it was taking me so high that I just couldn't help myself. I even asked him if he wanted to suck me – imagine that! He did it, holding my boobs up one by one and putting my nipples in his mouth to suck on, while this horrible bristly moustache he had was tickling my breast-flesh.

'While he was sucking me he got his cock out and put my hand on it. That was such a shock. Just to touch him made my flesh crawl. But I'd promised to toss him off and I did, tugging away while he drooled over my boobs, kissing them and fondling them and sucking on my nipples, calling me his booby-baby and his titty-tart, of all things. It didn't take him long, fortunately, or I might have really disgraced myself by going down on him to suck him off or something. He just came all over my hand, without the slightest warning, sticky stuff running down my fingers as I tossed him off and going all over my tummy and my trousers too. Never, ever, have I done anything so utterly disgusting – or so exciting. I learned an important lesson too. Always get the money first – the bastard went off without giving me my fiver.'

# Tales from the Strange Ones on the Outside – Titty Whipped

I feel the weight of my breasts come forward as I bend over to touch my toes. It is a sensation with which I've become very familiar over the last few months, ever since meeting Alan. Always it's my breasts that I'm made to focus on, however much I might like it to be other parts of my body or what is going on in my head. Like now. I'm in my school uniform: black shoes and white socks that reach to my knees, full-cut white panties, a red tartan skirt so short that as I bend over I show my behind, a plain white blouse, a black and red striped tie, and no bra. I have no bra because Alan says schoolgirls shouldn't need bras, although in my case I've needed one since long before I left school, needed one badly. The real reason why I have no bra is so he can enjoy the movement of my naked breasts under my blouse and the way my nipples poke up through the cotton. Also so that as I bend down for my punishment I am especially conscious of the way my breasts hang heavy and bare underneath my chest.

Alan comes closer and I feel a shiver of anticipation run through my body. Will he expose me to make my punishment more humiliating? Will he pull down my panties all the way and tell me that he can see my bumhole and my pussy lips from behind? Will he make me count the cane strokes as I'm beaten? Of course he will, and more.

'You are a sight, aren't you?' he says. 'I'd have thought you'd have learned your lesson by now, that this is how naughty girls end up. No? Obviously not. Well then, there's only one thing for it: six of the best, again.'

'Yes, sir,' I respond, and there's nothing false about the tremor in my voice.

I do love it, I really do, but that doesn't stop it hurting, or mean that the humiliation of my exposure isn't genuine – far from it. There are times, when I'm trying to break through the pain before the pleasure kicks in, or maybe when I'm having my bottom cheeks held apart for my anus to be inspected, when I really do wonder what the hell I'm playing at. I still come back, though – always.

'Skirt up,' Alan says. 'Can't have that getting in the way, can we? Oh yes, and I think we'd better have these down too, don't you?'

As he speaks he has lifted my tiny skirt and tucked it up into its own waistband, exposing my panties, but only for a moment before they too have been removed, jerked down over my bum to leave me bare behind, the air cool on my naked pussy and my anal star. The humiliation of it brings a lump to my throat, but I hold my pose, rather wishing that he'd taken more time over getting me stripped so that the full implications of what was being done to me could sink in.

'Very pretty,' he remarks as he admires my bare bottom. 'What do they say – nature's natural shock absorber, that's it, isn't it? So now that I've got your shock absorber bare, what do you think I should do to it? Do you think I should cane it quickly and let you cover it up? *I* don't, not at all. You see, I haven't got you bare just to make an easier target for my cane, not even to make sure it really hurts. I've stripped you to take your modesty away, Tina, because a naughty schoolgirl shouldn't be allowed any modesty, none at all. Which reminds me. Why should you be allowed to keep those nice big titties covered up when your bum's already bare?'

Alan gives a dry chuckle as he ducks down beside me. I close my eyes, trembling with humiliation as he begins to open my blouse. It is nice – it does make my punishment more intense to have my breasts naked as well as my bottom. I just wish he'd pay a bit more attention to my rear view and a bit less to my front. He knows, but he doesn't care. My buttons are undone one by one, agonisingly slowly, and between each button he takes a moment to grope me, squeezing my breasts and pinching my nipples, until both of them are hard and I'm gasping in reaction.

With the last button undone my school blouse is opened and turned up over my head, leaving me unable to see anything in front of me except the curtain of my hair and the back of my blouse, while my breasts are hanging down almost in my face. Alan continues to feel me up, amusing himself by making my breasts slap together and pulling at my teats as if I am a cow and he's trying to milk me. I know that's what is going through his mind, because he's told me his fantasy about keeping pregnant girls naked in a barn so that he can have fresh girls' milk every day and fuck them between their swollen breasts whenever the fancy takes him, with their milk squirting all over his belly as he pumps and mixing with his spunk when he comes. I'm not pregnant, I'm not in milk, but I am naturally big, so big that he never seems to be able to get enough of me.

'Such lovely big udders you have, Tina,' he says, now with one breast cupped in each hand as he squeezes my teats between his fingers and thumbs. 'Lovely and big, the way a girl's tits should be – smooth too, and so heavy.'

He's lifting them in his hands and rubbing my skin, making me gasp and shiver. But my position is getting uncomfortable and I badly want my bottom attended to. Not that he cares, ducking down lower to take one of my nipples in his mouth and suck. This is not the sort of thing a sadistic headmaster would do to an errant sixth-form girl, but I put up with it because it's not easy to find a man who'll beat me properly and not get hung up about my fantasies.

I let him fondle me, trying to resolve my own feelings about what he's doing. Maybe a really perverted headmaster *would* expose a girl's breasts for a caning, and if he did maybe he *would* lose control and touch her up. If she didn't protest maybe he would grow bolder, milking her as if she was a cow and sucking on her nipples. Maybe he'd go further still, caning her hard until she's whimpering and tear-stained, beaten into utter submission so that he can fuck her and spunk all over her bruised, aching bottom. Now I want it, I really want it, but Alan is still engrossed in my breasts, making them wobble as he suckles me.

'Beat me,' I sigh. 'Beat me and fuck me.'

He stops and my stomach twitches as I wonder what I've let myself in for. If there's one thing he hates it's being disturbed while he's playing with my breasts, and when I'm being punished I'm supposed to do as I'm told and not to speak unless I'm spoken to. Sure enough, he reacts with fury.

'How *dare* you speak to me like that?' Alan demands. 'I'll do as I please with your body, when it pleases me.'

'Yes, sir,' I whimper.

'Not good enough,' he snaps angrily. 'You get twelve.'

My tummy goes tight with fear, but there's no denying the sudden jolt of ecstasy at the thought of having to take twelve strokes. They'll be hard. They'll hurt. They'll leave me in tears and ready for his cock, slid right in up my soaking pussy, ready for me to be fucked with his hard belly pumping against my well-thrashed bottom cheeks. Now he's behind me, the cane in his hand. I take a firm grip on my ankles and shut my eyes, genuinely scared and trying to imagine how it must have felt for a real eighteen-year-old schoolgirl to be made to adopt such an intolerably humiliating position, waiting for the bite of her headmaster's cane with her skirt lifted and her panties pulled down, her virgin sex and her tiny neat bumhole revealed showing to the man about to punish her, her naked breasts dangling heavy and quivering from her chest.

The first stroke hits me and I cry out in a raw emotion that is so much more than mere pain. It stings. It stings like fire, but that's only part of it. I am being punished, and that is everything. I call out the number of the stroke and again the cane cuts in, and again, making me gasp and sob, my dignity stripped away as surely as my clothes. The fourth stroke hits me, smacking into my bottom with a meaty sound, and the fifth, the sixth, and then it stops, leaving me sobbing and gasping for breath, with the first of my tears rolling slowly down the bridge of my nose.

'Halfway,' Alan declares calmly, so much the master, cool and aloof, immaculate in his suit while

I'm snivelling and near-naked with my bare bottom criss-crossed by the marks he's put there with his cane.

Again he strikes, and again, each cut driving me higher, into that state of helpless, grovelling wantonness that I can only achieve through punishment. With the ninth stroke I'm crying freely, sobbing out Alan's name as I open my eyes to watch myself thrashed around the side of my school blouse. He's looking down on me, his stare fixed to my upside-down breasts, and as the cane bites into my bum-flesh they jiggle in reaction and a cruel little smile appears on his face.

I am ready, ready to be made his plaything, to have anything done to me that takes his fancy. There are two strokes to go but I don't need them. I've already been beaten into complete sexual obedience. I stay in position anyway, like a good girl, holding my ridiculous pose to let him thrash me once more, and again, the last cut of the cane. Now he will use me – but still I stay in position, knowing better than to move without permission.

'Get down on all fours,' Alan orders.

I obey promptly, down into one of his favourite positions, and mine, my palms planted flat on the floor, my knees apart to make sure that my pussy shows, my back pulled in to make my bottom cheeks spread and show off my bumhole, my breasts hanging down like a pair of substantial udders. He comes close and prods one breast with his shoe, making it swing and slap against its neighbour. My blouse is grabbed and pulled roughly up over my head and off my arms, leaving me naked from the waist up.

'Crawl around the room,' he says.

Again I obey immediately, crawling on all fours with my breasts swinging and slapping beneath me as

Alan watches with that same cruel smile. Now I want to be made a human cow and milked, even made pregnant so that I'll have milk to give – anything to please him.

I crawl around the room twice, while he watches, now seated in a chair. He has taken his cock out and is masturbating lazily as he watches. It should be my job to get him hard and I come to him, my mouth agape in expectation of being filled with hot penis. Instead, he continues to play with himself, his cock growing swiftly hard and his stare fixed on my breasts.

'Kneel up,' he tells me, 'and put your hands on your head.'

I obey promptly, shuffling close on my knees. For the first time in what seems like ages my breasts are as they should be, but the torment isn't over. As Alan masturbates he touches me, squeezing my tits and pulling at my nipples, cupping my breasts to feel their weight and slapping them to make them wobble. I don't feel like a cow any more, I feel like a slave, kneeling naked on an auction block while a prospective buyer tests me for quality, to see how much fun I'll be walking topless around his house. Or maybe he wants to fuck my tits, or even make me a wet nurse. Whatever it is, what matters is not me at all, only the size of my tits. Me, I'll do as I'm told, an obedient little slut, too dirty and too scared to disobey, but even my natural submission is worthless without a big fat pair of tits for him to use.

Alan's cock is fully hard now and my breasts are going red from the slapping and scratching, with both my nipples sticking out hard and urgent. He begins to pull at them, tugging and twisting, until they're more swollen still and I'm whimpering and gasping in pained reaction. I move closer, making it easier for him to torment me, and his slapping and squeezing grows rougher still. I want his cock, desperately, but he wants my breasts, and I quickly shuffle in between his feet, hoping that he'll titty-fuck me and come in my mouth or my face.

He grins to see me so eager, and speaks. 'One day, Tina, one day I'm going to cane those fat tits of yours.'

My answer is a sob, compounded of longing and fear, and at that Alan's face grows slack with ecstasy, spunk erupting from the tip of his cock, all over my breasts and into my mouth as I lose control and snatch at him, sucking down his sperm as I pull him off down my throat and swallowing again and again until he's finished. Only then do I turn to my own pleasure, rocking back on my heels as I start to masturbate in front of him, my fingers busy with my pussy as I rub his hot sticky jism into my nipples.

It is a month before I see Alan again. That is our agreement, that I should come to him once a month to have my demons worked out of me with a cane, and for him to do as he pleases with my body. On that day, and only on that day, normal life is suspended.

As always, my need grows as the days tick by, each much like the last, and as always my head is soon full of thoughts of how it will feel to be beaten again. In particular I think of his promise to cane my tits. I'm not at all sure about it. Bottoms are made to be beaten, girls' bottoms in particular, with plenty of flesh-padding. Tits are different, altogether more delicate, and yet part of me wants to give in to his desire.

It occurs to me that, if I am to have my breasts beaten, then perhaps it could be done with something other than the school cane. Maybe a whip would be better, a small one, appropriate for when a girl needs to be punished across her titties. The idea intrigues me, and I experience an exquisite thrill at steering myself towards my own pain and humiliation.

I often browse in junk shops in the hope of finding an original school cane or maybe a tawse, and it is in a junk shop that I find the perfect titty whip. It is an old-fashioned fly whisk, with a horn handle and a foot-long hank of horsehair attached. Just to touch it makes me shiver and I'm sure that the man in the shop knows exactly what's going on in my head, so that I'm blushing hot as I pay him for it. All the way home I'm thinking of how it will feel laid across my breasts, softly at first, to tease and tickle my nipples to erection, then harder, until my skin is flushed pink and I'm wriggling in pain and excitement.

At home I even try it a few times, with my top and bra lifted as I flick the whisk over my naked chest. It feels nice, but it's not the same. I need Alan to do it, first to strip me and humiliate me, then to whip me. That doesn't stop me masturbating, using the whisk to flick my titties as I rub myself before finishing off with the rounded end of the handle pushed in up my pussy.

His e-mail arrives as usual, telling me to come to him on Sunday. The choice of dress is mine, the choice of punishment his, but I know that I'll be bringing the fly whisk. My outfit is hard to choose, because I'm not at all sure what sort of girl would traditionally be punished with a fly whisk. Schoolgirls are caned. Horsy girls get the riding crop. For cheerleaders it's the paddle. But who deserves a fly whisk across her tits? A maid at some country house? Maybe. An Indian servant in the days of the British Raj? Perhaps.

Knowing that it's going to be my tits makes a difference. It is at least possible to pull a girl's panties down for a beating and pretend that she's only being laid bare to humiliate her and make sure it really hurts, but to expose a girl's breasts is undeniably erotic. When Alan strips me so that I'm bare-chested I always have to imagine him not so much as the cold, heartless authoritarian of my spanking and caning fantasies but as a pervert using a girl's punishment as an excuse for access to her body.

Now it's the same. I see him as an upper-class Englishman, keen to get some unfortunate girl stripped and whipped across her chest. Who would he choose – a naive maid, some dollymop from the streets or the local village? Maybe some hapless milkmaid who could be tricked into taking the punishment? That appeals, and it fits Alan's own fantasy of having me in milk.

I buy myself the costume at my local fancy-dress shop: a blue dress with a full skirt and a low neckline, along with a white apron. Dressed up, with petticoats under my skirts, big lacy knickers and a matching bra, I look a bit like a grown-up version of Alice in Wonderland. It's easy to pop my tits out of my bodice, which leaves them looking very big and very vulnerable in my mirror. For the second time I manage to turn myself on so strongly that I end up masturbating, this time on the floor in the hall as I watch in the mirror my bare breasts jiggle to the motion of my fingers.

Before I met Alan I would never even have considered doing such a thing, but he has turned me on to my breasts in an extraordinary way. I even travel to my assignation in my milkmaid's costume, acutely conscious both on the bus and as I walk through the streets of the amount of cleavage I have showing. Almost everybody I pass looks at me, with surprise or lust, disapproval, even envy, and every glance makes me more self-conscious still. By the time I reach Alan's place I am already strongly aroused, also full of apprehension at my forthcoming titty-whipping. As soon as I arrive I give him the whisk, which is neatly wrapped in shiny red paper with a black ribbon.

'A prezzie for you,' I tell him.

Alan takes a moment to respond because he is still admiring my chest. But rather than take the present from my hands he reaches out and with one quick motion my tits have been popped out of my bodice to sit fat and heavy on my chest, right there in the doorway of his flat. All day they had felt big, and now that they are naked they feel bigger still, huge balloons of flesh on my chest, blatantly exposed to the man I have made my master. He takes the present and shuts the door, chuckling at my blushes as I put my hands over my breasts and quickly take them away again, feeling foolish.

'What's this, then?' he says, pulling at the wrapping paper.

I curtsy, pathetically eager to please. He pulls out the fly whisk, his expression puzzled for an instant before understanding dawns.

'You said you might like to whip my breasts,' I explain.

He laughs. 'You're a slut, Tina. What are you?'

'A slut,' I answer, and for him it is the truth.

'So I'm supposed to be the cruel country squire?' he asks.

'Please, yes.'

'I can do that. Come here.'

Alan slaps my bottom, urging me towards his living room which is usually where I'm punished so that merely entering it gives me a fresh touch of fear. Using the fly whisk on my back and bottom, he drives me close to one of the windows and quickly draws the curtains.

'Turn around,' he orders, 'and put your hands out.'

I obey, already trembling a little. Normally he takes it slowly, running through what is going to happen to me over a coffee before I'm sent to change. Now I've only been in the flat a minute and already my breasts are bare, while it seems that he's going to tie me up as well. Sure enough, he uses the rope from the curtains to bind my wrists together and throws the end up over the rail, leaving me on tiptoe with my breasts thrust out towards him, naked and completely vulnerable, my nipples already hard.

Alan plays with my buds for a moment, then goes. I'm left hanging there, exposed and helpless, my naked breasts feeling huge and vulnerable, also very sensitive. I'm scared, as any girl would be who is tied up and about to have her breasts whipped – and, as always, with that fear comes excitement. Soon I'm wriggling in my bonds and I can barely control my breathing, thoughts of my humiliating exposure and my coming pain running hot through my head. The urge to touch myself is growing stronger too, but I'm bound, so I can't, which makes my feelings stronger still.

When Alan comes back he's in a Norfolk jacket and cords, with his walking boots on his feet and with a rough shirt open at the neck. It looks right, good enough for me, and of course he is completely covered, while I am already partially naked and will probably soon be completely nude. He is grinning as he steps close, and the fly whisk is in his hand.

'So you want your tits whipped, do you, you little trollop?' he asks.

'If it pleases you,' I tell him, hoping that he'll take full control and do as he likes with me rather than what he knows I want.

'It does,' he responds. 'It pleases me very much. Now let's see them.'

He already can see every private detail of my chest. What he really wants to do is *feel*, and he does, reaching out to take my breasts in his hands, cupping them and weighing my flesh, stroking my skin and running his thumbs over my nipples until I'm biting my lip in blended pleasure and frustration. He takes no notice, casually fondling me until he has had his fill and only then stepping back to heft the fly whisk in his hand.

This is it. I'm going to have my tits whipped. I'm whimpering already, before he's even struck me, and shaking so badly that it's making them quiver, which sets him smiling and chuckling. Alan lifts the fly whisk and I'm biting my lip again, hardly daring to look but unable to shut my eyes. It comes down, smack across the upper surface of one fat globe of girl-flesh, stinging enough to make me gasp. He gives a complacent nod and lashes the whisk down again, this time harder and across both my breasts. I cry out in pain and his smile immediately grows broader and crueller.

'Push them out,' he orders and I struggle to obey, just in time to catch a yet harder blow of the whisk right across my nipples.

Again I cry out, and again when I'm given my fourth blow. It stings crazily, and as Alan sets up a rhythm with the whisk lashing back and forth across my breasts I'm soon jumping on my toes and shrieking with pain. The motion makes my breasts bounce, making him laugh and encouraging him to whip me harder still, until I'm screaming and writhing on my rope, with my breasts two huge balls of burning flesh on my chest, my nipples so swollen that it feels they must burst. Already I want his cock thrust up me, preferably while I'm still being whipped. But he stops.

'You're being very noisy today, Tina,' he says.

'It hurts,' I pant. 'I can't help it.'

'You're so selfish,' he tells me. 'What about my neighbours? Do you think they want to be disturbed by your bawling?'

I shake my head.

'Are you going to shut up, then?' he asks.

'I'll try, sir.'

'Not good enough.'

As Alan speaks he ducks down to rummage under my dress and petticoats. Taking hold of my panties, he jerks them over my hips and bum, wrenching them down to the floor and off. He stands up again, sniffs the gusset and shows it to me. The material is wet, soaked with my juice.

'Open wide, Tina,' he orders.

I obey, my mouth agape as my soiled panties are crammed in until just a wisp of lace is left hanging out. Now I won't be screaming any more. I can't even close my mouth. It's right, too, just the sort of thing I can imagine being done to a milkmaid to shut her up while her breasts are whipped. Having my mouth full of the taste of my own sex adds to my humiliation, too.

'That's better,' Alan says, and goes back to whipping me.

I'm not really ready, and the first stinging blow sets me writhing in pain again and makes my titties jiggle. The second one comes harder and he has set up his rhythm again, lashing the whisk back and forth across my tits to send me into a squirming, wriggling dance of pain, jumping on my toes and thrashing my body from side to side so that my breasts are bouncing crazily on my chest.

He's laughing as he whips me, his eyes shining with delight as the lash strikes down on my naked breast-flesh again and again. I'm crazy with pain, completely out of control as I buck and thrash on my rope. If my panties hadn't been stuffed in my mouth I'd be screaming the house down, but if my hands hadn't been tied I'd have been on my knees with my fingers busy between my thighs.

Again Alan stops, and I look down. My breasts are red and swollen, my flesh covered with tiny weals, my nipples standing up like corks. Both fat boobs are rising and falling to the rhythm of my breathing, which is deep and hard to control. I want him to start again, for all the agonised stinging in my chest. But he has dropped the fly whisk and is pulling out his cock, fat and turgid in his hand, its head already sticking out from his foreskin.

I try to plead with my eyes, but he begins to masturbate, indifferent to my needs. Or so I think. His stare is fixed on my whipped chest as he brings himself to erection, but as soon as his cock is hard he stops, stepping close to me with it sticking up from his fly like a flagpole. He adjusts my apron so that it supports my breasts and makes them more prominent still – and more vulnerable – almost every inch of my flesh now on display. For a moment he plays with me, caressing my hurt flesh and suckling on my nipples until I'm writhing on the rope once more and whimpering through my panties-gag.

At last Alan stops and moves away, leaving the room. Again I'm left hanging, only now I'm in an agony of frustration, my whipped, swollen breasts stinging furiously, making me desperate to touch them, to stroke them and soothe them, to pull at my nipples as I masturbate, to fold them around Alan's cock and let him titty-fuck me, despite all the pain that it will cause. I get nothing, just left to hang there alone, but when he steps back into the room I'm not sure I wouldn't rather be alone, even tied up and half naked. He is carrying the school cane.

I'm wriggling immediately, shaking my head and pleading with my eyes, trying to get my panties out of my mouth with my tongue. But all to no avail – I have never seen Alan's grin so cruel as he steps up to me and carefully, deliberately measures the cane up against my chest, pressing the cold hard wood to my burning flesh. I turn to him, my eyes wide with fear, my breasts quivering against the cane.

'Just six,' he says. 'But if you don't stop dancing around like that it will be twelve.'

All I can manage is a pitiful whimper, deep in my throat, but I'm doing as I'm told, too much the slave and too much the slut to disobey. Bracing myself, my eyes shut tight, I stick out my tits.

'Good girl,' he says, and the cane leaves my breasts.

To swish back down immediately, full across the underside of both tits to set me kicking crazily in my bonds, jumping up and down and shaking my head. The stroke is nothing like the ones he applies to my bottom, but it hurts so much more, impossibly much more. Even so I find myself getting back into position, despite my sobbing, despite my fear, with my tits stuck well out, fat and naked and ready to be beaten.

Again the cane lashes down, biting into my flesh just above my nipples, and again I go into my frenzied, stupid dance of pain, bringing myself under control again only with the greatest effort. My tears have started, streaming down my cheeks, while my panties are a soggy ball in my mouth and twin streamers of snot hang from my nose where I've begun to snivel.

'You do make such a fuss over it, don't you?' Alan says, his voice full of laughter. 'What a baby you are!'

I can't answer, and I don't need to. He's right. I *do* make a fuss. I can't help it. It's the way I am, a pathetic, cowardly little rag doll who can't even cope with her own needs, and yet I'm sticking out my fat tits for another stroke. The cane hits and I'm writhing again and jumping on my toes to make my boobs bounce. Now I have three thick red welts across my breasts to add to the even pink glow produced by the fly whisk, and there will be three more before I'm put on my knees to suck cock, or be titty-fucked, or just plain fucked.

My boobs are stuck out again and I get my fourth stroke, this time right across my nipples, which hurts far more than before, more than I could possibly have imagined. My cheeks blow out around my panties-gag and I'm shaking my head in a desperate effort to contain my pain, but I can't. It's too much – my control is completely gone as I writhe on the end of my rope, gasping and sobbing, a pathetic, wretched mess.

Alan waits patiently until at last I manage to recover. I really can't take another stroke like that, but I have two more coming and I'm going to get them anyway. I stick out my tits, trying desperately to be brave but sobbing bitterly and uncontrollably with fear. The cane lashes down, lower this time, but it still hurts enough to set me mewling in my throat and dancing. He watches, caressing his cock, the cane trailing in his hand, until I'm ready once more.

This is the last one, and then I'll be used. But there is regret mingled with my relief as I get into my lewd pose, breasts thrust high for the cane. He nods, lifts it, and brings it down, harder than before, and striking right across my nipples for the second time. I scream, my panties finally fly from my mouth, my bladder opens, and as my breasts and face are spattered with my own snot and spittle, so my thighs and my dress are sprayed with piddle.

I can't stop it. I piss everywhere, into my pretty petticoats and my dress, all over the floor. I've filled my shoes too, my stockinged feet squishing in my own urine as I tread up and down in my awful pain. My panties are in my cleavage and slither slowly down as I jiggle about, to fall to the floor with a wet plop, right at Alan's feet. He is looking at me, cool and amused, the massive erection sprouting from his fly the only evidence that he finds exciting what he has done to me.

Me, I'm broken, tear-stained and snotty, wet with my own piss, my breasts a mess of hot red lines. When Alan releases the knot that holds my wrists I simply slump to the floor, kneeling defeated in my own pee puddle as I gape for his cock. He puts it in, letting me suck, and my hands are burrowing up under my soggy petticoats to find my cunt. I start to rub and he doesn't stop me, just easing his cock in and out of my mouth while he holds me by my hair to stop me trying to swallow him whole.

I cradle my breasts, feeling my bruised and beaten flesh, already in an ecstasy close to orgasm, on my knees in a puddle of piss, masturbating my sopping cunt as I suck the penis of a man who has just beaten and humiliated me, had me dress up as a milkmaid and whipped and caned my tits, brought me so high that I want to spend the rest of my existence sucking his lovely cock while I masturbate my dirty cunt and my boobs burn with pain.

Alan pulls out a moment before I come to jerk at his cock, right in my face. Then he grabs my breasts, squashing them hard around his shaft and pumping furiously in my sweat-, snot- and spit-slicked cleavage. It hurts crazily, and I scream, just in time to get a mouthful of spunk as it fountains from his cock. More goes in my face and all over my tits, and the instant he's finished I'm masturbating with it, rubbing his spunk over my bruised nipples and snatching at my dirty little cunt, at my breasts too, clawing at my flesh and screaming as my orgasm rips through me, spasm after violent spasm, until at last I can take no more and the world turns red around me, then black as my senses slip away.

nexus

## The leading publisher of fetish and adult fiction

## TELL US WHAT YOU THINK!

Readers' ideas and opinions matter to us. Take a few minutes to fill in the questionnaire below and you'll be entered into a prize draw to win a year's worth of Nexus books (36 titles)

Terms and conditions apply – see end of questionnaire.

**1. Sex:** Are you male ☐   female ☐   a couple ☐?

**2. Age:** Under 21 ☐   21–30 ☐   31–40 ☐   41–50 ☐   51–60 ☐   over 60 ☐

**3. Where do you buy your Nexus books from?**

☐  A chain book shop. If so, which one(s)?

_____

☐  An independent book shop. If so, which one(s)?

_____

☐  A used book shop/charity shop
☐  Online book store. If so, which one(s)?

_____

**4. How did you find out about Nexus books?**

☐  Browsing in a book shop
☐  A review in a magazine
☐  Online
☐  Recommendation
☐  Other _____

**5. In terms of settings, which do you prefer? (Tick as many as you like)**

☐  Down to earth and as realistic as possible
☐  Historical settings. If so, which period do you prefer?

_____

☐  Fantasy settings – barbarian worlds

- ☐ Completely escapist/surreal fantasy
- ☐ Institutional or secret academy
- ☐ Futuristic/sci fi
- ☐ Escapist but still believable
- ☐ Any settings you dislike?

_____

- ☐ Where would you like to see an adult novel set?

_____

## 6. In terms of storylines, would you prefer:

- ☐ Simple stories that concentrate on adult interests?
- ☐ More plot and character-driven stories with less explicit adult activity?
- ☐ We value your ideas, so give us your opinion of this book:

_____

_____

_____

## 7. In terms of your adult interests, what do you like to read about? (Tick as many as you like)

- ☐ Traditional corporal punishment (CP)
- ☐ Modern corporal punishment
- ☐ Spanking
- ☐ Restraint/bondage
- ☐ Rope bondage
- ☐ Latex/rubber
- ☐ Leather
- ☐ Female domination and male submission
- ☐ Female domination and female submission
- ☐ Male domination and female submission
- ☐ Willing captivity
- ☐ Uniforms
- ☐ Lingerie/underwear/hosiery/footwear (boots and high heels)
- ☐ Sex rituals
- ☐ Vanilla sex
- ☐ Swinging
- ☐ Cross-dressing/TV

☐ Enforced feminisation

☐ Others – tell us what you don't see enough of in adult fiction:

_____

_____

_____


8. Would you prefer books with a more specialised approach to your interests, i.e. a novel specifically about uniforms? If so, which subject(s) would you like to read a Nexus novel about?

_____

_____

_____


9. Would you like to read true stories in Nexus books? For instance, the true story of a submissive woman, or a male slave? Tell us which true revelations you would most like to read about:

_____

_____

_____


10. What do you like best about Nexus books?

_____

_____


11. What do you like least about Nexus books?

_____

_____


12. Which are your favourite titles?

_____

_____


13. Who are your favourite authors?

_____

_____

14. **Which covers do you prefer? Those featuring:**
    **(tick as many as you like)**

☐ Fetish outfits

☐ More nudity

☐ Two models

☐ Unusual models or settings

☐ Classic erotic photography

☐ More contemporary images and poses

☐ A blank/non-erotic cover

☐ What would your ideal cover look like?

_____

15. **Describe your ideal Nexus novel in the space provided:**

_____

_____

_____

_____

16. **Which celebrity would feature in one of your Nexus-style fantasies?**
    **We'll post the best suggestions on our website – anonymously!**

_____

## THANKS FOR YOUR TIME

Now simply write the title of this book in the space below and cut out the
questionnaire pages. Post to: Nexus, Marketing Dept., Thames Wharf Studios,
Rainville Rd, London W6 9HA

Book title: _____

### TERMS AND CONDITIONS

1. The competition is open to UK residents only, excluding employees of Nexus and Virgin, their
families, agents and anyone connected with the promotion of the competition. 2. Entrants
must be aged 18 years or over. 3. Closing date for receipt of entries is 31 December 2006.
4. The first entry drawn on 7 January 2007 will be declared the winner and notified by Nexus.
5. The decision of the judges is final. No correspondence will be entered into. 6. No purchase
necessary. Entries restricted to one per household. 7. The prize is non-transferable and non-
refundable and no alternatives can be substituted. 8. Nexus reserves the right to amend or
terminate any part of the promotion without prior notice. 9. No responsibility is accepted for
fraudulent, damaged, illegible or incomplete entries. Proof of sending is not proof of receipt.
10. The winner's name will be available from the above address from 9 January 2007.

Promoter: Nexus, Thames Wharf Studios, Rainville Road, London, W6 9HA

## NEXUS NEW BOOKS

*To be published in June 2006*

### UNEARTHLY DESIRES
### Ray Gordon

When Alison comes into money, she uses the small fortune to buy a country home. A house unlike any other she has ever experienced. From the discovery of a sinister playroom in the basement, to the strange men who call upon the house and request unusual and bizarre services, Alison begins to wonder about the previous owner. And herself, when she is compelled to oblige the visitors' demands.

Both the mystery, and Alison's alarm, ratchets up another notch when she realises her country retreat was once a house of ill-repute, run by an elderly madam. And as she and her friend, Sally, sink further and further into committing depraved sexual acts with their guests, she becomes certain that the previous owner is still in control . . .

£6.99   ISBN 0 352 34036 3

### EXPOSÉ
### Laura Bowen

Lisa is a successful book illustrator with a secret that could ruin her reputation. The two sides of her life – the professional and the erotic – have always been strictly separated. Divided until mysterious events begin to act powerfully on her imagination. And when her secret is discovered, she is drawn inexorably into circumstances ruled by her own unrestrained desire in which her fantasies, however extreme, become real.

£6.99   ISBN 0 352 34035 5

# THE DOMINO TATTOO
## Cyrian Amberlake

Into this world comes Josephine Morrow, a young woman beset with a strange restlessness. At Estwych she finds a cruelty and a gentleness she has never known.

A cruelty that will test her body to its limits and a gentleness that will set her heart free. An experience that will change her utterly. An experience granted only to those with the domino tattoo . . .

£6.99   ISBN 0 352 34037 1

If you would like more information about Nexus titles, please visit our website at www.nexus-books.co.uk, or send a large stamped addressed envelope to:
  Nexus, Thames Wharf Studios,
  Rainville Road, London W6 9HA

## NEXUS BACKLIST

This information is correct at time of printing. For up-to-date information, please visit our website at www.nexus-books.co.uk

All books are priced at £6.99 unless another price is given.

Please send me the books I have ticked above.

Name          ................................................................

Address      ................................................................

................................................................

................................................................

............................................. Post code ...................

Send to: **Virgin Books Cash Sales, Thames Wharf Studios, Rainville Road, London W6 9HA**

US customers: for prices and details of how to order books for delivery by mail, call 888-330-8477.

Please enclose a cheque or postal order, made payable to **Nexus Books Ltd**, to the value of the books you have ordered plus postage and packing costs as follows:

  UK and BFPO – £1.00 for the first book, 50p for each subsequent book.

  Overseas (including Republic of Ireland) – £2.00 for the first book, £1.00 for each subsequent book.

If you would prefer to pay by VISA, ACCESS/MASTERCARD, AMEX, DINERS CLUB or SWITCH, please write your card number and expiry date here:

................................................................

Please allow up to 28 days for delivery.

**Signature** ...................................................

**Our privacy policy**

We will not disclose information you supply us to any other parties. We will not disclose any information which identifies you personally to any person without your express consent.

From time to time we may send out information about Nexus books and special offers. Please tick here if you do *not* wish to receive Nexus information.      ☐